PASSAGE OF CRIME

By:
R. Michael Phillips

1

Additional books by R. Michael Phillips in

The Ernie Bisquets Mystery Series

ALONG CAME A FIFER

ROOK, RHYME & SINKER

DEDICATION

Thanks to all the wonderful people I've met
through life, which have stimulated my imagination
in such a way as to populate these pages
with unforgettable characters.

ACKNOWLEDGMENTS

A special thank you to Maya Bogaert, for graciously allowing me to use her photograph for the cover of my latest mystery. It truly sets the mood for the story.

1/ An Angel of Mercy

Cold as charity. That's the best way to describe the raw night air in Whitechapel that spring evening. A sudden afternoon chill had caught most people by surprise, convincing them winter was not about to be brushed off so quickly, or at least without having the final word on the subject. The wispy grey curtain that fluttered over the city had stiffened into a dense charcoal blanket by late day, settling quietly over the dun-colored buildings along Brick Lane. By the supper hour, a sliver of the moon peeked out briefly from behind the billowy folds, then hastily disappeared without warning as if frightened by something below. Small clusters of people scurried by the dingy brick facades, their collars cinched tightly to their necks, unaware of the murderous act playing out in the shadows of a nearby alley.

Most people don't give their walking commute a second thought. They are distracted along the way by emails, tweets from people they are at odds to remember, or the latest album download. It's routine to them. They pass the same shops and scurry across the same zebra crossings as they traverse the city to their flat, exhausted from a days labor and lost in a digital world. The next morning, as they sit picking at their fry-up, wrapped comfortably in flannel, the newspaper strewn about on the table, they'll gradually realize their walk home was anything but routine. Something in a headline will catch their attention. The street mentioned is quite familiar. Curiosity draws them to the article beneath the headline. It hints at an otherwise unremarkable alley, an alley they possibly pass by daily without thought of what might lie deep within its bowels. The location won't register at first, and then they'll read it again. Suddenly, something too familiar about the location and the details will startle them like hot tea on their lips. A quick gasp will freeze the moment in time. Their eyes will dart about their flats, reassuring themselves the nightly routine of bolting doors and fastening windows had been completed. A sigh of relief will follow. As they continue reading, sipping at their tea and pondering the terrible fate of that poor woman mentioned in the article, the cold touch of death from a series of similar murders begins to raise the hairs on the back of their neck.

Death's shadow has a way of lingering long after the tears have gone, long after faces have become locked in the memories of those left behind. The years can never fully scrub away the stain left from a murderous act, and Inspector Flannel's meeting was about to prove that turn of phrase correct.

Inspector Flannel was walking at a brisk pace. The call that came into the station asked for him specifically. The caller gave no details, only his name, where he could be found, and a plea of urgency. Normally he would have sent a constable round to handle such an ambiguous request, leaving it to the officer's discretion as to whether there was an actual need for the inspector. But this call was different. Though the request itself was annoyingly vague, the name was enough to warrant his attention without the customary vetting process. He turned off Fournier onto Wilkes Street, stopping in front of an alley on the left.

"What's all this about, Brown?" barked Inspector Flannel. He was prickly on a good day, so being taken away from his supper wasn't about to add anything positive to his disposition. He stopped a few steps into the alley, allowing his eyes a moment or two to adjust from the bright street lamp to the darkness. "I've no time for your foolishness, Brown! Show yourself, or it's back to my sausages and beans for me."

For a moment, all was quiet. The muffled sounds of traffic and pedestrians merged together into a deep growl, eventually being absorbed into the thick night air. A mild stench wafted out from within the depths of the alley, adding yet another layer of displeasure to the inspector's evening.

"No. Wait," a timid voice called out from behind a large, rusted and well-used rubbish bin. "Down here, sir. Horrible thing it is. Horrible thing. No reason for it. Not again, sir, not again. This way, Inspector. This way."

Flannel's eyes were not yet fully adjusted, but he recognized the voice and twisted silhouette of Prophet Brown as he emerged from behind the bin. Disfigured from palsy–his right arm curled up on his chest, rendering his hand all but useless–he was further recognizable by the labored clubfoot stride and a repetitive head motion when he spoke.

Prophet was making his way toward a dim light flickering at the far end of the narrow alley, just where it turned round to the left behind a Thai take-away shop. Flannel started after him, kicking aside the assortment of discarded boxes and refuse strewn about, quickly gaining on the limping figure that was slowly leading him deeper into the alley.

Prophet Brown mumbled to himself, repeating his plea to the inspector over and over, muffled in part by the sound of his left foot dragging through the rubbish. "Horrible thing, just horrible. You have to stop him. Not again, sir, not again."

"I'll ask you once more, Brown, what's this all about?"

The harsh tone of the inspector's voice had little affect on the man he was following. He caught up to Prophet

Brown just as they turned the corner. Reaching out, he clapped a hand on his shoulder. "I've asked you a question, lad, and I expect an answer. Now, what have you done?"

"I . . . I didn't do anything," whimpered Brown. He looked back over his shoulder at the inspector, never making eye contact. Instead, he cowered before the imposing figure, wincing as he tried to yank his shoulder free of the inspector's grasp. It was a pitiful sight, and a reaction known all too well by the inspector from his years in Scotland Yard dealing with domestic cases. Unable to pull himself free, Prophet Brown wrenched his shoulder up, tucking his face down as far on his chest as possible in an attempt to protect himself from what he anticipated to be a backhand across his face.

"Sorry, Prophet," said the inspector, in an uncharacteristically soothing voice. He withdrew his hand slowly, brushing at the shoulders of the trembling man before him. "You know me, son. You have no reason to fear me. I'd not raise a hand against you. It's been eight years, so I was surprised to hear from you. That's all." The inspector gave a warm smile and a wink. "I'm a bit grumpy when I'm taken away from my sausage and beans."

Prophet slowly relaxed his tense posture, nodding as he looked up into the sympathetic eyes of the inspector.

"So, what have we got here?" Flannel continued. "I assume you called me because you need my help?" The inspector paused, catching a momentary glimpse of Prophet Brown's bruised face. His tone turned from compassion to one of anger. "Did Raventhorn do that?"

Inspector Flannel reached out in an attempt to acknowledge what appeared to be a fresh bruise on Prophet Brown's face. Prophet reacted with an apprehensive jerk of his head. It was a conditioned response, even though he knew the inspector wouldn't hurt him. After a moment, Prophet lowered his eyes and unconvincingly shook his head.

It was eight years ago Prophet Brown, then a lad of 22, first met Inspector Flannel. He introduced himself as the domestic servant to Lord Alfred Raventhorn. London society knew Raventhorn as a charismatic and well-respected Member of Parliament, but the inspector had his own opinion of the man—one supported by the scars and bruises on a young man the MP kept somewhat isolated from his affluent circle of friends. On those occasions of being questioned about the injuries, Raventhorn insisted they were a result of Prophet's propensity for dust-ups at the local pubs. Prophet did little to confirm or deny the explanation. Instead, he chose to manufacture his own version of the truth, owing his unsightly bruising to the result of a careless step on a staircase.

It was during that first meeting in the spring of 2002 that Brown approached Inspector Flannel. He claimed to have information implicating Raventhorn in the *Brick Lane Slasher* case–a rather theatrical moniker coined by the London Telegraph to further enforce their front-page coverage of a series of five sensational murders in the Whitechapel section of London.

As reported at the time, over the course of three months five women were found dead in alleys around London's East End. There were no indications the women knew each other, and they were all working in different parts of the city. Each time, the women were found dressed in a white choir robe, their hands clasped in prayer on their breasts. All were attacked from behind with their skulls crushed from a single blow. After being positioned on the pavement, as if thoughtfully laid out for a viewing, their throats were slashed and a red scarf was wrapped around the wound. On the wrist of each woman was a garish white plastic watch with a cracked crystal, a detail never released to the public. The only common link the police were able to establish, although it was not considered relevant at the time, were claims that all five women were engaged as gentleman's companions at some point in their early careers with reputable agencies.

According to an unsigned statement in possession of the inspector at the time of the murders, Prophet Brown claimed to have seen three of the women in the company of Raventhorn at different times during the year prior to their deaths. Inspector Flannel understood he needed to advance cautiously. Accusing an MP of anything was a serious matter and could easily end the otherwise brilliant career of the accuser. Despite feeling certain Raventhorn was skillfully keeping a dark side tucked away from the public eye, he wasn't about to rush to an indictment with little more than circumstantial evidence and the testimony of a battered servant. While he was gathering evidence to substantiate Brown's claim, a story broke in the London Telegraph. An unidentified source indicated Detective Inspector Flannel was about to accuse Lord Alfred Raventhorn as the *Brick Lane Slasher.* The MP vehemently and publicly denied any and all associations with the murdered women, challenging the inspector to produce his evidence in the matter.

After Flannel's suspicions were leaked to the media, Brown recanted his testimony, leaving the inspector at the mercy of the headlines and his superiors. The case he had been building against Raventhorn was pieced together from clues he obtained at the crime scenes and statements given to him by Prophet. The clues were circumstantial at best, so without Prophet's testimony to tie the pieces together, any case there might have been against the MP would never withstand the assault Raventhorn's legal team would mount against it in court. Within a week, the inspector's case quickly fell apart. He was chastised in every form of social media for bungling the investigation and removed from any further official involvement in the case.

Infuriated at the digital maelstrom of accusations and innuendo, Raventhorn left London to spend the summer months at his country home in Worlington. He never confronted Prophet about his involvement with the inspector's case, though he left little to the imagination about his displeasure. Instead, he left Prophet behind to tend to the house in London during his absence.

Inspector Wynne Godfrey, a piercing young Scotsman new to Scotland Yard, took over the investigation. When first assigned to the Yard, Flannel was assigned as Godfrey's mentor. Important cases usually went to Flannel, so the grooming of bright new recruits, such as Godfrey, was also something his superiors relied on. As a result, a friendship developed, with Flannel pulling Godfrey in on every case of merit he was assigned. Flannel had an exceptional conviction record, notwithstanding the unexpected shortcomings of the *Slasher* case, so it was extremely difficult for his superiors to justify removing him from the case. They finally bowed to the pressure, handing the investigation over to Godfrey–a move that raised more than a few eyebrows, with some going as far as to hint his assignment to the case was more an arrangement rather than coincidence to keep Flannel's finger in the pie.

Over the course of two years, a few additional suspects were questioned, but no one was ever formally charged with the murders. Flannel remained steadfast in Raventhorn's guilt, blaming himself for allowing the murderer of those five young women to escape justice. Ignoring his removal from the official investigation, Flannel leveraged his friendship with Godfrey to discretely follow up on potential leads either one or the other would uncover. The years went by without another similar murder. It was as if the *Slasher* vanished, something often mentioned in conversation as reminiscent of another individual known to frequent the dark alleys of Whitechapel.

Despite a formal reprimand from his superiors, and the abuse he took at the hands of the media, Flannel never held any hard feelings toward Brown. He was not a man known for any outward display of emotion or tenderness, yet when it came to Prophet Brown, the tough inspector was always willing to put aside his case-hardened exterior and extend a hand of kindness when needed. That kindness would be needed if they were to get through the events of this evening.

In the flickering light, the inspector could see Prophet Brown was visibly shaken. He waited patiently for him to regain his composure and then noticed something else. There was blood on Brown's left hand and sleeve.

"What is it, lad? What's happened?"

"It's a young girl, sir," Prophet replied, quivering as he spoke. He looked up momentarily at the inspector, his eyes blinking rapidly from the glare of the light overhead, his head bobbing as he spoke. He pointed toward a doorway, partially in shadow from a teetering stack of wooden lettuce crates. "Poor thing . . . blood everywhere . . . it's starting all over again."

Flannel rushed over to where the girl lay. There was no sign of life. Pulling his mobile phone from his pocket, he called into the station. Prophet Brown watched from a safe distance as Inspector Flannel examined the body. His head twitching as he mumbled words of comfort, wiping at the tears on his cheeks with the stained sleeve of his coat.

The woman appeared to be in her late twenties, neatly dressed in an elegant white pantsuit beneath a white choir robe, with no visible signs of a struggle. She lay peacefully on the cold pavement, a Coach purse tucked neatly under her arm. Her thin fingers clasped together on her breast as if in prayer; her soft green eyes were open, staring up to heaven in search of a reason for this horrendous act of violence. Flecks of silver and gold from her dangling earrings shimmered in the pool of blood beneath her head, casting an angelic halo around her tightly curled blond hair. A red scarf was wrapped around her slender neck, concealing the deep slash that delivered this young woman to the hands of God.

Flannel checked for a pulse. The young woman was gone. A shiver came over him as he crouched next to the body, drawing up the left sleeve of the white robe. This murder scene was all too familiar to him. Looking down at the young woman's wrist, he saw a white-faced, square watch with a red plastic band. The crystal was cracked, the hour hand was missing, and the minute hand was stopped at quarter past the hour. This one accessory was certainly out of place, especially when compared to the other obviously expensive and coordinated diamond and gold jewelry adorning the neck and wrists of this young woman. The existence of the jewelry and the Coach handbag dissolved any remaining thoughts he had of labeling this as just a simple robbery gone terribly wrong. At best, he was dealing with a perverse copycat, at worst, the return of an old nemesis.

As the inspector stood up, he could hear the sirens of the approaching emergency vehicles. Prophet Brown had slowly inched his way over to where the inspector was standing, his shadow falling across the body.

"She's dead, isn't she?" asked Brown. His voice cracked and he began to shake, his head twitching more than usual. "It's him again, isn't it? Poor girl. You must stop him this time."

Inspector Flannel looked at Brown, his dark eyes doing little to mask his anger at the pathetic little man before him. The pain of his last encounter with Raventhorn would pale in comparison to what his superiors would do if he even suggested the MP might be involved with this poor girl's death. Flannel had his chance eight years ago. A chance he watched slip through his fingers when Brown recanted his testimony. He had every right to lash out at Brown, something he wouldn't think twice about if it were anyone else, but his overwhelming sympathy for this battered shell of a man held the words back. Instead he took a deep breath, slowly put his arm around Brown, and turned him away from the murder scene.

"We don't know who killed this woman," said the inspector bluntly but with compassion. "And I'll ask that you refrain from making any unfounded accusations."

Prophet Brown slowly nodded his head.

"I'll need you to tell me what you were doing here, starting with how this blood got on your hand and sleeve."

"I . . . I didn't do it," stuttered Brown. He pulled his shoulder away from the inspector's hand, turned, and motioned with his head toward the body. "I found her like that. I tried to help. Her pretty curls there in the puddle of cold water. I lifted her head. It wasn't water. It wasn't water at all. It was blood. Her blood."

Brown began to shake uncontrollably. He paced back and forth, mumbling to himself. The inspector stepped in front of him, clasping a hand on each of his arms in an attempt to calm him down. It took a moment, but Brown regained his composure and Inspector Flannel released his grip on him.

"No one's blaming you," said the inspector. "I just need to know what happened."

Before Brown could answer, a wave of EMTs and constables washed through the alley. The inspector motioned for him to stand out of the way while he spoke with one of the officers. Prophet slowly backed away from the crowded scene, taking a seat on a wooden crate nestled amongst a group of dented and rusted rubbish bins. Spotlights flickered on, illuminating every dark crevice and rubbish pile, causing a flurry of vermin to scatter in all directions. Prophet shielded his eyes from the bright lights with his arm, squinting as he peeked out to confirm Inspector Flannel was still present. Flannel had concerns of his own, occasionally looking back over his shoulder to confirm Prophet was still waiting for him.

"I got your call," said Inspector Godfrey walking up to Flannel. He was hastily dressed, but alert. "What's happened?"

Flannel pulled Godfrey aside, quietly filling in the basic details. Godfrey listened intently, directing his attention from the young woman's body to the crate where Prophet waited. When he finished his explanation, Flannel walked over to where Brown was seated.

"There's no need for us to remain here," said the inspector, helping Prophet up from his seat. He pointed back toward Wilkes Street. "We can talk down at the station and then I'll have one of the officers take you back to Raventhorn's residence."

"I can't be late," said Brown with a short gasp. "I can't. He'll not stand for it."

"Don't worry, lad," replied the inspector. "I'll not keep you long."

Prophet Brown reluctantly nodded his head. An appreciative smile came to his face, though his sad eyes told more of the story about his frame of mind. He gave one last look at the young woman who lay motionless in the alley, lowered his head, and followed obediently behind the inspector.

* * *

A shaft of light pierced the darkness, scaling the brick facade as a late model sedan made its way down Lower Sloane Street. It slowly navigated the narrow passage through the affluent Kensington neighborhood, pausing at the corner for just a moment. The light entered a second floor window, following along the frayed silk wall coverings. A gaunt figure of a man seated at a desk was cut from the darkness, his intense stare challenging the assault on his privacy; a portrait even Caravaggio would hesitate to capture.

"Where is that wretched excuse for a servant?" Raventhorn grumbled under his breath, his eyes burning holes through the clock face on the mantle. He sat motionless in the dark, slumped back in his chair, drumming his bony fingers on the worn desk blotter. "He's at it again, I'll wager. I'll not stand for it this time."

2/ Away From the Maddening Crowd

It was close to eleven thirty as they emerged from the alley on Wilkes. A Prussian blue sky was tearing at the charcoal gray blanket of evening, dotted here and there with twinkling stars doing their best to draw attention away from the bloodstained edges of the city. Fournier Street was quiet, with just the usual locals walking about and the clattering of a light stream of taxis and buses, as was typical for a Friday evening. The slight drizzle had given up for the time being, leaving behind a glittery sheen to the otherwise bland pavements. Not enough water to puddle, but enough to cause Prophet to take extra care with each step as he followed along behind the inspector. Prophet Brown and Inspector Flannel turned the corner onto Brick Lane. The familiar blue lantern of the police station was up ahead in the middle of the block.

Prophet hesitated for a moment when the inspector opened the door to the station. The grim look of the desk sergeant gave him pause, but a reassuring nod from the inspector was enough to calm his fears. Inspector Flannel was well known on the force, and this wasn't his first visit to the Brick Lane station. The desk sergeant gave a nod and directive glance toward the hallway leading to the interrogation rooms–which Flannel was quick to reply with a nod of thanks–and then returned to his paperwork.

Prophet Brown followed the inspector down the dark hall and into one of the empty rooms. He sat down in the steel chair on one side of a well-worn green table, his head lowered and left hand resting in his lap. Prophet continued to shake slightly as he looked around the room. Eight years is a long time, but not so long that it erased the memory of sitting nervously across from the inspector at that very table, detailing his suspicions about Lord Raventhorn.

It was information supplied by Prophet that connected three of the murdered women as gentleman's companions. Before Inspector Flannel could corroborate the facts, the story had been leaked to the newspaper, resulting in a firestorm from Raventhorn's legal team. Flannel's superiors fought back determinedly against the governmental pressure to make an example of him. In the end, it was their confidence in his skills as a detective, and his otherwise exemplary record of service with Scotland Yard, that ultimately spared his job.

Through it all, Inspector Flannel harbored no ill feelings over the incident, only regret. Five women were dead, the trail quickly went cold, and the Internet talking heads seemed more interested in hypothesizing on how his misstep allowed a murderer to go free. Too many questions were left unanswered, including who tipped off the media.

Inspector Flannel watched Prophet carefully. He could sense the concern in his expression over the position this latest incident had put him in. He did what he could to make the situation as un-confrontational as possible, pulling over a chair next to him instead of taking a seat across the table.

"I thought this would be more private than the two of us walking into Scotland Yard," the inspector said with a slight wink. "Too many eyes there, even at this time of night."

"Thank you, sir," came the hushed reply. "Thank you. But I really shouldn't be here."

"Rubbish," said the inspector. He quickly dismissed Prophet's concerns with a wave of his hand. "It was a terrible thing you stumbled on this evening. Better you regain your composure here than have that sorrowful look on your face come under the suspicious eye of Raventhorn."

Just the mention of his master's name was enough to unravel Prophet's attempt at composure. "He'll not be happy about this. Not at all. I really shouldn't be here."

Prophet started to rise but the inspector gently put his hand on his shoulder, directing him back into his seat.

"I'll not keep you long. A few questions, that's all. This is just between you and I. There's no need for His Lordship to find out we spoke."

Prophet halfheartedly nodded his head and settled back into his chair.

"Now, what were you doing in that alley off Wilkes? That's quite a walk from Sloane Square." The inspector took a small pad and pencil from his waistcoat and placed them on the table.

Prophet's eyes were fixed on the pad. "It's Friday. I go to the late mass at Christ Church. Not many folks there. Been doing that since I was a young lad."

"That's right, you grew up a few blocks from there. Torn down, isn't it?"

"Yes." Prophet glanced up at the inspector briefly to answer, and then lowered his head again. His head twitched, but slightly less dramatically as he replied, "It's a car park now. Not much left of the old walkups. All glass and metal now. There was a nice bookstore down the block. Open late on Fridays. Had all the latest magazines. Stopped in every week after mass, regular as clockwork. The owner let me read them without charge. Decent man, he was . . . at least to me."

The inspector was accustomed to Prophet and his tendency to ramble on about nothing when he was nervous. He let him ramble for a bit then followed up with another question to bring his attention back to the matter at hand. "So you were on your way back to Raventhorn's from mass? That's the opposite direction, isn't it?"

"Off to Truman's for a pint. Don't like the main road–too many people. Always pity in their smiles."

"Why not the Ten Bells? It's right there on the corner."

This innocent question seemed to puff new life into the nervousness Prophet had stifled. He pulled at the seam on his trouser leg, and his head twitch becoming more pronounced. When he noticed the inspector watching him carefully, he tensed up in an effort to control his shaking and then answered.

"Don't like the crowd. Tourists think I'm part of the show. The *Ripper* and all that. Always staring. No way to have a peaceful pint without—"

"Understandable," Flannel politely interrupted. "So you went up Fournier Street and then cut through the alley off Wilkes?"

Prophet nodded his head. "Poor girl. Found her there. Like an angel. I just couldn't let her lay there like that."

"You did the right thing for her by calling me." Inspector Flannel paused for a moment, allowing Prophet to relax. "Are you alright?"

"He'll tell them I did it," Prophet Brown snorted. He looked up at the inspector and then leaned over to one side, peering over his shoulder toward the doorway. He pulled his crippled arm up and held it out as best he could, continuing in a hoarse whisper. "He'll have his way this time. Look at me. Who would believe me? Young girl dead. Her blood on my hand and sleeve."

Before the inspector could answer, he became aware of a presence at the door behind him. After giving Prophet a reassuring nod, he turned his head. One of the constables the inspector had spoken to in the alley was standing there. The constable motioned for the inspector to follow him.

"What is it?" asked the inspector once they walked down the hall back toward the front desk.

"Preliminary report says blunt force trauma to the back of the head. Her throat was cut, but she was already dead."

"Do we know who she was?"

"Identification in her wallet shows her as being Mary Walsh. She had a flat on Newcomen Street." The constable tore a page from his notepad and handed it to the inspector. "All the information is on there. Is he a suspect?"

The inspector paused, looking from the note to the room where he left Prophet sitting. "No. He found the body. Like that poor wretch doesn't have enough problems."

The inspector turned and walked back down the hall. Prophet didn't look up when he entered.

"They think I did it, don't they?"

"No one thinks anything at this point," the inspector curtly replied. "I know finding that poor girl was upsetting, but you need to stop portraying yourself as the pathetic wretch everyone's looking to blame for the ills of the world. I'm sorry for the position you're in, but there's nothing we can do about that now. Just tell me what you know and you can go back about your business. As long as your story checks out, I'll do what I can to keep your name out of the papers."

Prophet nodded his head obediently.

Inspector Flannel sat back down in his chair and leaned back. "Does the name Mary Walsh mean anything to you?"

"Mary Walsh," Prophet repeated quietly. He sat pondering the question for a moment. "Was that the young girl he killed tonight?"

"We don't know who killed her," Flannel grunted impatiently, knowing full well whom Prophet was alluding to. He was close to the end of his patience. "You'll not do either of us any good by conjuring up old ghosts."

Prophet Brown slowly nodded his head, but in a less than convincing way, continuing to pick at the inspector's patience. "It's him, you know. Say what you will, but I saw it on your face in the alley."

The inspector slammed his fist down on the table, startling Prophet and almost knocking him out of his chair. The noise also brought the desk sergeant running down the hall. As he got to the room, he was met at the doorway by the inspector. He quietly muttered a few words to the sergeant, who responded with a quick look in Prophet's direction and promptly returned to his desk. With great restraint, Flannel calmly closed the heavy steel door.

"Now you listen to me, Brown," said the inspector, drawing out each word slowly through clenched teeth as he walked back over to the table. With one hand on his chair and the other on his notepad on the table, he leaned in close and continued. "I'll not walk down that path again with you. If that *is* the case, you have only yourself to blame for that poor woman's death."

Prophet Brown cowered beneath the inspector, pulling away to a defensive posture and whimpering like a whipped dog.

Inspector Flannel snatched the pad and pencil from the table and stuffed them into his pocket. With a grunt, he walked around to the other side of the table and began to pace along the mirrored wall.

"May I go?" said Prophet between short breaths. "I don't want to make him angry."

The inspector stopped. He looked over at Prophet who was back to pulling at the seam on his trouser leg. As angry as he was, sympathy still held the upper hand on the inspector's emotions when it came to Prophet Brown. He shook his head, followed by a sigh of regret for his abrupt outburst and the affect it had on the poor man.

"I'll have one of the officers drive you back."

Prophet looked up at the inspector and quickly shook his head to refuse.

Inspector Flannel interrupted his attempted refusal with a raised hand. "It's not open for discussion. I'll have the officer drop you a few blocks away. Raventhorn will never know we talked. Off with you now."

The inspector walked over and opened the door. The two men walked back down the hall to the front desk. The inspector gave instructions to the sergeant, who relayed them to one of the officers at a desk behind him.

Following behind the officer, Prophet Brown stopped before exiting the station. He looked back at the inspector who was leaning against the desk. "It's him, you know. You have to stop him. More women will die if you don't."

The inspector folded his arms, gave a frustrated shake of his head, and let out one last heavy sigh. "Enough of that. Off with you now."

As the glass door slowly closed, Inspector Flannel caught the faint reflections of the original five murdered women looking back at him. Their once vacant eyes were now looking at him with a hopeful stare. Maybe this time? He stood motionless for a minute.

"You all right, inspector?" asked the desk sergeant.

It took Flannel another moment to respond. "Thanks for the use of the room," he replied gruffly, ignoring the question as he left the station.

3/ The Five Original Links

Fear is an endless chain our minds are burdened with, seeing fit to forge new links when just the right experiences are gathered. These experiences, both real and imagined, are extracted from our inner soul and wrought into shape by the heat of sensational headlines. It was early autumn, eight years ago now, that the residents of London were horrified by a series of five murders in the Whitechapel section of the city. To many the headlines and speculations were all too reminiscent of a dark time long past. The faint echo of another series of horrific crimes committed against women in that same area in the late 1800s lingered between the lines. There were certainly similarities, skillfully linked within the descriptive articles that followed the case, but with a subtle difference. The original murders were committed against women of a certain profession; these murders were committed against professional women.

The first link forged seemed unique in itself, needing little help from the press to sensationalize the appearance of the murder scene. A young, attractive woman dressed in a white choir robe, her hands clasped in prayer on her breast, lying in peace on the dark pavement, her eyes open and staring up into the heavens. The diamond studded necklace and bracelet peeking out from the edges of the white satin robe glistened in the early morning sun, adding to the angelic appearance of the woman. The peaceful façade was fleeting. The blood trailing down her neck onto the pavement from beneath a red scarf wrapped around her throat quickly brought you back to reality. The only adornment out of place was a cheapjack plastic watch with a red band on her left wrist.

Her name was Cindy Paige, a tall brunette of thirty-five years, with a severe countenance emanating from her piercing green eyes. She was abrupt in both manner and speech, with little tolerance for anyone she deemed below her station in life. She was a Senior Research Manager with Wensley Ltd., a well-established British firm specializing in advanced consumer insights and performance analytics. Although she was working out of the main office located in Henley-on-Thames, Miss Paige spent most of her time at client meetings in London, affording her the luxury to make use of the firm's flat on the top floor of a prominent new high-rise on Primrose Street.

Her social life was dotted here and there with short-term relationships, mostly long distance, and none that ever took root. These were casual affairs with little relevance to her desire to become a leading presence in British society. Her catwalk poise, along with what was considered by some an outrageous investment in haute couture, was never to be overlooked by the paparazzi. She left little to the imagination about her fondness for everything posh. Fashion editors referenced her style regularly, though some saw fit on occasion to poke the lioness with a stick, making casual inferences that her cutting-edge tastes were the offspring of an acute ability with stock futures and a cold, ferocious determination in societal elevation. Such conjecture was one of the few things that brought a smile to her face, much like her favorite Oscar Wilde quote, *"There is only one thing in the world worse than being talked about, and that is not being talked about."*

Later in the investigation into her murder, it was discovered, but not released to the media, that when Cindy Paige first arrived in London, she was briefly engaged as a gentleman's escort with Kelly & Kemp, Ltd. After one engagement the first month, she and the managers of the agency mutually agreed to take her off the books. An abrasive temperament left her less than desirable for a second engagement with those she determined would have little or no influence in raising her *endroit dans société*.

About a week after her twelfth anniversary with Wensley Ltd., on a remarkably dry and cool final Friday evening in September, Cindy Paige eased back into her chair, sipping a rather mischievous Bordeaux and basked in the glow of a lengthy and fruitful client dinner meeting in the Lecture Room at Sketch. Afterwards, and with the proper parting words cordially exchanged, Cindy Paige found herself out front on Conduit Street in want of a taxi. The driver remembered picking up a fashionably dressed woman and dropping her off at the corner of Primrose Street at Bishopsgate just after midnight, a fact verified by the dispatcher and the interior camera in the taxi. It was the last time anyone saw her alive.

Cindy Paige was found dead around 6:15 the next morning off of Brick Lane behind two large, plastic rubbish bins by a ticketing agent on his way to work at the Aldgate East tube station.

Two weeks later, a second victim was claimed. It didn't take long for the media to link the first crime together with the second, wrapped up neatly on the front pages of the papers, and tied tightly together with the blood-red string of sensationalism. JACK IS BACK was the dramatic headline flashed across the afternoon edition of one paper to introduce the second victim to the residents of London, forging the next link in the chain.

Margaret Morris was of medium build, pleasant smile, soft green eyes and a compassionless resolution to secure funding for a lifestyle she determined was owed to her as payment for a miserable and deprived childhood. She started life in a family of little means, eventually scratching her way out of a council house district that had yet to see any promised government investment. An aversion to filth remained with her as a reminder of the life she was speeding away from. She curiously retreated to any nearby sink when stressed, repeatedly washing her hands until the feeling passed.

Starting at the age of sixteen, spanning a long twenty plus years, Margaret Morris worked tirelessly in multiple situations, mostly of a legitimate nature, but not always. At a low point in life, she used her remarkable talent for persuasion to fleece a number of prominent men in Bath, the last mark almost landing her in front of a magistrate. Realizing a tainted reputation would inhibit her ability to move on to the next funding source locally, she quickly packed up her skills and left for London, never looking back.

Margaret Morris interviewed favorably in any situation, having a pleasant and convincing way about her, so securing a new position in London was immediate. She carried herself with a positive attitude and a well-manicured CV, allowing her to ease right into the position of Corporate Fundraiser with the British Heart and Lung Foundation. Her unassuming nature and enjoyable disposition opened every door she rapped upon. It also served her well by masking a ruthless ability to leave every meeting with a check in hand and a promise of continued support. She became a well-known and well-respected name in the upper floors of corporate Britain.

This new life suited her well enough, though she couldn't resist the urge to keep a hand close to the pockets of affluent London gentlemen. Being incredibly articulate and well versed on current affairs, she leveraged these two traits during a brief employment with Chamber Escorts, a gentleman's companion service.

At the time of her death, rumors of impropriety and manipulation of funds were rising and nipping at the heels of the foundation. A complete audit of the foundation's funds was assigned to an outside accounting firm, with indictments pending at the conclusion. Before the findings were made public, the body of Margaret Morris was discovered on Back Church Lane at 6:30 in the morning, beneath the railway flyover that runs along Cable Street. It was well noted in the papers how she was found dressed and posed identical to the previous victim, though the irony of being surrounded by the rubbish she spent years distancing herself from was completely overlooked.

It looked as if the media's attempt to resurrect "Jack the Ripper" wasn't getting the attention they had hoped. Undaunted, and never at a loss for words or a dramatic headline, the *Brick Lane Slasher* was born.

Tina Aldebourne most likely read of the tragedy on Back Church Lane as she sipped her morning coffee, never realizing she was to be the next victim. Miss Aldebourne was a very private librarian type and the Social Secretary for the Norwegian Consulate in London on Belgrave Square. Her long, light brown hair was neatly pulled back, braided and wrapped into a bun. Thin, gold-framed glasses resting high on her slender nose all but disappeared as a result of captivatingly bright green eyes. She had an engaging figure, with shapely legs hidden beneath modestly long skirts and dresses of a lackluster palette. Stylish heels were her only extravagance, hinting at the alluring femininity that could be.

She worked directly for Vice-Consul Bjørn Bersen, arranging special functions at the consulate, dinner parties for visiting dignitaries, and coordinating social affairs requiring the vice-consul's appearance. An invitation to attend all the consulate functions went without saying, though she graciously declined all in favor of a light meal with a glass of chardonnay, leading quietly into an evening lost in the pages of a tawdry romance novel. She enjoyed a satisfying and completely uneventful life with Sir Edward, an overfed and lazy tabby cat. It was reported in a subsequent article that early in her working career she was engaged as a gentleman's companion with one of the smaller escort services in London, but found the demands of the London social scene too exhausting.

On the evening prior to her death, a last-minute discussion with an irritating French chef held Tina Aldebourne captive in the kitchen area close to an hour and a half past her usual 5:00 departure. He was refusing to prepare his Brandade de Morue Canapés with the addition of potatoes, as suggested by the vice-consul, to a point of stamping his feet and refusing to continue with any of the required hors d'oeuvres. She reluctantly consented. They were being served during the cocktail hour that evening. The vice-consul would have little time to notice or enjoy them, as he ate very little during this type of event.

Miss Aldebourne kept a third floor flat within walking distance of the consulate on Ebury Mews. It was otherwise a pleasant Friday evening, suggesting a walk home might be more in order than the usual taxi to shake off the last remaining crumbs of a bothersome late afternoon. The idea became more exciting remembering the small cluster of boutiques and eateries she passed on her way home each night on Elizabeth Street. She decided Sir Edward would be perfectly content to sleep another hour or so before being fed if she stopped for a quick meal and maybe a little shop gazing on her way.

Exactly twenty-four hours after the discovery of the body of Margaret Morris, the choir-robed body of Tina Aldebourne was found. She was laid out in the same peaceful, angelic form as the others, in a gated parking area behind Christ Church off Fournier Street. Her head was propped up slightly by the braided bun, the first golden rays of the morning sun reflecting in the halo of blood beneath. A deep red scarf and the red band of the watch on her wrist were the only other signs of color on her pale figure.

At this point, most of London had been whipped into a frightful lather by the press. The angelic way the bodies were posed afforded the media an endless array of adjectives to describe the horrible events. They stayed at it for another nine days when the next link was forged.

Nancy Makepiece was a tall, bright, willowy woman with an engaging smile and eyes the color of an afternoon summer sky. She was a graduate of London College of Communication—starting her career as a graphic artist with Bullen & Wake, a London-based communications firm located in one of the newer corporate centers on Commercial Street, and elevating herself to Account Director within nine years. Her client list was an envious assortment of leading British-based pharmaceutical firms, anchored with two major international names in the industry.

Nancy Makepiece was self-conscious about her looks to a point of keeping her blond hair pulled up into a bun atop her head. Her rationale was to keep the focus directed more toward her acute marketing acumen, with a secondary objective doing what it might to desexualize her otherwise striking overall appearance. She was polite but direct when addressing clients, with an equestrian posture and focus. Dark rimmed glasses and business suits were her usual daily attire, a complete contrast to the elegant flowing evening gowns adorned when hired out as a gentleman's companion.

Miss Makepiece maintained an excellent relationship with Kelly & Kemp, Ltd., enjoying the nightlife and affluent circles afforded her when attending political or royal affairs. Being attractive and optimistically opinionated on all things British, she was a magnet for conversation. One of her more remarkable characteristics, the one that took most first-time admirers by surprise, was her fluency in Mandarin. She was often requested by embassies for her linguistic skills unrelated to social events.

She kept a flat on Artillery Lane, and was well known and liked by the staff at Williams Pub down the street. A regular at the Women's Library during the week, she preferred to spend most weekends and holidays, when not engaged, at her family's home in Saint Osyth. The only relationship of note was her involvement with a bank executive, but she broke it off about a month before her death when she found out he was married. He didn't take the breakup well at all, showing up at inappropriate times and making a bloody nuisance of himself. The directors of Bullen & Wake eventually called in the police on her behalf.

To get her mind off the breakup, she started chatting with a man she met through an online dating service who was in a similar situation. It was just killing time at first, a sounding board for her troubles, but eventually she became intrigued and then interested. At his suggestion, they arranged to meet on Saint Katharine's Way, across from the Tradewinds. When the police questioned the staff, two waiters remembered seeing a woman by her description talking to a man sitting on the bench across the road. Neither could give an accurate description of the man.

Just after two o'clock the following morning, a pensioner, out walking her Yorkshire terrier during a sleepless night, found the body of Nancy Makepiece off Goulston Street in a small, overgrown garden area. Like the others, she was dressed in the white choir robe, hands clasped in prayer, the red scarf and watch in place.

At this point, the *Brick Lane Slasher* had a firm foundation in the minds of Londoners. Headlines like POLICE BAFFLED, as one newspaper saw fit to print in blood-red letters across the front page of the Sunday edition, only stoked an already growing flame of uncontrolled fear. Nervous women, who routinely walked to the tube and then home from the station, were now scurrying for taxis or hiring car services to get around London. Obscure alleys, unnoticed for years along narrow streets, took on ominous characteristics. Men and women alike hastened their step as they walked past, a quick breath and a darting glance over the slightest noise emanating from the dark recesses. A week went by, then two. The absence of another victim became just as unnerving as the discovery of the next body.

Amber Flower, a single woman of twenty-eight, was the fifth link in this chain of terror being rattled in the dark alleys of Whitechapel. She was the youngest of all the victims; a bright, enthusiastic Irish lass, with an athletic build and endless charm. Her pale red hair, turned under in a bob at the shoulder, framed a cheery disposition highlighted with an adventurous cluster of freckles on each cheek.

Originally from Cork, she was a transplant to London via her position as a Program Installation Manager with Baines Software International. Sean Baines, founder of the company and, as discovered later, a one-time love interest of Amber, made his fortune with the development of integration software used to decipher CAT scans and reconfigure the data into a three-dimensional image. He was not at all the stereotype nerd expected with such development; instead, he was charming, an above average dancer, and somewhat aloof. The break-up was a mutual decision, according to a close friend of Amber's, but she hinted Amber was suspicious of his sudden display of irritability over the smallest issues.

Amber coordinated all software installation and training programs for the staff of London-based hospitals and their satellite clinics. Her effervescent personality and passionate enthusiasm was contagious, adding an overall pleasantness to what would otherwise be a dry and tedious classroom experience. Most training was accomplished during business hours, though at times a second grouping was required at night to accommodate additional shifts.

Health conscious and an advocate for greater government emphasis and commitment to the needs of children living below the poverty level, Amber Flower was a well-respected participant in foundation-sponsored marathons. To keep in shape, twice weekly she ran the Inner Circle in Regent's Park in the evening after work. The park was within walking distance of the flat she shared with her over-protective sister, Grace, on Fitzhardinge Street, just off Manchester Square.

On a dusty brown Monday evening, thirty-eight days after the first *Slasher* victim was discovered, Amber Flower prepared for her run in Regent's Park. She tied her running shoes, took a water bottle from the fridge, and called up to her sister that she was going for a run. Normally she would walk the ten or so blocks to loosen up, but the sky was threatening to drench the city one more time that day before heading for the channel, so she decided to take the car. She looked up at the second floor window as she opened the car door and waved. Her sister returned a stern governess look as she pointed up at the dark clouds forming overhead. Amber gave a nod of acknowledgement, a mock salute, and waited for a reply before getting into the car. Grace shook her head, her pursed lips retreated to an understanding smile, and she waved back. She watched as her sister disappeared around the corner. It was midnight when a very concerned Grace decided to call the police and report her sister missing.

Amber Flower's choir-robed body was found within a small, bricked garden area between dun-colored brick flats on Ashfield Street, in the shadow of the Royal London Hospital. Two nurses walking down the street to work passed the open blue door of the garden area and noticed what they thought was a woman sleeping in the grass. Curious to her condition, they entered. Realizing what they were looking at, a sudden terror froze them both where they stood. The woman was dressed and posed exactly how the newspapers depicted the *Slasher* victims. One nurse screamed, running back out to the street. The other, more compassionate than afraid, knelt down next to the body. She was careful not to touch anything as she dialed 999 on her mobile phone. The *Slasher* had claimed his fifth victim.

Tension remained high for some time afterwards. For weeks a frightened mass scoured the papers for word of his capture. Those with a more morbid curiosity waited patiently for details of another victim. With neither rhyme nor reason, the murders stopped.

4/ What Prophet Had to Say

Inspector Flannel took his time walking back to his flat facing Arnold Circus on Calvert Avenue. He was immersed in quiet reflection over his first encounter with Prophet Brown.

It was a week prior to the discovery of Amber Flower's body that Prophet Brown approached Inspector Flannel. The timid, disfigured lad was a wreck, mumbling about how he was certain his master was behind these murders. His head twitched erratically as he spoke, repeating his personal fears over and over.

The inspector was patient and took great interest at first, until Prophet explained that his master was Lord Alfred Raventhorn. Flannel knew the name as an important Member of Parliament and was quick to dismiss Prophet's allegations. Prophet Brown was not about to be dismissed so quickly. The facts he provided about the MP's whereabouts on the evenings of the murders caused Flannel to reconsider his opinion of the allegations. Those facts now rushed back as if it were just yesterday Prophet nervously rattled them off.

He remembered Prophet wincing as he described the demeaning manner he tolerated from Cindy Paige on at least two occasions, dropping her back at her flat after a social engagement attended by her and Raventhorn. It would be a week after Inspector Flannel was released from the case before Inspector Godfrey could place Raventhorn and Cindy Paige in attendance together at three separate functions, though not in each other's company.

Prophet had only a vague memory of Margaret Morris. He remembered a woman of her build and hair color speaking with Raventhorn outside Parliament at least once. On a second occasion, and if it was the same woman, he remembers Lord Raventhorn in an animated discussion, getting in the car afterwards flush with color and barking orders as they drove off. Neither Flannel nor Godfrey could find anyone to corroborate Prophet's recollection of a heated discussion involving Raventhorn and a woman at any time.

Prophet continued, mentioning the close proximity of Tina Aldebourne's flat on Ebury Mews to Raventhorn's residence. It was the first solid connection Inspector Flannel made during his investigation. The sting of dismissal from the case was still lingering with Flannel when he discovered Raventhorn had attended the dinner party at the consulate the evening of Miss Aldebourne's death. According to Prophet Brown, who was waiting in the car outside the consulate, he saw Raventhorn leave after cocktails. Raventhorn refused the car, explaining a walk was needed to clear his head, and returned an hour later.

Nancy Makepiece had the only direct link with Raventhorn. He requested her on three occasions while he was the British Ambassador to The People's Republic of China. Prophet had exact dates, which were easily verified. Inspector Flannel was quick to introduce this fact in his defense when questioned by his superiors. The accusation was quickly dismissed as ludicrous by Raventhorn's legal team, as the encounters were two years prior to her death. Inspector Godfrey questioned Adam Staverton, the man harassing Nancy Makepiece, with no positive result or indication of his involvement in any of the crimes.

Prophet was most convincing about Amber Flower. He smiled as he remembered her Irish lilt when she spoke and her bright green eyes. She was one of the few to witness Raventhorn's verbal abuse of Prophet. Miss Flower accidentally walked into a private room during a fundraising event at the Royal London Hospital. Realizing what was happening, she intervened on Prophet's behalf, much to the anger of Raventhorn who promptly stormed off. She was a fighter; a fact further attested to by the medical examiner that determined Amber Flower tried desperately to fight off her attacker. Unlike the others, whose torsos showed no signs of a struggle or defensive wounds, Miss Flower had bruises on both hands and along her right arm. It was determined she was strangled, receiving the signature blow to the back of the head afterwards.

These were five attractive, affluent women, with only one of a somewhat questionable background. The connection of them all being employed at one point in their careers with an assortment of posh gentleman's escort services wasn't accepted as relevant. Services such as these are an acceptable function in affluent society, providing intelligent companions to wealthy men of power for social engagements they would otherwise attend alone. Women like these would pretty up an otherwise stuffy event. Inspector Flannel thought differently. Despite his insistence, the decision was final. However, Inspector Wynne Godfrey was in agreement with the inspector and intended to discretely follow up on it as time allowed.

One strategic request Inspector Flannel insisted on before his removal from the case was agreed to without resistance. The police would not release any information regarding the specifics around watches found on the wrists of all the victims. It was a fact he felt should be kept from the public, a fact that could be used to determine if any additional murders were the work of the same person or a copycat.

5/ Turning the Page

Saturday morning brought with it the promise of a warm spring day; reminiscent of the colorful postcards you see lining the racks along Regent Street. An early morning fog left a shimmering gloss on the white sandstone façades standing majestically along Conduit Street. The shops were just waking up. One by one the doors slowly yawned, eager to greet the visitors who were just as eager to experience everything the shops had to offer. Traffic had already rubbed the sleep from its eyes as a steady hum rose from the pavement. London taxis darted about like little children playing at their parents' feet, trying not to get stepped on by their large, red, double-decker relatives. This bright morning was in complete contrast to the dark, murderous events of the hours preceding it.

Lord Patterson Coats was seated at his usual spot at the dining table, sipping his coffee and catching up on the headlines. One article caught his attention. A low, mournful groan resonated from his gut as he digested the details.

Patterson Coats was the former HM Chief Inspector of Prisons, now retired. He's a tall, handsome man, with chiseled features, a sun burnt face and windswept, grey curly locks. At 67 he was still as strong as a bull and not one to be trifled with in a disagreement. His military background was evident in his commanding stature and penetrating steel-grey eyes.

With his East London group he carved out a respectable career locating and excavating significant archeological sites for the sundry museums throughout the British Isles. Around a dig site he would be found properly attired in a white cotton twill shirt, tan riding breeches and knee-high, laced field boots. But in London he dresses more refined and appropriate to his station in life. That morning he was comfortably dressed in a somber black suit, shirt and tie and a red waistcoat. A short paddock boot completed the outfit.

Antiquities weren't his only interest. Over the years he had secured the confidence of those around him through his discretion and extraordinary analytical skills. He consulted with the police when their investigations stagnated, and was called upon by members of the Royal family when a delicate hand was needed. His social standing afforded him access through many doors and commanded the attention and cooperation of those he spoke with. It was understood having Patterson Coats in control of the situation also assured tight management of the information related to the problem. His calculated release of details assured them the public would be informed of the result without the public embarrassment of the problem being drawn out for weeks in the papers. He would have progressed well in uniformed police service. Instead he chose to observe crime at arms length, and only when it knocked upon his door on Conduit Street.

There were footsteps coming from the hall. He glanced back over his shoulder, forced a smile, and pushed out a chair for Ernie.

"Anything interesting in the papers, sir?" asked Ernie. He sat down across from Patterson, turned over his cup and filled it with coffee.

Patterson folded the paper to obscure the headline and placed it down on the table. "Nothing of interest really. Just the usual dustups and political posturing. So, what have you planned for the day?"

"Not sure really. I'm still getting use to my freedom. Maybe just a coffee to get me started."

"Nonsense," said Mrs. Chapman, a silver tray in hand as she burst through the kitchen door. "I've a proper fry-up for you. You'll have a better day with a bit of food in you."

Patterson smiled. "Not as free as you think."

Ernie Bisquets had just recently become part of Patterson's household. It was only in the fall of the previous year that His Lordship intervened on Ernie's behalf, securing an early release for him from Edmunds Hill Prison. Patterson became his sponsor, affording him a place to live and a paid position within his group.

It wasn't for the main occupation of the group regarding antiquities where he would be of use; it was for the more private investigations that he was called on from time to time where his talents could be leveraged. When not drifting in and out of someone else's pockets he had a very unassuming manner and could just disappear into the crowd. His skills as a pickpocket were unequaled, legendary actually in some of the darker corners of London. It was for this talent, and a somewhat selfish intent, that Patterson Coats recruited him.

Ernie felt this opportunity would enable him to make amends for his less than saintly life by using his talents for a greater good. His past was not something he was proud of, but he was by no means a hardened criminal either, just a pickpocket. There was a strict code of ethics he lived by, the main rule being not to steal from those less fortunate than himself. To underline that, it was just like him to give part of the day's take to the local soup kitchen. His idea was: if those toffs strutting around London were too busy to drop a few pounds off to the needy, he was obliged to do it for them. It was a service he was happy to provide.

On rainy days, when the pickings in Grosvenor Square were lean, he would volunteer at one or the other kitchens. He was never comfortable about his future. One day he could need a meal or a place to lay his head, so his thought was to do what he could, when he could, to pay in advance. For the time being fortune seemed to by smiling on him, though he never completely let his guard down. It was one thing to put the past behind you, but that doesn't always guarantee you'll be able to outrun it.

"Thank you, mum." Ernie said taking the plate from her hands. "I'd be a right fool to pass up a meal like this."

Mrs. Chapman looked at Patterson's half eaten breakfast and then at him. Before her one eyebrow reached the final height of its destination, Patterson quickly stabbed one of the sausages and took a healthy bite. With a satisfied nod of her head, Mrs. Chapman tucked the tray under her arm and retreated into the kitchen.

"Looks like neither of us are completely free," said Patterson, giving Ernie a wink.

When they finished, Patterson excused himself from the table. He had mentioned during the meal he intended to look over the notes from an old case.

"Could I be of any help?" asked Ernie.

"No." Patterson softened the abrupt response with a pleasant but vague follow up. "Just an old case I happen to be thinking about. No sense us both wasting this brilliant day."

"Well, I've a mind then to enjoy the rest of this beautiful morning with a walk up to Regent Street and maybe a chat with a new friend."

"A new friend? Well, an even better reason to exclude your participation in what is going to be nothing more than a dusty bit of the gloomy past. Go on, we'll catch up later."

Ernie soon found himself on the pavement taking in a deep breath of the morning air. After a long exhale, Ernie gave a wink and a nod to a group of tourists who passed him on their way up Conduit Street. He followed along behind them. In the old days he would be sizing them up, determining which pigeon he would pluck first. He laughed a bit to himself noticing a half-opened purse dangling from the shoulder of one of the women in the group in front of him. When they stopped at the corner he intended to suggest she consider a few basic security measures while walking about London. His attention shifted when he noticed a familiar face looking back at him. It was Inspector Flannel. Ernie's first thought was to cross over and avoid adding a sour note to an otherwise splendid morning, but the inspector seemed to be making an uncharacteristic attempt to secure his attention. Ernie continued up the street.

"Nice to see you again, Inspector Flannel," Ernie said, holding out his hand to greet him.

"You'll not need bother yourself with forced pleasantries," the inspector grumbled.

"I can assure you–" started Ernie, but his attempt to persuade the inspector otherwise was met with a wave of the inspector's hand and a grunt. This was followed with a jerking motion of his head, indicating Ernie was to follow him.

Ernie quietly followed along next to the inspector, waiting patiently for some indication or reason for his cloak and dagger behavior. It was too nice of a morning to worry about what might be on the inspector's mind; Ernie was quite certain he would find out in due time.

Inspector Flannel was about six foot, with a long drawn face. Bushy eyebrows hung over two slits where his eyes were assumed to be. His hair was short, receding and as coarse as his demeanor. A thick gray mustache concealed his thin lips and curled down at the ends giving the appearance of a perpetual frown. A gruff, casehardened man, he was the last of the traditional breed of inspectors that helped establish the untarnished reputation for justice that is synonymous with Scotland Yard.

Inspector Flannel was well known for his austere countenance. He had no interest in the common man, save a portentous nod in response to a greeting on the street. Even his most casual of statements carried with them a bristling effect, leaving the recipient at odds whether to answer or retain legal council before confirming something as innocent as the time of day.

The inspector saw things in black and white. You were either a citizen or a criminal; there was no grey area. Reformed or not, in the eyes of Detective Inspector August "Derby" Flannel, once a criminal, always a criminal. His long years with the Yard only served to reinforce his belief, so amending it to accommodate collaboration with Ernie was going against every fiber of his being.

Patterson and the inspector were long time friends, having shared military service attached to the Green Howards. They have since worked together on many occasions- Flannel in an official capacity and Patterson as a consultant. He did his best to soften him up about Ernie. For every bit of progress he would make, the harsh cruelty Flannel was exposed to in the course of executing his duties as a police officer chipped away at his arguments. Still, progress was being made and the possibility of redemption was close at hand, as Ernie was about to find out.

"This will do," grumbled the inspector. He pointed to a small café with tables spilling out onto the pavement. The inspector indicated his desire to take a table tucked back in the corner of the shop, but Ernie had other ideas. He slowly sat down at an empty table outside, an action that was met with a piercing stare. There was dead silence between the two men.

An attractive young woman with raven black hair, sporting an assortment of bangle bracelets, walked up and broke the silence; in effect making up the inspector's mind about the seating arrangements. "There's a good bloke. Too nice to be inside a stuffy old shop. Seems your friend here has the right idea." She finished by giving Ernie a wink and nudging the inspector back toward the table where he was seated.

"Two coffees, Luv," Ernie said through a flirty smile. "And maybe a couple of those cranberry scones."

The young woman returned an inviting smile, turned and retraced her steps back toward the kitchen area as she wrote the order.

"I half thought you might not wish to be seen with me," said the inspector, grudgingly taking the seat across from Ernie.

"Why ever would you think that?" Ernie was genuinely confused, as the look on his face must have expressed. "I have a great deal of respect for you, inspector."

"No reason," Flannel replied. For an instant there was a glimmer of appreciation in the inspector's eyes. He opened his mouth to begin, but then looked about the café as if searching for another alternative to what he was about to ask. With a deep breath he finally got around to the point of their meeting. "I'll be blunt, Bisquets. I need your help with a very delicate matter."

"My help?" Ernie puffed. "Shouldn't you be talking to His Lordship? After all, Patterson Coats is your friend."

"That's exactly why I can't ask his help," replied the inspector. He pulled a newspaper from his coat pocket and placed it down in front of Ernie.

As the coffee and scones arrived, Ernie scanned the headline and the accompanying story. He shook his head as he read; the tragic end to such a young life had an unsettling affect on him. When he finished, he leaned back in his chair, pushing the paper back over to the inspector.

"This is horrible," said Ernie tenderly. "But why come to me and not His Lordship?" He paused for a moment. A thought rushed into his head, leading him to continue with a rather indignant tone. "You can't possibly think he could have had something—"

"Easy now, Bisquets," interrupted the inspector. "Nothing at all like that."

"Well if it ain't that, then what?" Ernie's tone had tempered to a polite sharpness.

The inspector looked around, making sure he could continue without fear of being overheard. "I'm going to tell you something, but I'll need your assurance you'll not breathe a word of this to Patterson. I'm not looking to raise any trouble between you and he, but this is a police matter, and for the time being, I would appreciate this staying between us. I'll tell Patty what's going on when the time is right, but for now, it needs to be this way. Have I your word?"

The confused look was back below Ernie's furrowed brow. "His Lordship has been right kind to me. I'll not spoil that by going behind his back, police business or not."

"I'm not asking you to do anything behind his back. I'm only asking for your help in verifying a few facts concerning this young woman's death." The inspector underlined his point by tapping on the headline facing Ernie.

Ernie glanced back at the paper, drawing it closer for a second look. One item in the article caught his attention. Ernie turned the paper back toward the inspector, underlining an additional point by tapping his own finger on the article. "It says here the investigation is being handled by Detective Inspector Wynne Godfrey?"

"That's right," replied the inspector. "There are circumstances involved that are keeping me at arms length for the time being. I can assure you, I'm keeping Godfrey informed of everything I'm doing, including this little chat with you. He's a good man, Godfrey, and he understands what I have to do. Now, have I your word?"

Ernie slowly rested back in his chair, looked up, and reluctantly nodded his head.

"What I'm going to tell you should make clear my reasoning for enlisting your services without Patterson's knowledge." The inspector leaned in close and continued in a hushed tone. "He and I have a mutual acquaintance, though we have very different opinions of the man. Years ago, there were a series of murders I was investigating. My suspicions concerned this mutual acquaintance, though I was never able to prove anything. Due to an unwelcome political intrusion, I was abruptly removed from the case. As a result, those murders remain unsolved to this day."

Suddenly, Ernie put the pieces together, as was evident by a gasp and the startled look on his face. The inspector raised his hand and nodded his head, indicating Ernie's understanding of the circumstances was accurate and that he should allow him to continue.

"You see," the inspector continued, leaning back in his chair, "this is why I can't involve Patty in this matter."

Ernie thought the matter over for a few minutes. "But what can I do?"

Once again, the inspector leaned in close before speaking. "The victim's name was Mary Walsh. All I need from you is to find out if she was ever connected with an escort service. It would be a high-priced group, with a very elite clientele, if that's any help?"

"You still think that MP had something to do with those young women murdered years ago? I remember those crimes. Terrible they was. Wasn't right what they did to you in the papers. *Just doing your job*, I thought back then. Still do."

The inspector slapped his hand down on the table in frustration, startling Ernie and a half dozen sleepy coffee drinkers seated at the surrounding tables. The inspector just glared at the people now looking at him until they went back to their quiet conversations, affording him a moment or two to regain his composure.

"Sorry, Bisquets," said the inspector. "Some old wounds have a tendency to fester."

"Quite alright, Inspector. My fault, really." There was a short silence between the two men while Ernie contemplated the inspector's situation. "Of course, I'll help if I can. Quite frankly, I'm a bit proud you'd ask my help."

The inspector nodded his head in gratitude. He reached into his pocket, pulled out a folded piece of paper, and handed it to Ernie. "All her particulars are on there."

Ernie took the paper, briefly glanced at the contents, and tucked it into his pocket. He took one last sip of coffee and stood up, an action followed quickly by the inspector.

"Bisquets," said the inspector, stopping Ernie from turning away by taking his arm. "Thank you."

A smile came to Ernie's face. He was surprised by the genuineness in the inspector's eyes. "I've not found anything yet, Inspector, but rest assured, I'll do everything I can."

"I have every confidence you will." The inspector tucked the newspaper back into his pocket, put a £10 note down for the coffee and scones, and bid Ernie goodbye.

Ernie started on his way back to Conduit Street, looking back only once. The inspector was gone, but he caught the eye of the young girl clearing the plates from the table. Her bright smile reminded him why he needed to help the inspector–that might have been her in that article. He was keen to chat her up, the main reason he ventured up for coffee in the first place, but this business with the inspector was now going to delay that plan. She gave a modest wave, promising another day might bring with it the opportunity to get to know her better.

6/ A Table for One

Not everyone found the bright sunshine of interest that Saturday morning. On a picturesque street facing Sloane Square stood a proud row of 5-story, redbrick, Victorian town homes, highlighted with tan bricks between stories and ornate terra cotta friezes to further enhance the grand structures. On the second floors, delicate wrought iron railings wrapped around slender oriels, which rose up from beneath the pavement below. White marble stairs led visitors up to the front doors, tucked neatly back from the street within small, pillared porticos. Window boxes, overflowing with petunias in an assortment of colors, gave further definition and a sense of warmth to the majestic row of homes.

In one such home, at the end of a dining room table cast in shadow by heavy tapestry curtains still pulled tightly shut, sat Lord Alfred Raventhorn impatiently tapping his long skeletal-like fingers. Below the table, hidden beneath a bump in the rich oriental carpet, was a large button. The top of the mound had been worn smooth from use. It could be reached with the outstretched foot of the person sitting at the head of the table, and, once pushed, rang a bell in the kitchen. The proper use would be to discretely signal the desire for having the next course served during a dinner party, but that morning it was being used to repeatedly summon Prophet Brown from the kitchen. More coffee. More toast. More juice. More sausages. More of anything Alfred Raventhorn could think of, one miserable thought at a time.

A Tiffany lamp on the sideboard between the two curtained windows cast barely enough light to read by on the table. It was enough though to make out the sharply defined features of Lord Raventhorn. He was a tall man, of thin but grand presence, a feature that served him well through his many years as an MP. His thick, gray hair curled out from his head, allowing only a slight glimpse, in the right light, of a small bald spot developing in the back. Course, black, bushy eyebrows hung heavy over dark eyes, held in place by high cheekbones. A pointed jaw competed with an equally pointed nose, separated by thin lips curled down in a perpetual scowl. In complete contrast to his severe countenance, he was well liked in Parliament and considered a charismatic addition to any social function. A crisp, white shirt and regimental tie peeked out from a blood red dressing gown with black velvet lapels.

Raventhorn was a relic of the Victorian era, steeped in long since amended traditional values, and compounded by his own revised version of proper social behavior. He held tightly to the rigid line of authority of the past, keeping a well-defined line between himself and those beneath him. The hosts of a social event would find him a charming and eloquent conversationalist, while the wait staff would find him a contemptuous snob. The latter traits were not unfamiliar to Prophet Brown.

A determined stare swung back and forth like a tree swing from the kitchen door to the clock on the mantel. His nostrils flared with each short, labored breath. As the seconds ticked by, his tapping became louder, adding dramatic percussion to the measured tone of the clock. Add to that the continuous muffled buzz of the bell coming from the kitchen and you have the baleful tempo of a dark orchestral intro for a tragic opera whose curtain was about to rise on act one.

"Sorry! Very sorry!" huffed Prophet Brown, his timid voice obscured by the rattling of china on the silver tray he carried to the table. His deformed hand and clubfoot further enhanced the task, lending a Dickensian texture to the scene. "Broke the first two eggs. Had to make new ones. Here now. Everything hot."

Prophet Brown placed the tray down on the table between the first two side chairs of the long dining table. Leaning over the first chair, and stretching out his arm so as to keep his face out of reach in the event his tardiness was met with a hand of disapproval, he carefully placed the breakfast plate on the charger in front of Lord Raventhorn.

Raventhorn continued to tap his fingers until Prophet had finished setting his place and refreshed his coffee. "Sorry you will be when I deduct the cost of those eggs from your pay packet this week."

"I'll not waste them, sir," Prophet replied, his nervousness exaggerating his head tic as he slowly drew back from the table. "They'll be my breakfast. Not a bit of waste."

Raventhorn casually brushed at the napkin on his lap. "It's a wonder I haven't found myself in the Welfare queue having supported you all these years. Instead of applauding my beneficence, the Fates have seen fit to punish me day after long laborious day with these antics of yours. And what do I get from you for my charity?" He pierced the yoke of his egg with the pointed, tobacco-stained nail of his bony index finger. "Cold eggs and burnt sausage."

"Sorry. They came right from the pan. Hot they were, very hot. I'll just—"

Prophet leaned over the chair as he spoke, attempting to remove the breakfast plate, an action that was abruptly halted when his wrist was grabbed. Raventhorn squeezed tightly as he pulled Prophet closer, the carved chair back pressing hard against the crippled arm curled up on Prophet's chest.

"You waste any more food," Raventhorn said, his words drawn out slowly, allowing the sharp edges of the chair back to administer a fitting punishment, "and you'll be owing *me* money by the time this meal is finished."

"Yes, sir. Yes," Prophet winced, never once looking up into the eyes that stared coldly down at him. "I'll just heat this up. Only take a minute."

"Don't bother." Raventhorn pushed him away, releasing his grip. "I've gotten quite used to your inept domestic abilities, so I'll suffer through yet another meal."

"As you wish, sir." Prophet picked up the tray and started back toward the kitchen, his clubfooted stride more awkward as he backed away from the table. He timidly continued, "Very sorry."

"Prophet," Raventhorn called out, never looking up from his plate. "Where were you last night? I was out late and came home to a cold house."

"Went to the late service at Christ Church," Prophet said. "Spitalfields. Long walk back. Stopped for a pint."

Raventhorn responded with a harrumph, "You'll have nothing for yourself when you reach my age if you continue to frequent the pubs. I thought I told you to stay away from that section of London? You bring nothing but trouble to yourself there. Those pubs are filled with the wrong sort, looking for any dust up to impress the shameless tarts clinging to their arms. You're an easy mark for that lot and those bruises only invite more."

"Sorry, it's my old parish. It won't happen again. I'll find a church close by."

"See that you do." He looked over at Prophet and continued, his eyes drawn into long slits. "I have guests coming this Wednesday evening. We'll have dinner for 3. You'll serve promptly at eight o'clock. I've left the menu on the counter in the kitchen, so I suggest you purchase what's needed. You'll dress accordingly, serve the meal, and then stay in your room until my guests have left. I may be going out afterwards, so I'll expect a warmed brandy on my return. Is that understood?"

"Very good, sir." Prophet nodded his head briskly, eager to please His Lordship. "Promptly, sir. And warm it will be. I'll not disappoint."

"As if that were at all possible," Raventhorn mumbled slowly to himself, turning back to his breakfast. With no further comment on the meal, he opened the morning paper Prophet had placed on the table alongside the place setting. The toast made it to within an inch of his mouth when an article in the paper caught his attention. He read the particulars with great interest, pausing twice to confirm he was alone in the room. When finished, he folded the paper, rose from his chair, and walked over to the fireplace. He unfolded the paper, taking one last look at the headline and committing the reporter's name to memory. Satisfied, he tossed the paper into the flames. The fire flared up as the paper combusted.

Raventhorn leaned on the mantel, staring into the flames as the account of the murder was reduced to ash. "He'll think twice this time before pointing a finger at me. It just might be time for him to suffer a loss of his own."

Slowly, across the room, the door to the kitchen that was slightly ajar silently closed.

In the quiet of the darkened room, Lord Alfred Raventhorn returned to his breakfast, staring in contemplation between the fireplace and the kitchen door Prophet had disappeared through.

7/ Splitting Hairs

"You wanted to see me, sir?" asked Flannel, taking a seat in front of the Chief Detective Inspector's desk.

CDI Hardgrave looked up from his paperwork and nodded toward a newspaper on the desk in front of Flannel. "I suppose you've seen that?"

Flannel knew exactly what Hardgrave was alluding to. He casually nodded.

Hardgrave rested back in his chair. "So. I have no need to worry about you stirring up the dregs of an old, sour case?"

"I was first on the scene, but after realizing the similarities with that other business, I was quick to call Godfrey in on the case. I've no reason to wrap that noose around my neck again for no reason."

"I've known you a long time, August," replied Hardgrave, not completely convinced with the response. "It would give me no pleasure being forced to take your badge. If you step over the line this time, you'll be hoist with your own petard. Do we understand each other?"

8/ The Copper Needle Pub

"Bisquets? Is that you?"

"Why sure it is," said an older woman to the man behind the bar. She was a cheery, stout woman, dressed in black with a white apron. She looked over from a table where she was placing empty glasses on a wooden tray and continued, "Who else could such a handsome lad be, John?"

It took a moment for Ernie's eyes to adjust from the bright afternoon sun, but he quickly recognized the familiar voice and large presence of the woman in front of him. He gave her a wink and a nod, an action prompting the woman to rush over and respond by wrapping her arms around him as if she had years ago left him for dead. She took Ernie by the arm and walked him the rest of the way to an empty seat at the bar.

"How long's it been?" said John, placing a pint of beer down on a coaster in front of Ernie. "Heard talk you gave up the old trade. Not Bisquets, I says. He's a fondness for pockets which ain't 'is. Ain't that right, Fie?"

"Right you are, John," replied Fiona through a laugh. She gave Ernie one more hug, catching him by surprise and almost spilling his beer. "They'll be stitching their pockets shut one day if they want to keep what's theirs out of yours."

John cheerfully wiped the bar down in front of Ernie. "Two years if it's been a day. You're a sight for these tired eyes, you are. Ain't that right, Fie?"

"Two years? Maybe two." Fiona leaned in close, an action drawing her husband in as well. "Heard you took residence up at Edmunds Hill for a stretch. Rumor said that nasty bloke set you up for a few quid." The two paused, looking at each other with a reassuring nod, then returned to Ernie. "Don't blame you. He ain't one to cross, that one. Either way, you're 'ere now and don't look a bit worse for the wear."

"Not at bit," said John, returning to the glasses he was drying when Ernie came in. "Ain't right doing such a thing for a few quid, treating you like he did. Ain't that right, Fie?"

"Don't be too hard on him," said Ernie. To anyone else asking, Ernie would have dismissed the conversation, but John and Fiona were like family. "Turns out he did me a favor. Can't say as I like the way he did it, but a favor none the less."

"It's a forgiving man you are, Ernie Bisquets," replied Fiona. "Always a good word for everyone, even those what don't deserve it. We don't get many like you in here. Ain't that right, John?"

"Right you are, Fie."

Ernie's stay at the prison in Suffolk was more a badge of honor in their circle, certainly nothing to be embarrassed about. Where it becomes an issue is the lingering shadow it casts to the rest of society, and in particular, Inspector Flannel. He smiled and gave a nod of thanks to his old friends. There was no reason to explain the rest of the story, so he left it at that for the time being.

John and Fiona Grimbald have owned and operated the Copper Needle pub on Fashion Street for as far back as the locals could remember. It was always a pub, nestled into the Southeast corner of the first floor of what used to be a leather tanner and boot factory. As urban decay crept up the narrow street, John and Fiona reluctantly acquiesced to a life of serving pints and meager meals to a handful of locals oblivious to the current state of the neighborhood. On occasion, young tourists, looking to get away from the more commercial pubs and higher prices of London proper, would stumble upon their little establishment. Fiona cheerfully welcomed everyone equally; John was more reserved with his acceptance.

The main building, a two-story, redbrick factory, ornamented with sandstone Moorish arches darkened with age, was long past its value as a local employer. It sat abandoned for years, with only the dim, flickering light from an Abbot Ale neon sign in the curtained window of the Copper Needle expressing any form of life.

Over the last two years, a chattering of young entrepreneurs were eager to breathe new life into the once proud building. They power washed the neglect of the past from its mortar and swept out the rusted piles of hobnails. The long empty shell was quickly divided into workshops occupied by artisans engaged in ornamental ironwork, expressive pottery, and elegant handmade jewelry made from precious metals and stones. The street was alive again with the tinkling of hand tools and the chatter of travelers congratulating each other for their good fortune in finding such a brilliant treasure in a most unlikely place.

John and Fiona were quietly enjoying the new income generated by the artisans moving in around them. Some of their regulars, mostly those of questionable character, were not so fond of the intrusion. To them, this little slice of the past was a safe haven, too obscure to be a blip on the radar of the local police. New faces meant new awareness, and new awareness brings with it temptation for others looking to plunder the once safe haven.

For the time being, a pleasant nod passed from face to face, as the old and new harmoniously, yet separately, shared a pint within the brick walls of the Copper Needle.

"We've baked cod if you fancy a meal," said John, taking a glass from the bar sink and drying it. "Fie's special recipe you know. 'Course it comes with chips . . . and I was just about to fry up a new batch." John slid open the door of the refrigerated glass case at the end of the bar where the food was kept. "I've got one thawed fresh this morning I was saving for meself. Wouldn't be right, it wouldn't, not to offer it to you."

Ernie smiled, waving off the offer. "Thanks, but I had a bite earlier."

"It's there if you change your mind . . . unless I get a bit peckish, aye." John was as solid as a brick, with a squeaky laugh that always made Ernie smile. His ruddy complexion glowed in the dim light of the pub, his light green eyes sparkled when caught at the right angle, and then disappeared into deep slits when his cheeks drew out a smile. He picked up the bar towel and went back to drying the glasses. "Now, what brings you here on this bright Monday afternoon?"

"I'm pretty sure he's here to buy a pint for his old mate."

All three looked up to find a bulky chap with dark, short-cropped hair staring at the group from the open door of the pub. He shared the same solid structure as John, blocking out most of the bright sunlight behind him, but carried an expression that assured anyone contemplating crossing him he knew how to handle himself. Not many crossed Dragonetti, at least not a second time. He walked over to the bar and brushed at the sleeves of his coat as he spoke. "John, I'll have what Bisquets here is having. Fiona, always a pleasure to see your smiling face."

Fiona had anything but a smiling face on as she watched the huge man take the seat next to Ernie. She wasn't one to intimidate easily. "The way I sees it, you should be putting a few quid on the bar to cover Ernie's pint. Wasn't right what you did, and don't think I don't know it. Sent him up to Edmunds Hill, you did . . . and for what, a few quid? I've half a mind to show you the door."

"That's a bit harsh, Fie, isn't it?" Dragonetti's sincere response was soft and in complete contrast to his large frumpish appearance. If they didn't know better, it might even have seemed remarkably convincing. "I've done this lad a good turn. He wouldn't be enjoying the life he has now with that little group of toffs he's taken up with if it wasn't for me. And mind you, I've asked nothing in return for my trouble."

"You've asked nothing, *yet*," replied Fiona sharply.

Dragonetti answered with a quiet laugh, sipping at the pint John placed in front of him. An awkward silence hovered over the group. With a slight jerk of his head, John suggested Fiona meet him at the other end of the bar. Fiona wasn't keen to the idea, but a wink and nod from Ernie assured her she had no reason to expect any trouble.

Satisfied they could speak privately, Dragonetti began, "So, I heard you wanted to see me? Usually the Guv'nor calls me directly when he needs my services. I know it ruffles his collar having to call me, but I'm surprised he would send an *employee*. Least he could do is send a good-looking bird."

"He doesn't know I'm here."

Dragonetti stopped in mid-sip, put his glass down and looked over at Ernie. "What is it you're up to, Bisquets? You'd be a right fool to bugger up that nice little situation you got going. Mind you, I've a great deal of respect for your employer. He pays well and never asks about my methods. I've a stake in this too, so I'll ask you politely again, what is it you're up to?"

The idea of dealing with Dragonetti was bad enough, but being scolded like a petulant child was quickly eroding the civility Ernie promised himself he would maintain. He took a deep breath and forced a smile. "I just need a little information, that's all."

"What kind of information?" Dragonetti asked, running his finger slowly around the rim of his glass.

"You know that young girl they found in the alley?"

Dragonetti hesitated for a moment, but then continued to circle the rim. "Friday night, over there off Brick Lane?"

"That's the one."

"What is it you want to know?"

"I believe her name was Mary Walsh, at least that's what the police think."

"Pretty thing, she was. Chatted her up a few times."

Ernie looked up with surprise. "You knew her?"

"That's not what I said, Bisquets. Go on."

"The police think there is more to this than just a random attack on a young woman."

Dragonetti shot his hand up, abruptly stopping Ernie's explanation. "By *police*, do you mean old Derby Flannel?"

Ernie just nodded his head. Dragonetti had no love for the inspector, or a desire to help him in any way. He pushed his pint toward the back rail of the bar and stood up. "This is a new low even for him, sending the likes of you to extract information from me. You might be in bed with Flannel, but I'll not soil my sheets with the likes of him. You'd be wise to do the same."

"Wait," Ernie pleaded, as Dragonetti lumbered to the door. He strained to keep his voice from attracting any more undo attention than Dragonetti's size already had. "I'm not doing this for the inspector. It's about this *Slasher*, that's all. I'm afraid he'll strike again if something isn't done."

This last statement stopped Dragonetti. *Slasher?* He turned, returning to his seat next to Ernie and pulled his glass back over. "This is more about those murders 8 years ago than it is about that young woman the other night, isn't it?"

"Yes, I'm afraid so. The inspector has always felt responsible for letting that murderer slip through his fingers."

"As well he should," said Dragonetti through a contemptuous smile. "Buggered it all up, he did. Flannel still thinks that MP, Raventhorn, had something to do with all that business? Bit of a Jekyll and Hyde is it?"

"Something like that." Ernie paused for a moment, confused about Dragonetti's sudden interest. "It was his man Prophet Brown that found the body Friday night."

"Well, that's a bit much of a coincidence, even for Flannel." Dragonetti took a few large gulps and finished his beer.

"Prophet Brown thought the same thing. He's scared to death. If Raventhorn is murdering young women again, what's to stop him from doing the same to Prophet?"

Spying the empty glass, John started back to where the two men were seated. Dragonetti looked over, waved him off and turned his attention back to Ernie. "So what is it you want from me?"

"Mary Walsh. Flannel thinks she's hiding a past, a past that might link her to the MP and perhaps those old murders." Ernie fumbled a bit looking for the note Flannel gave him. He pulled the piece of paper from his pocket and read the particulars from it. "He says she had a flat over on Newcomen, right by the Kings Arms. He can't officially look into this, not without raising suspicions around Raventhorn again. He's also afraid Raventhorn might murder again and use the past accusations by Flannel to keep the police at arms length."

Dragonetti sat quietly for a few minutes staring at his empty glass, ignoring the paper Ernie held out to him.

"You say Prophet Brown found the body?" Dragonetti spoke softly, staring at the bottles on the shelf in front of him.

"Yes. It really upset him. He called the inspector first thing."

"Does Raventhorn know about this?"

"Not that we know. Inspector Flannel isn't in charge of the investigation. He's quietly conducting his own without the knowledge of his superiors. For the time being, there is no suspicion being cast on Raventhorn. I've not even told the inspector I was going to ask your help."

Dragonetti sat quietly contemplating the last few facts. "Right. I'll see what I can find out about Mary Walsh. If there's a past, I'll find it." Dragonetti stood up and finished with one last question. "So why hide all this from the Guv'nor?"

It took a moment for Ernie to answer, surprised by the sudden change in the attitude and willingness of Dragonetti to offer his help with such little persuasion on his part. "He and Raventhorn are mates."

Dragonetti laughed. "It's a dog's breakfast for you on this one. I'll contact you in a couple days."

"Thanks," said Ernie, holding out his hand.

Dragonetti glanced down at the outstretched hand, ignoring the gesture, then up at Ernie. "Just pay for the pint. Don't think this makes *us* mates, Bisquets. I've got my own reasons for doing this. I've known Prophet Brown since he was a young lad. Think what you might, Bisquets, but I'm not without a heart. Ain't right how he treats that lad. Ain't right at all. If he wasn't an MP . . . " Dragonetti finished his thought by clenching his fist and pounding it down on the bar.

Ernie gave a nod of appreciation and turned back around, watching Dragonetti's reflection in the mirror as he walked out. John and Fiona waited to be sure he was gone before they came back to where Ernie was seated.

"What did he mean about enjoying the life you have now with that little group of toffs?" asked John. His normal jovial look was replaced with a serious, contemplative stare.

Ernie didn't wish to lie to his friends. Although he was quite proud of his transformation to the right side of the law, he worried what effect this news might have on his old mates. He didn't want them to think him a snitch. His ability to walk the streets of his past life was an important aspect of his new position. It was certainly something he couldn't jeopardize. On one hand, he felt he was betraying their trust, but on the other hand, he knew what he was doing could help bring the murderer of that young woman to justice. He did his best to mask a doleful expression as he started to explain.

"An important swell approached me after my release from prison. He's in the antiques business. Travels a bit, he does—him and his group that is. On occasion he handles 'delicate' matters for other swells, even the Royals at times, who would rather not have their business put about. The Guv'nor even helped me with an early release from prison. It seems my particular talents come in quite handy in this line of work."

A big grin returned to John's face. He leaned in close, an action that drew Fiona in as well. "So, you're stepping up in the world, aye. Working for a top fence is nothing to be ashamed of. Why, I always said old Bisquets would make a name for himself. Ain't that right, Fie?"

"Quite respectable, I'd say, John."

"That's it, respectable." John gave a sharp nod of his head to confirm his approval. "Just the right situation for a man of your talents. I often mentioned to Fie I always knew you was all class."

John and Fiona's misconception of his new situation brought relief and a smile to Ernie's face. "You'll keep this between us?"

"Like he has to ask," John replied looking over at Fiona and rolling his eyes. "Ain't that right, Fie?"

Fiona responded by once again wrapping her arms around Ernie, almost pulling him off his stool. "You'll not be a stranger, now, will you?"

"I forgot how good it was to share a pint with you two." Ernie pulled a £5 note from his pocket and placed it on the bar. "You'll forgive my absence then?"

"Nothing to forgive, Bisquets," John replied, pushing the fiver back at Ernie. "Stop by again on a Friday night and you can buy your old mates a round. You know we still see some of the old crowd. Always asking about you, they are. For now, put that back in your pocket."

Ernie smiled and picked up the fiver. Before he could do anything with it, John took hold of his arm.

"I worries about that Dragonetti," said John, careful not to be heard by a few of the regulars who had sauntered in. "You watch out for him. He's trouble that one. He sold you out once for a few quid, no telling when he might do it again. Ain't that right, Fie?"

Fiona had one last hug left over which she quickly wrapped around Ernie. "John's right, you know. His sort can't be trusted."

"I'll be careful," said Ernie. He gave John a wink and nod. "I'll be back later in the week. Keep a bit of that cod handy."

Ernie shook John's hand. He gave Fiona a peck on the cheek, tucking the fiver into her apron pocket; a gesture he was sure would bring a smile to her face later when she found it. The bright daylight cut a bold slice through the pub as he opened the door and headed back to Conduit Street.

9/ Getting Things in Order

It was that quiet time between lunch and the dinner meal when Ernie returned to Conduit Street. The flat was remarkably somber, almost churchlike. The second floor foyer was sun-dappled, with the muted colors reflecting through the cut-glass dome above drifting down the satin covered walls, finally being absorbed into the intricate pattern of the Fereghan Sarouk rug. A particularly soft orchestral tune floated gently on the air through the flat, so soft to obscure any attempt to identify the actual opus, and leaving the individual with no other choice but to just enjoy the serenity of its presence.

Patterson was busy cataloging notes and sundry artifacts that had been cluttering his desk for months since his return from Cairo. The small, white museum boxes that occupied one corner of his study were now visible on his desk, being fitted one by one to hold the delicate artifacts his group painstakingly sifted out of the sand. He heard Ernie come in, followed by the echo of his footsteps in the cavernous hall. Catching a glimpse of him passing by the door of the study, Patterson paused only long enough to call out a quick, "Hello."

Ernie returned the greeting and continued down the hallway. In the kitchen, Mrs. Chapman could be heard singing one of her usual Irish ditties, accompanied by a symphony of clattering china and a chorus of copper pots and ladles.

Ernie was helpful by nature, a trait often commented on by one or the other of his mates. Not offering assistance to Patterson with his cataloging wouldn't raise an eyebrow. It was something that had been explained to him in the past as being a solitary endeavor and one that required concentration. But scurrying past the kitchen door, like a child hoping to conceal his muddy trousers, would surely raise the alarm with Mrs. Chapman. Not wanting to draw any unwanted attention to himself, Ernie pushed open the kitchen door just enough to poke his head in. "Anything I can do to help, Mrs. Chapman?"

She turned and greeted the offer with a bright smile, giving a lyrical response. "It's always a kind one you are, Ernie, for asking. I'm just relining the cupboards. No need to trouble yourself. Dinner's in the oven. All's right with the world."

"I'll just have a look at the paper then and see what the world's been up to. Or maybe close my eyes for an hour or so. I didn't sleep well last night."

Mrs. Chapman put the pot she was polishing down on the counter and looked over at Ernie. "Nothing wrong, I hope? I'll put a pot on if you're in the mood for a chat."

Mrs. Chapman was more than just the housekeeper and was very protective over her charges. She had incredible intuition and could sense the slightest ripple of concern. Knowing when not to intrude was also one of her finer traits. She was particularly attentive to Ernie's moods, being aware of the past baggage he brought with him.

Ernie, realizing he slipped, smiled and waved off the offer. "No need to trouble yourself, just a bad dream. Besides, I wouldn't think of interrupting your concert."

Ernie finished with a reassuring wink, but had his doubts about whether she believed him.

In her best motherly fashion, she accepted the explanation, drawing out a soft smile beneath understanding eyes. Picking up the pot in one hand, and waving the polishing cloth about like a conductor with the other, Mrs. Chapman returned to her song. Ernie laughed and slowly withdrew his head.

Ernie made his way up the stairs and down the hall to his room. He was still struggling with the decision to hold back his recent activities from his benefactor. Dragonetti's warning, though brutish, played over and over in his head. Despite the promise he made to the inspector, if asked a direct question by Patterson Coats he resigned himself to the fact that he was not going to lie. If that meant suffering the wrath of Inspector Flannel, then so be it. He was prepared to accept whatever consequence might arise from his action. With the goose down pillows propped up against the carved headboard, Ernie kicked off his shoes and stretched out on top of the comforter to think things through. It wasn't long before he drifted off to sleep.

* * *

Patterson Coats was enjoying this well deserved down time from the international travels, dusty crypts, and hot hotels rooms that were usual to his professional life. Getting twenty or thirty small artifacts cataloged is a tedious, but relatively easy, task, unless curiosity gets the better of you. Patterson invited curiosity's intervention. He had no reason to hurry, intending to take full advantage of the situation. Having the time to take a second and more deliberate look at these treasures from the past was an opportunity not often afforded.

The day waned on. The two London Philharmonic CDs Patterson had put on earlier were on their third encore. What was once a bright, sunlit room was now cloaked in an evening shadow, except for the desktop. The clutter was awash with the soft glow from a matched set of bronze Tiffany lamps with caged amber glass shades. An illuminated magnifying lamp clamped to the edge of the desk added additional light and accommodated a closer inspection when needed. With its arm extended, the lens hovering between Patterson's face and the priceless objects below, the cataloging continued without interruption.

It wasn't difficult to lose all track of time inspecting each one of those remarkable objects in such a manner. Marveling at the craftsmanship. Questioning its use or significance. Collectively, these artifacts help define a civilization long past, but, individually, they are the sole remaining evidence of the artist who created them. This artist, whose existence may have been insignificant to his contemporaries, used nothing more than rudimentary tools and transcended time. Though his name may never be known, his skill as an artisan will secure him a place of honor in one of the British museums. Over time, millions will admire the work he intended for the eyes of only a select few.

With his sleeves rolled up, a fresh supply of index cards and small museum boxes, and a journal filled with copious notes relating to the particulars of each of the objects at hand, Patterson went about his task. One by one, he inspected each object, confirming then transferring his notes onto a card—adding any additional findings his inspection may have uncovered. He finished by tearing away pieces of foam inside the box to allow a somewhat form-fitted resting place for the artifact. Each object had its own story to tell, with a promise not to disappoint. Patterson listened intently as each dusty narrative unfolded before him. With the story revealed, he slid the top onto the box and moved on to the next story.

The phone rang, startling Patterson, causing him to clumsily mishandle the faience ushabtis he was inspecting. With his grip quickly restored, and his attention still engaged with the small funerary object, he tapped the speaker button on his desk phone and gruffly said, "Yes?"

"Bonjour, Patterson," a low, sweet voice answered. "Have I called at a bad time?"

Patterson paused, very much surprised by the caller, but recognizing the soft-spoken voice and slight accent immediately. "No. No, not at all, Marie. I was just cataloging a few objects we brought back from our last dig. Usual nonsense, nothing I can't put aside. This is a delightful interruption."

Marie Bussière was the acting curator of the Musee d'Orsay in Paris. She was attractive, intelligent, and shared the same intense interest in archeology as Patterson, though she was confined to an office at the museum. The twenty-year difference in their ages had little affect on their feelings for each other. She adored Patterson, and he, her. The romantic journey they had mapped out for themselves so many years past, filled with the anticipation of a lifetime of joy, had been derailed by the long months of absence his work demanded. She was content and patient in awaiting each return, but this was not the life he wanted for her. In gallant fairness, but struggling with great regret, Patterson broke off their engagement. Marie was reluctant to accept this fate at first; assuring him his concerns were unfounded. He insisted. The decision wounded both in the beginning, but over time was healed by the devoted friendship they vowed to maintain.

Each went their separate ways, promising to stay in touch as often as possible. A few years later, Marie married an academic named Marc Lafarge. They kept a flat in Paris, enjoyed the theater and fine wine. Both loved children, but they were never able to conceive a family of their own. Marc became a teacher at a respected primary school in the La Rive Droite quarter of the city. Marie accepted a position with the Musee d'Orsay on the Rue de Lille, eventually elevating herself to her current position of acting curator.

Patterson became more involved with his work for the museums, interspersed with the occasional delicate matters brought to him by the Crown or the police. There were many times over the years when business brought him to Paris. Each trip was filled with eager anticipation of calling Marie, but each arrival brought yet another reason why he felt it was best to leave her to her new life. To compromise, he would call her at the museum on his return, never mentioning the trip.

Through it all, Patterson's feelings for Marie never diminished. He was afraid, if given the opportunity, he would not give a second thought to ruining another man's marriage if it meant getting back the woman he still loved so deeply. And what of Marie's feelings? Did she share his desire to rekindle their love? Would she be just as willing to walk away from her husband of so many years? These questions and more drove back his desire to pursue her. Keeping a safe distance between them was his only chance if they were to have any type of relationship.

He buried his feelings for Marie deep inside, hidden away from the temptation to rekindle what they once shared. Marie believed it was love she and her husband shared, and perhaps in the beginning it was. Unbeknownst to Patterson, the passing of time was relating a different story, the final chapter of which was about to unfold.

There was hesitation in Marie's voice as she answered. "I was just thinking about you, that's all. You're busy. We'll talk later."

"Not so fast, young lady," Patterson quickly replied, reacting to the tug of an underlying current he felt prompted the call. "Is everything all right?"

A brief pause.

"I'm fine, mon amour. I just wanted to hear your voice."

Compassion tempered his concern. "Fine, is it? You know I adore the sound of your voice, it whispers at your every thought, your every mood. As flattered as I am over the idea of you longing to hear the course tone of my voice, we've known each other far too long to act like bashful schoolmates alone for the first time. You never need a reason to call, but I sense there is one today."

Another pause.

"I've left him, Patterson. I've left Marc." Her voice crackled as she spoke. She was unable to hold back the tears.

Patterson waited to respond, giving her time to collect herself. He understood from previous conversations with Marie that she and Marc had problems, but nothing that seemed out of the ordinary for a married couple. What he wasn't aware of was the extent of Marie's unhappiness. With each passing year, Marie and Marc shared less of a life together, with Marc finally taking a position at a small university outside of Paris. He kept a flat near the school, spending the weekdays there. At first, he was back in Paris for the weekends, taking the late afternoon train in on Friday's from Aubergenville. It slowly progressed to every other weekend, a result, he explained to Marie, of added class responsibilities. After six months, he was coming into Paris only one or two days a month. Marie was accepting at first, her work at the museum kept her occupied through the week and they spoke often. As time wore on, and the phone conversations became less frequent, she began to not care if he made it back to Paris at all.

"What can I do?" Patterson replied softly.

"I don't know. You'll think me foolish, crying like this over a man for whom I have such little feelings left."

"Not at all, Marie. You were married for twelve years. Walking away is not an easy decision. I would be more concerned if it didn't affect you this way. I assume you've told Marc."

"Oui. He was in Paris Saturday. I told him over lunch."

"How did he take the news?"

There was another pause, followed by quiet sobbing.

Patterson didn't wait for an answer. "Maybe we should put this aside for now. What's done is done. My concern is you. I have nothing holding me here in London at the moment. I can be in Paris on the morning train. Perhaps the shoulder of an old friend will help ease this pain?"

"I want to see you, but not in Paris. I have an important installation going on right now in the museum. It will be completed by Wednesday. I have a symposium I am to address in London on Thursday evening. If you could put up with the teary eyes and runny nose of a foolish girl, I can be in London by nightfall on Wednesday?"

"I'll let Mrs. Chapman know you'll be arriving then. You'll find an ample supply of tissues and a large rubbish bin waiting." This last remark prompted a small laugh at the other end of the phone. "That's better. Wednesday it is. You let me know when you'll be arriving and I'll meet you at the station."

"Au revoir, mon amour."

"Au revoir, Marie."

The phone went dead. Patterson rested back in his leather chair, lost in thought, all but forgetting about the little statues waiting patiently amidst the papers and boxes on his desk. A light tapping at his office door broke his concentration.

"Pardon, sir," said Mrs. Chapman, "I've a knife-and-fork tea waiting. Will you be coming out?"

"I'm sorry, Annie, I didn't realize you were there. Supper you say? Yes, I'll be right there."

"Very good, sir." Mrs. Chapman smiled and turned away from the door.

"Annie," Patterson called out. "Marie will be coming on Wednesday and staying for a few days. Would you mind making up the guest room tomorrow?"

"Oh, it's a lovely child she is. A pleasure to have her here in London with us."

"I'm afraid life has been less than kind to her this past year."

The bright smile drifted from her face. "Nothing serious, is it?"

"Serious enough. She has left her husband."

"The poor child. Not to worry, I'll make her stay a pleasant one."

Patterson smiled and rose from his chair. He walked over to the doorway and put a hand on each of Mrs. Chapman's shoulders. "How could anyone have less than a pleasant stay here with a wonderful woman like you to look after them?"

Mrs. Chapman blushed, her rosy cheeks drawing a large smile out across her face. "It's ever so kind you are, sir."

"Well, let's not waste another moment standing here when we could be enjoying the meal at the other end of that delicious aroma. I saw Ernie a few hours ago. Will he be joining us?"

Mrs. Chapman looked up toward the stairs and then back at Patterson. "I was just about to wake him. Said he didn't sleep well last night and thought a nap was in order." She lowered her voice and continued. "He says all is well, but I've a notion there's something troubling the lad."

Patterson raised an eyebrow and smiled. "I'm sure you'll get to the bottom of his sleep disorder, soon enough."

"Why, whatever do you mean, sir?" replied Mrs. Chapman as innocently as she could.

10/ Coffee, Scones and Bisquets

For the most part, the evening meal was filled with conversation centered around the artifacts Patterson had been working on all day. His enthusiasm was not lost on Ernie and was a welcome diversion. Despite a lack of formal training in antiquities—and an accumulated knowledge drawn only from participation in a 3-month dig in Cairo—Ernie was quite pleased with his education to date. He considered himself a quick study, and was pleasantly surprised at how genuinely interested he had become in Dynastic Egypt.

Patterson also filled in the basic details about the upcoming visit from Marie. She met Ernie not long after his arrival from prison. She originally chastised Patterson for his method of enlisting his services, especially for throwing him headlong into the Musee d'Orsay affair, which almost cost him his life. By the time it was resolved, and after spending a little time getting to know Ernie, Marie realized Patterson's intentions far outweighed her concerns.

The conversation concluded with Patterson mentioning the article he had read in the paper concerning the murder in Brick Lane. Ernie gave only a brief acknowledgement of the facts and made a hasty retreat to the coming weather.

With coffee served, and Mrs. Chapman occupied once again with her pots and pans, Patterson settled back into his chair. It didn't go without notice that Ernie seemed a bit uneasy during breaks in the conversation, fidgeting with his napkin, brushing at crumbs that weren't really there. With just the two of them at the table, his actions were that much more conspicuous. He would now and then sit upright in his chair and take a deep breath, giving every appearance of intending to interject something important into the conversation. Each time, nothing more than a refrained exhale came out, followed by a relaxed lean back into his chair.

Patterson waited patiently, giving no indication of concern for Ernie's erratic behavior. To ease the situation further, Patterson would toss an odd fact or two into the conversation about similar figures he had uncovered over the years. Ernie smiled and listened intently, but the cause of his concern tugged endlessly at his brow, hinting at the overall uneasiness beneath.

The nervous fidgeting displayed in Ernie's actions was very out of character for an accomplished, though recently retired, pickpocket who relied on steadiness. To a lesser man, the commanding presence of Patterson Coats could be extremely intimidating. If it was anyone else fidgeting at the table that just might be the case, but not so for Ernie. Ernie was as comfortable with Patterson Coats as if he had known him since he was a wee lad. They quickly gained a mutual respect for each other. Ernie was filled with gratitude also, commenting often to himself on how kind the Fates had been to provide such a fine benefactor. Even the embarrassment he once felt over his incarceration in Edmunds Hill had diminished. Patterson understood how difficult the transition could be for Ernie. One doesn't just drift from one side of the law to the other. It's a commitment to a course correction, steering away from the known world, and heading toward an unknown point just beyond the horizon. Patterson summed it up nicely during their dig in Cairo over a cheeky glass of port, " . . . a past is nothing more than the notes life scribbles in the margins of a map. It's the final destination we set for ourselves, and what we learn along the paths of that journey, that determines the person we eventually become." All of these lofty thoughts and ideals Patterson had shared with Ernie were now tugging at his conscience.

Ernie kept telling himself he had no reason to feel he was being deceptive, though his outward appearance fought back every attempt. With the exception of his first few days at Conduit Street after his arrival, Ernie had never felt this uncomfortable with anyone. This was *just another meal*, he said to himself. Just another of many meals and conversations he and Patterson had shared since taking up residence on Conduit Street.

"You know, she's on to you," said Patterson.

"S . . . Sorry," Ernie stammered, realizing he had been staring off into the room. "Someone's on to me?" Ernie paused for a moment to collect his thoughts. "I'm very sorry, sir. It's just that—"

Patterson raised his hand, interrupting Ernie's would-be confession that longed to burst forth from his lips. "I said that just to make you aware that the devil himself couldn't hide his intentions from Mrs. Chapman. Nothing more. You're entitled to your privacy, and she wouldn't think of intruding on that. Nor would I. If, or when, you feel compelled to share whatever has your attention, we are both at your disposal. Don't do it out of some foolish idea you are obligated to answer to me. You've earned your place at this table; you owe no one for that, including me. If you are indeed the man I know you to be, I trust you will determine what's right and act accordingly. Now, if I go on any more we'll have to move this conversation to Speaker's Corner."

Ernie smiled. He once again sat upright in his chair, a look of relief returning to his drawn face. Before he could respond, Mrs. Chapman came in from the foyer. Her purposeful gait, and the troubled expression, was enough to gather the attention of both men.

"There's a man at the door—big one he is—asking to see Ernie. I asked what it was in reference to, but he said it was of a 'private nature'." She leaned in close between the two men and continued in a whisper, "He's a gentle voice, though he has the look of a brute. Don't like the look of him one bit. Says his name is Dragonetti. What should I tell him?"

Ernie did what he could to hide the surprised look on his face.

Patterson leaned in close himself, amused by Mrs. Chapman's impression of their visitor and a sudden desire to hold the conversation in secret. "Well, Dragonetti, is it? A bit of a brute you say? Your instincts serve you well, Annie. Not to worry though, Ernie and I are very familiar with the gentleman in question."

"Gentleman?" Mrs. Chapman huffed. "You calls him a gentleman, I calls him trouble."

Patterson smiled and rested back in his chair. "Ernie, why don't you run down and see what brings him to our door? I would say it's most important if it has brought him here unannounced."

Ernie nodded his head, and quickly made his way through the doorway, down the stairs, and out the front door. There, waiting patiently with his hands tucked into his coat pockets, was Dragonetti.

Mr. Hayball, from the stationary shop next door, was just closing up for the evening. He was taking in his sign when he noticed Ernie coming through the arched doorway next to his shop. He was already suspicious about the large man lurking about with no particular interest in exchanging common pleasantries, so much so that he hastened his step to get back inside and lock the door as quickly as possible. Upon seeing Ernie, he slowed down his pace. Suspicion quickly turned to curiosity. It was certainly a pleasant enough evening. The type of evening one might fancy polishing up a storefront. Mr. Hayball decided this would be an opportune time to brush away the dust and grit thrown up by the traffic that settled along the ledges below his front windows. He was particularly concerned with the window closest to Ernie and his rather dubious visitor.

"What are you doing here?" asked Ernie coarsely. He kept his voice low so as not to be overheard by Hayball. "What will I tell the Guv'nor?"

"You're a clever lad, I'm sure you'll think of something. Now, you asked for my help, so do you want it or not? I've a mind to go about my business before I regret getting involved with this nonsense of yours."

Ernie looked over and saw Hayball had been inching closer to where they were standing. Hayball was a large man himself, so he had little chance of being inconspicuous. Ernie gave a quick jerk of his head at Dragonetti. "I think it would be best if we take a walk up the street."

"Up the street it is. I'd fancy a nice cup of coffee up at that little café. I don't get over this way much, but when I do, I makes it a point to stop in there for a cup."

The two men started on their way up towards Regent Street. Mr. Hayball, disappointed in the results of his intelligence-gathering maneuver, decided the ledges were just fine and closed his shop for the evening.

Ernie was very familiar with the coffee shop he mentioned. It was the small café just around the corner where he and Patterson made regular visits for coffee on Saturday mornings, and the very place where Inspector Flannel lighted the fuse to this little matter. As anxious as he was to hear what Dragonetti had to say, he wanted to wait until they were at least on Regent Street before getting into the details. The traffic noise would certainly drown out the conversation, making it impossible for anyone to eavesdrop. Ernie knew he was being overly cautious, but he thought better cautious than having something in their conversation end up on a city editor's desk. On top of that, his idea to quietly look into this matter for Inspector Flannel was starting to unravel. Getting Dragonetti involved was beginning to look more like a mistake.

They were soon standing by the tables on the pavement in front of the café. Ernie's new problem was the attention Dragonetti's size was calling to the two men. Fortunately, Dragonetti was quite adept at mustering a piercing stare when needed. It was quite handy at keeping the curious from taking a second look. The two men took a seat at a table set back against the windows of the café, separating themselves from the other patrons with a few empty tables.

"I'm seeing quite a bit of you lately."

Ernie turned and recognized the voice as the same young waitress from the other day, smiling, ready to take his order. Her hair was black as a raven's breast, with bangs cut straight across. Resting just below were kind green eyes, an impish nose and deep red lips. Ernie nodded, returning the smile, as did Dragonetti. Neither accepted the offer of a paper menu.

"Two coffees, is it?" Her bracelets jingled as she scribbled the order, not waiting a moment for any confirmation. "Where's your other mate? You know, not the policeman, the older, handsome one? But don't tell him I said so, he's ever so polite and I certainly wouldn't want to give him the wrong idea. Besides, given the choice, I'd rather see more of you than him."

The remark brought a blush and a smile to Ernie's face. "That would be Patterson. He's been busy with his museum work. I'm afraid you'll have to settle for me."

The waitress winked. "Maybe I can find a couple of fresh cranberry scones you like to go with those coffees?"

"That would be delightful, young lady," replied Dragonetti, laughing a bit to himself over the awkwardness of Cupid's latest targets. "I can see now why Bisquets here finds this fine establishment so irresistible."

Dragonetti's size and somewhat threatening appearance had little affect on the young girl. She acknowledged his remark with the same cheerfulness and without the least notion of uneasiness. There may also have even been a blush of pink in her cheeks over the remark.

She turned her attention back towards Ernie. "Bisquets?" she said, tucking her order pad into her apron pocket. "That's a bit unusual, innit. I like it. It fits a distinguished looking gent like yourself. I'll just get those coffees."

"I think that bird kind of fancies you, Bisquets," said Dragonetti with a smirk. "Twenty-five I'd say. A bit old for my tastes, but attractive just the same."

Ernie looked into the café where the young girl had disappeared and then back at Dragonetti. The same touch of pink lingered for a moment on Ernie's cheeks, then quickly vanished. "I'd be much happier if we confined our conversation to whatever you've found out about Mary Walsh. It's bad enough you showed up like you did. I don't need dating advice, just a few answers and we can go about our separate lives."

"There, there, now Bisquets, just an observation." Dragonetti seemed genuinely hurt by the dismissive tone in Ernie's voice. "I thought a little chitchat might be nice while we waited for our coffee. You seem like an okay sort, thought it might be nice to just share a bit like a couple of mates. We'll have it your way then. Lets get to it and I'll be on my way."

"Sorry," Ernie replied, leaning forward and resting his elbows on the table. "You're doing me a favor and I've shown little appreciation for it. It's not your fault this mess I'm mired in."

Dragonetti waved his hand and shook his head, dismissing the thought. His sour expression softened to one of charity. "You know, Bisquets, you ain't such a bad lad. Mind you, I don't do favors for just anybody. We're not so different, you and I. Despite our chosen *professions*, we both have a moral code we live by. When something ain't right, it's unsettling. I sense your problem ain't this girl's death old Flannel has you looking into. It's the Guv'nor, isn't it?"

Ernie just nodded his head in response.

"Take this for what it's worth. I wouldn't lift a finger to help anyone on *that* side of the law—anyone except the Guv'nor. He's a fair man, that one. He's done me a good turn or two, and I him. You just do what's asked of you and he'll understand."

"Here you go, gents." The waitress had returned, placing two coffees down on the table. She grabbed the creamer and sugar from a table near by. "I'll just see about those scones."

She lingered at the table for a moment, giving Ernie another smile, and then she was off to retrieve the aforementioned baked goods.

The big man smiled at the look on Ernie's face. Even Dragonetti wasn't immune to the affect a young girl's smile can have on a man's heart. "I'll tell you this, if you don't chat her up, I will. Mates or not, that's a bird one of us should get to know better before the week's out."

Ernie stammered a bit, trying to conceal the obvious attraction and making some feeble excuse about how he had to take care of this business about the murder first. Dragonetti responded with a restrained laugh, falsely furrowed brow, and patronizing nod of his head.

"Well, I guess we better get down to it then," said Dragonetti, retaining the same determined glare. He looked over Ernie's shoulder and saw the waitress was making her way through the tables. "Far be it from me to stand in the way of cupid's arrow. Just one last thing before we start."

Before another word was said the waitress had returned, placing a plate down in the center of their table. "Here you go." She leaned in close, whispering into Ernie's ear. "They're the fresh ones. The ones the owner takes home to his wife." She stood up and gave Ernie a playful wink. "Will there be anything else?"

"Thank you," replied Dragonetti, holding back his amusement. "I think we're just fine now. These look delicious."

The young waitress started to turn away when Dragonetti tapped her gently on the arm. "There is one other thing. We were wondering, that is, my friend here was wondering what your name is?"

Her eyes lit up at the question. She looked right at Ernie and blurted out the answer. "Vicki. Victoria, actually, but my friends all call me Vicki."

Ernie was flush with embarrassment, struggling to get a few words out in response. "Thank you, Vicki. It's a pleasure to meet you."

Vicki smiled, patted Ernie on the shoulder in a, I-hope-I-see-you-later way, and moved on to a couple at another table who had spent the last few minutes waving to get her attention.

11/ The Curious Tale of Mary Walsh

Dragonetti shook his head and laughed as he waited for Ernie to drift back down from the cloud he was resting on. "Mind you," Dragonetti started, adding a fifth package of sugar to his coffee, "you're not to ask me how I came about this information. You take it for what it's worth and do with it as you please. I don't want any of this to wash back on me. The last thing I need is your new inspector mate getting the idea I'm involved in this somehow. Understand?"

"You have my word."

Ernie pulled his chair closer to the table as he waited for Dragonetti to continue. The big man stirred his coffee slowly, as if divining the proper way to begin.

"She's a puzzle this Mary Walsh," said Dragonetti, content his thoughts were in order. He picked at one of the scones as he spoke, examining each tiny morsel for the small bits of information he was seemingly extracting from each. "She was well known around Spitalfields as Mary Walsh, but her full name was Mary Walsh Trevor. She came to London from Cornwall about a year ago and settled in Southwark, not far from Guy's Hospital. A quiet sort, but always a kind word or a smile for those she passed."

"Trevor, you say?" Ernie took out a small notepad and pencil, making notes as Dragonetti continued.

"Miss Trevor was in her late twenties, and quite a looker I might add. She attended Cornwall College, eventually graduating with a journalism degree from Falmouth College of Arts. From what I gather, she traveled a bit after college, writing essays for various magazines under the name of Mary Trevor. I did manage to come across a few articles she penned for one of those crime magazines. You know the type, speculation on sensational murders, stirring up rubbish about unsolved crimes splashed across the headlines. The ones the old crows like to read and gossip about over tea. Details are a bit sketchy about exactly what brought her to London, but I've been pondering my own theory on that."

This last morsel captured Ernie's attention. He looked up, his eyes wide, his brow raised in eager anticipation of the forthcoming theory. But Dragonetti was not ready to oblige. He was methodical when investigating a problem, examining and cataloging each fact for its relevance, storing away the bits and bobs to be assembled later. As a result, Dragonetti was not a man to be rushed. When he was ready, and not before, he would slowly expose each bit of information, much like a workman would carefully peel back layers of old wallpaper to reveal the character and tastes of the previous owners. Accurate and precise, there was never a question about the certainty of the facts he presented, though he had a flare for the dramatic when finally reciting the collected work. In that regard, he fancied himself a bit of a raconteur. When he was fully prepared, each fact neatly threaded together with the next, he would rest back in his chair, sip at his coffee and casually disclose the details of his story.

Under any other circumstances, Ernie would be amused over such a bizarre behavior as Dragonetti's flare for dramatic recitation, but not this time. He'd been wrestling with regret from the moment he consented to help Flannel. His patience was fast approaching its limit and he wanted more than anything to bring his participation in this business to a close as quickly as possible. These thoughts were all tied together with a neat little determined stare and the rhythmic drumming of his fingers on the table.

Dragonetti continued at his own pace, ignoring Ernie's impatience. "Like I said, the best I can determine is she took that flat on Newcomen about a year ago. It was about that time she found a situation as a secretary for Hanson and Bloom, an accounting firm over on Bishopsgate. It's situated not far from where her body was found. From all outward appearances, she led a pretty quiet life, contradictory to the usual hectic social life of an attractive, intelligent woman her age. She had regular habits, so says the old woman in the flat next to hers. Out for work everyday by eight, back with a bag of fresh groceries by six. Never any how's-your-father going on, never any noise or trouble. Didn't see her much on the weekends though, claimed she was a homeminder out in the Lake District. On occasion, usually once maybe twice a month according to this woman, your girl would step out on Saturday night dressed to the nines."

Dragonetti took a long draft of coffee, gave a slight laugh and continued. "Played havoc with the old crow's sleeping habits. Kept her up to all hours, peering out the window, hoping to catch a peek at who her suitor might be. Each time, she came home alone. Here's where it starts to get interesting. I happened to mention her name in passing to a couple ladies I know in the escort business." Dragonetti leaned in close, raising an eyebrow in defense of what he thought was a hint of disapproval on Ernie's face as he explained. "Here now, Bisquets, don't think they're on the knock. Nothing sordid about their dealings, mind you, all top-shelf birds with looks and brains. It's a respectable service what provides important gents with attractive companions for social events. These ladies knew

Mary, and I can tell you, they are a bit unnerved by her death. It seems Flannel ain't the only one connecting her death with those other women murdered eight years ago."

Dragonetti returned to a more relaxed pose, contently sipping at the cold remains of his coffee as he watched Ernie hurriedly jot down these latest facts.

"So, there is a connection," Ernie mumbled, not looking up from his notepad. "Is this the same agency the other women were connected to?"

Dragonetti closed his eyes, pondering the question for a moment. He lowered his head, slowly brushing at the table with his fingertips as if paging through a dusty old book for the facts. "If I remember the details correctly, there were three escort services connected with those other murders—Kelly & Kemp, Littlebury Associates, and Chamber Escorts. That last one's the one you want. That's the one what employed Miss Mary Walsh Trevor, and two of those previous victims. My two lady friends also hired out for them on occasion. You can see why they've had the screaming abdabs since reading about this business off Brick Lane."

"This is brilliant!" Ernie cried. His outburst drew a few curious eyes in their direction. A quick, threatening glare by Dragonetti sent the lingering stares back to their own business. "Was she ever hired out to Raventhorn?" Ernie continued, lowering his voice to just above a whisper. "If we can make a connection between her and the MP, it might be enough for Inspector Flannel to make a case to get himself reassigned. Then I'll be done with this."

"That's for you to find out. I've done my part."

"What do you mean?" asked Ernie, surprised at the abrupt halt in the flow of information.

"If there's a connection to be made, those ladies I mentioned would know. I asked, but I didn't get much change out of them. I believe you may have more luck when you meet them at the George Inn." Dragonetti gave a wink. "Money for jam for a bloke with your talents."

"Meet them at the George Inn?" Ernie's voice once again drew a few admirers. "What do you mean?"

Dragonetti laughed. "Would you rather they show up at your flat? That certainly would leave you snookered with the Guv'nor, wouldn't it?"

Ernie was gobsmacked by the suggestion. Having the women show up at Conduit Street was beyond the scope of anything he could possibly imagine. Dragonetti's appearance at their door was bad enough–the plausible explanation of which will certainly be keeping him busy on his walk back–but he was paralyzed over this new suggestion and the absolute mess such an unexpected visit would leave in its wake. So preoccupied was he that he didn't even notice Vicki standing next to him, or her polite inquiry regarding the untouched and cold state of his coffee.

She smiled at Dragonetti and walked back toward the kitchen area, only to return a moment later with a fresh pot of hot coffee. She replaced Ernie's cup with a fresh one, making another attempt to engage him in conversation. "Everything all right here, luv?"

Ernie looked up with a sociable but confused grin and nodded.

Dragonetti felt obliged to offer his own explanation, though not at all related to the actual cause or reason for Ernie's confused look. "I made the mistake of mentioning to my friend here that such a lovely creature as yourself would most surely have a boyfriend. As you can see, he didn't take to the idea very well at all."

Dragonetti's cheeky remark slapped the confused grin off Ernie's face, quickly replacing it with the flush look of embarrassment and casual innocence. He managed to stammer out a few words in reply, attempting to retain at least a small portion of the unassuming nature he walked in with. "I'm sorry, Vicki. My friend here is–"

Vicki laughed, the blush returning to her cheeks. She bent over close to Ernie's ear and softly replied, "No worries, luv. It just so happens I'm between blokes." She turned to walk away, then stopped and turned back. "And I love a good stage play, if you feel so inclined yourself."

For a brief moment a smile returned to Ernie's face as he watched Vicki make her way through the tables and back to the kitchen area.

Dragonetti responded with a hearty laugh. "There you go. Get this mess in Brick Lane figured out and you'll have a nice bit of crumpet waiting for you."

Ernie just shook his head. He wanted to be angry with Dragonetti, but the idea of a date with Vicki defused any lingering irritation for the moment. Putting the suggestion aside for the moment, he addressed the original call to action. "So when are we meeting these lady friends of yours?"

"There is no *we*," replied Dragonetti, rising from his seat. "I'll give it a miss, thank you very much. It's a charmer you are, Bisquets. You don't need me. You'll do just fine with those two birds. They're real lookers, they are."

Ernie let out a deep sigh and shook his head. "So, when am *I* meeting these two women?"

"You've a 1:00 engagement tomorrow afternoon." Dragonetti drew out a serious look as he continued. "And don't be late. These birds have more important things to do than sit about a pub waiting for the likes of you."

Ernie nodded his understanding with just a slight sneer of irritation over the remark. "George Inn you say?"

"That's right. How I envy you. Nattering over a pint or two can be such a pleasure when in the company of two beautiful women. Independent, too, they've got a bit of dosh and aren't a bit shy about spending it. I'm sure they'll pick up the tab, so order the best. Like I said, you've a clinking good way about you. You'll have this business done and dusted in no time."

Ernie made one final note on his pad and tucked it back into his pocket. "You mentioned you had a theory?"

"Right you are, Bisquets. It seems Walsh's family has quite a bit of dosh themselves. I think it's a bit queer, it is, that Miss Mary Walsh would rather add a few bob to her income working as an escort than enjoy the family money and high life as Miss Mary Trevor. Then there's that penchant she has for writing articles about murders she has no business sticking her nose in. What say you?" Dragonetti reached into his pocket and tossed a tenner on the table. "The coffee's on me. Les Misérables."

"Les Misérables?" Ernie looked up, incredibly confused.

"Yes, Les Misérables. It's playing at Queen's Theater." Dragonetti nodded in the direction of Vicki. "Come on mate, I've done all the hard work for you."

Dragonetti laughed as he walked over to the curb where a few taxis were idling. He got into the first taxi in line. Ernie sipped at his coffee, watching the cab disappear into the stream of traffic.

"I see you brought *him* into it."

Ernie turned back with a start to find Inspector Flannel standing over him.

"I, uh, well I thought..."

Before Ernie could finish, the inspector waved off the attempt, taking the seat across from him. He pushed Dragonetti's cup aside and took out his notepad.

"No need to explain yourself," replied the inspector. "I've asked for your help and I'll not judge your methods. I just hope bringing him in doesn't muddy the waters. Well, what have you found out?"

"Dragonetti said her full name was Mary Walsh Trevor. She's been in London about a year and was a secretary for Hanson and Bloom." Ernie paused; looking around to ensure no one was listening. "You were right," he continued in a hushed tone. "She was an escort at one point. Worked for Chamber Escorts, just like a couple of those other victims."

"I knew it!" Inspector Flannel banged his open palm down on the table, rattling the china and toppling the cheese shaker. "If we can put her in the same room as Raventhorn my superiors will have to listen to me. You've done well, lad, and don't think I don't appreciate it."

Inspector Flannel began to rise, but Ernie took hold of his sleeve and pulled him back down. "There's more, and it's a bit queer. I think you should hear this before you take any action."

This surprised the inspector. He sat back down attentively in his seat, eager to hear the remaining details. "More you say?"

"According to Dragonetti, Mary Walsh Trevor came from a family with money. She had no reason to work as an escort. She had no reason to work at all."

A slight, patronizing smile came to the inspector's face, curling up the ends of his course gray mustache. "Some women do it for the thrill, Bisquets. They like mingling in the right circles. Maybe this Mary Walsh was just looking to find herself a rich husband and caught the eye of the wrong person."

"I don't think so. Tomorrow I'm going to meet with two women who knew Mary Walsh. They work as escorts, too. I'm told this latest murder has their nerves on edge, so I'll see what they have to say about their mate. Dragonetti believes they know more about this business than they were willing to share with him. He set up the meeting for me. I'll report back to you afterwards."

"Fair enough. I'll keep this in my pocket until I hear from you again. At this point we still need something that will to tie her directly to Raventhorn, otherwise she's nothing more than just a new random victim."

"You might think differently when you hear this last bit. Dragonetti put some of the pieces together on his own and came up with an interesting theory. If he's right, she wasn't random at all. He thinks she was poking about looking for the same thing you're looking for."

This last statement got the inspector's complete attention. "The same thing I'm looking for? Come on, Bisquets, out with it."

"She was a journalist."

12/ House of Commons

Second Reading
6.48 pm
Albert Raventhorn (Bermondsey and Old Southwark) (Lab): I beg to move, that the Bill be read a second time.

"As noted in the first reading of this Bill, I intended to draft regulations and procedures that would in no way encumber the Criminal Records Bureau with additional work beyond the basic staffing requirements dictated by their current workloads. This *burden*, alluded to by my honorable Friend in our previous debate, as it has been so interpreted, is not intended to be retroactive in any way, unless deemed prudent by the CRB. The provisions are to define appropriate steps to properly archive each conviction in a magistrate's court from the day forth when it is noted in the statute book, thus rendering this information available on demand to the public *without* burdening an already thinly stretched staff in the offices of criminal records. The Bill asks nothing more but to compile a proper digital archive of information currently residing in the public domain. It further asks that this basic information, and I say basic information because the archive will only record what the conviction dictates and in strict compliance with the Rehabilitation of Offenders Act

1974 and the Police Act 1997, be made available to the general public with substantial cause proven to be in the public interest. This archive, as proposed in my Bill, is not intended to be something casually perused like the agony columns and then gossiped about on the train platform."

Mr. Harris Saynesberry (Basingstoke) (Con): "Your intent is admirable, and I commend my honorable Friend for his grasp of the role technology can play in filtering and bringing forth such information as deemed important to the public safety. My issue with the Bill remains in the prejudicial information such access would grant. A young offender, convicted of a minor offense, can be disproportionately judged because of such a black-and-white database. His prospects of resuming a normal life and once again contributing to society can be stifled by such open access, if not denied completely. You have yet to satisfy this concern. As a result, I cannot yet fully support the Bill as written."

Albert Raventhorn: "To the point my honorable and learned Friend has voiced regarding spent convictions, I will state again that technology will allow the archive to *tag* each conviction with a date of expiry. Those who have been rehabilitated will suffer the yoke of conviction for no longer than dictated by law. Those seeking a second chance are free to do so, but must expect to atone for past sins. And those looking to resume a normal life will need to prove themselves worthy of the public's trust. Let us not forget, this is an archive of convicted offenses of all magnitudes, perpetrated against the laws of the United Kingdom and the subjects thereof. Its intent is not to step on the rights of one man in order to inform another, but to make such information available to the law-abiding public as a means of comfort in an ever increasing angry world."

It was 7:00 pm, and the Moment of Interruption was at hand. The Adjournment Debate, which followed, did little to hold Lord Raventhorn's attention. He was more concerned with how the weather was holding out. Throughout the session flashes of lightning filled every corner of the chamber, a myriad of color reflecting off the gilded surfaces above the viewing level, bringing about a deathly silence. A startling clap of thunder intensified the interruption, rattling every inch of the leaded windows it burst through, demanding the full attention of those assembled on the vibrant, red leather benches below.

Raventhorn gave little more than a grunt in response to each attempt to arrest his attention. After the session came to a close he found himself outside the main entry doors to Old Palace Yard, cursing the fact he had left home that morning without his umbrella. About seven very wet meters away, close to the bronze statue of King Richard I, Prophet Brown stood patiently by the door of Lord Raventhorn's sleek Jaguar. The umbrella he held over his head had little effect on the drenching rain.

Raventhorn was only a few feet away before Prophet noticed him walking toward the car and pointing at the rear door. As Raventhorn entered the backseat of the car, he mumbled something under his breath, intimating his now soiled Italian shoes were more the fault of Prophet than of nature.

Raventhorn sat forward for a moment, tapping his finger on the seatback near Prophet's soaked shoulder. "Sometimes I believe you deliberately ignore my attempts to gain your attention, especially when there is a soaking rain involved."

"Sorry, sir, I didn't see you there."

Raventhorn replied with a harrumph and settled back into his seat. "Have you acquired the items specified on the grocery list for the dinner tomorrow evening?"

"I have, sir."

"You have your instructions. I'll not have anything spoiled because of your incompetence in the kitchen. Do we understand each other?"

"I had the butcher cut and bind a fine rack of lamb. The salad plates are already chilling and I've polished the serving cart. They'll be aptly impressed, sir. I've taken care of everything as requested. All will be as you like. Not to worry."

"It's your ability to take care of everything that now leaves me with soiled leather Oxfords. I distinctly remember you mentioning this morning the bright clear day I would be enjoying. All is NOT as I like it, is it?"

Prophet glanced into the rearview mirror. A cold stare reflected back, sending a chill up his spine to compete with the one left by his wait in the rain. "Unexpected turn of weather in the North Channel they said. Couldn't be expected. Sorry. I'll have them over to the cobbler first thing."

"See that you do," Raventhorn responded, giving one last piercing glance into the rearview mirror. Not another word was shared on the ride back to Sloane Square.

13/ Tonic for the Soul

The threat of a rainy morning never made it past an ominous gray cloud cover, and soon gave way to a bright afternoon sky. On the south side of the River Thames, just beyond a lantern-topped, wrought iron entrance, the George Inn stood basking in the sunlight which now shone brightly overhead. For centuries, this lively place welcomed both locals and tourists alike, providing comfort without prejudice for those who might care to rest their tired bones. The rows of tables lining the square in front of the black and white façade were beginning to bristle with activity. Small clusters of people were gathering, sifting out slowly from the adjoining lanes and alleys like cats after a rain. Pints were plentiful, the atmosphere Dickensian, and the cod and chips a menu favorite with all who visited this well celebrated, galleried coaching inn.

Stepping inside transported you back in time. Its lengthy and colorful history hung on the walls beneath dark wooden beams supporting low ceilings. Light streamed in through the lattice windows, illuminating the Old Bar where coachmen and passengers once took respite from their long journeys. Arranged around two massive fireplaces were an assortment of tables and chairs, mismatched yet comfy. Voices and laughter intertwined to a level approaching what one might expect at any social function, but not so much as to be a bother. No need for concern over eavesdroppers. Talk as loud as you wish about whatever you wish without fear of being quoted. All the secrets of London melted into one incoherent hum inside the George Inn.

Ernie sat quietly at the corner table closest to the main door, nestled between the fireplace pilaster and the wall, patiently waiting for the two women he was to meet. He sipped at his pint, looking up each time the door opened. Occasionally, he would catch the eye of a young woman entering, only to receive a polite smile as she continued to scan the interior for whoever she was looking for. It was almost 1:00 pm when the room cleared out a bit. He noticed two women sitting at a table across the room staring at him. They spoke quietly to each other, as if deciding what to make of him, and then got up and casually walked over to his table. They glided across the room with an air of refinement, attracting a glance from some and outright stares from others. Both were incredibly attractive and enchanting in ways even a learned scholar would have trouble describing.

Ernie jumped to his feet, almost knocking over his pint. The chair fell back against the wall. He turned and reached to catch it, hitting his head squarely against a wooden plaque designating something or other historic about that particular nook. His clumsiness brought a smile to both their faces. Rubbing his head with one hand, he held out the other and said, "I'm Bisquets, Ernie Bisquets. Are you here to see me?"

The tall redhead whispered one last thought into her friend's ear and then shook Ernie's outstretched hand. "Are you all right?"

"Embarrassed, really. Not to worry; I've a hard head I'm told."

"I'm Diana," said the tall redhead through a cheerful smile, "Diana Parsons, but you can call me Dee. All my friends call me Dee. This is Jacque Laine."

"A pleasure to meet you, Mr. Bisquets," a charmingly shy Jacque added. "It's so good of you to meet with us."

"My pleasure, really," replied Ernie through a modest smile, his hand waving to gain the attention of the waitress. "Can I get you something to drink?"

"That would be delightful. Please allow us to take care of the refreshments," said Dee as the two women took a seat at the table, followed by Ernie. "It's the least we can do for your interest in bringing Mary's killer to justice."

Dee was tall with fiery red hair, straight as the bishop's staff, and held back with a delicate black and taupe pheasant feather, flower Alice band, highlighted with coque feathers. She had intense brown eyes that glistened from the light streaming in through the window and a genuine pleasantness about her that beamed from a bright smile. Jacque was blond, her hair turned in at the shoulders, and a head shorter than her friend; gaining what extra height she could from expensive patent leather heels. She had soft, inquisitive blue eyes, further accentuated by a slight pinkish hue to her cheeks. Both were fashionably dressed—Dee in a cream, Galliano newspaper print dress and Jacque in an off-white, ruffle layered dress by Chloé— both hinting at a longstanding relationship with Harrods and the finer shops Mayfair has to offer. Attractive. Intelligent. Courteous. They were, to all who gazed upon them, everything you would expect of British society.

It was a somewhat uncomfortable moment or two as they waited for their order of two Bombay Sapphire and tonics and a fresh pint of Abbot Ale. Ernie seemed hypnotized, much to the amusement of Dee and Jacque. When the drinks arrived, Jacque was the first to break the awkwardness.

"Terrible thing, this business about Mary Walsh. Just terrible. Did you know her, Mr. Bisquets?"

Ernie opened his mouth but nothing came out. He recovered quickly, taking a sip of his ale to cover the action. The two women waited patiently. They smiled and leaned in close, hoping that might help ease the words out. Nothing.

Dee gave it a go to help the situation. "Is there something wrong, Mr. Bisquets? You seem to be staring at us."

Ernie took another sip of his ale and gave it another try. He stammered a bit, but this time was able to form basic sentences and join the conversation. "Sorry. You're not what I expected. Ernie. Please call me Ernie."

"Well, Ernie," replied Dee cheerfully, "I can return the compliment by saying you're not what we expected either."

"It's . . . it's not that, miss. Sorry. I didn't mean to say . . . it's just that . . . you know . . . Dragonetti and all."

Jacque and Dee both laughed, settling back in their chairs in a more relaxed manner. Dee replied, her look shifting to one of repugnance, "Dragonetti. He makes my skin crawl, that one. He's handled *security* at a few functions we've attended and he thinks it gives him the right to chat us up like we're old friends."

"I can tell you this," Jacque chimed in, "we're not here because of any obligation to that brute. We're here because he said you were helping the police solve Mary's murder."

"Yes. Yes, that's correct." Ernie sat up attentively; his thoughts finally back on track. "Detective Inspector Flannel of Scotland Yard has asked me to help. He believes this might be more than just a random murder. I was hoping you could give me a bit of background about Mary Walsh Trevor."

This last fact raised an eyebrow on both women.

"How do you know about her last name?" asked Dee.

Ernie took out his notepad and read from the pages. "I have here her full name was Mary Walsh Trevor from Cornwall. She was a secretary for Hanson and Bloom for the last year, and I understand she worked for the

Chamber Escort service also." Ernie paused, closing his notepad and placing it back in his pocket. "It's a bit queer, the rest. Her family was well off, landed gentry they say. And it seems she had her degree in journalism. She didn't seem like a woman who would need two sources of income. For that matter, she didn't seem like a woman who would need one source of income. I was hoping you might have additional information about that?"

Jacque's expression changed to one of somber reflection. "She was a beautiful girl. Full of life. We met her right here, early autumn of last year. Dee commented on a hat she was wearing, very striking. It led to a cheerful conversation, lunch, and a new friendship. She lives— lived—on Newcomen Street, around from Guy's Hospital. She came from money. Old money." Jacque looked up at Dee and smiled sadly. "She tried to hide it, but we could tell."

"We feel somewhat responsible for her death," replied Dee quietly.

"Whatever do you mean?" asked Ernie, quite surprised by the remark.

Dee slowly stirred her drink. "Mary was intelligent, attractive, and very inquisitive about the service. We met her here a number of times for lunch. She always asked about our weekend engagements. Where did we go? Who were we with? She was well mannered, articulate and carried herself with grace and dignity. It was our idea for her to join the service, and now the poor girl is dead."

"You mustn't blame yourselves," Ernie replied thoughtfully. "There's no way you could have anticipated anything like that would happen. When she first introduced herself, did she use the name Mary Walsh Trevor or just Mary Walsh?"

"Odd you should ask that," replied Jacque. "At first, she said her name was Mary Walsh. After we got to know her a little better, she confessed her full name was Mary Walsh Trevor, daughter to Sir Harlan Trevor. His family made their money during the Industrial Revolution—invented some sort of bobbin used in the millinery trade I believe. Mary said she had a falling out with the family, or some such rubbish. That's when she moved to London."

Ernie cocked his head sideways, like a terrier confused about a command.

"Mary made it a point," replied Dee in answer to Ernie's puzzlement, "to convince us her motive for moving to London was driven by this falling out with her parents. The oddity of the circumstance was that she innocently spent a great deal of time doting over her parents and the privileged life she enjoyed in Cornwall. When she realized the direction of the conversation, and subsequent conflict in her feelings toward her parents, Mary was quick to change her expression from a warm smile to a grim sneer. It was all less than convincing, but we didn't want to press the issue. Mary was a pleasure to spend time with. If she had a secret, we were content to let her keep it or divulge it as she saw fit to do. We all have our little secrets, don't we, Ernie?"

Ernie smiled bashfully. "Some more than others."

"Mary was well liked at her office," said Jacque. "I had occasion to speak with the two managing partners over a legal matter a few months back. They were very complimentary toward Mary, remarking how fortunate they were to find such a levelheaded young woman with such meticulous work habits. Refreshing. Yes, refreshing, that's the word they used."

"One thing I did find a bit queer," Dee intimated. "Once Mary was hired by the service, she seemed obsessed with those murders that took place around Spitalfields eight years ago. I made the mistake of mentioning it one afternoon and she asked a barrage of questions. Her knowledge of the facts pertaining to the murders was eerie. I was quite surprised over the amount of detail she went into regarding the victims and their backgrounds. She was quite apologetic afterwards, but the incident still struck me queer nonetheless."

Ernie sipped at his ale as he pondered these last facts. "I'm not so sure your meeting was as much a coincidence as it was by design. As I mentioned, she had a degree in journalism. It wouldn't surprise me one bit if she was digging around at a story about those murders. It would certainly explain the otherwise random act that left her dead in that alley."

"Whatever do you mean?" asked Dee.

"If I understand you correctly," interrupted Jacque judiciously, "let's suppose Mary Walsh Trevor had uncovered information about those murders—information that could lead to revealing the identity of the person responsible for those murders. If that person made the same connection we did, it would certainly have put her life in danger." Jacque paused, looking over at Dee who was sheepishly ignoring the dotted line being connected before her. "What is it, Dee?"

"I believe there is a great deal of truth in your supposition. I feel just awful."

The waitress came with a tray of drinks, interrupting Dee's statement. All three waited until the empty glasses were replaced with fresh drinks and they could resume their conversation privately.

"What are you talking about?" Jacque asked.

"That's just it," replied Dee, placing her hand on Jacque's arm. "It's what I didn't say. Maybe if I had mentioned all this to you, Mary would be alive today."

Dee started sobbing. Ernie handed her his handkerchief, as he and Jacque waited for her to regain her composure.

Dee wiped away the last few tears and continued, "We were having lunch one day, about two weeks ago I believe. You were held up in court, so Mary and I enjoyed a glass of wine while we waited. Somehow, the conversation drifted into the facts surrounding those damn murders. I don't know what came over me, but I abruptly asked why she was so obsessed with that business. She avoided the question at first, dodging about with this or that. She could tell I wasn't buying it. There was an awkward pause, then, without warning, she confessed her true motives. Our meeting was deliberate and she was a journalist. I think she was relieved having someone to confide in. Somehow, Mary had uncovered a link to those murders eight years ago. In order to confirm her suspicions, she had to become an escort. It was the only way she could get close to the person she suspected without him realizing what she was up to. When she saw you come in that day, she made me promise not to tell you. She knew you would try to stop her. The last thing she mentioned was something about notes she was compiling in a journal. She said she was close."

"Close to what?" asked Ernie.

"I don't know," replied Dee exasperated. "I just don't know. When Jacque arrived, Mary quickly changed the subject."

"Why haven't you gone to the police?" asked Jacque.

"I had forgotten all about it until I read about her death. I'm ashamed to say, I was a bit afraid. Afraid if we got involved we might meet the same end. Whoever Mary suspected was responsible for this despicable business is still out there."

"You have no reason to be ashamed," said Ernie thoughtfully. "This person has proven they aren't to be trifled with. You've done right by Mary now by telling me what you know. I'll pass this along to Inspector Flannel. Just be careful, both of you. If you see or hear anything out of the ordinary, please call me immediately." Ernie handed her his card. "Call that number or come to that address. Even if I'm not there, someone will be able to help."

Dee took the card and placed it in her handbag. Both she and Jacque smiled and nodded their appreciation for Ernie's concern.

"What *did* you mean when you said we weren't what you were expecting?" said Dee to Ernie, signaling the waitress for the check.

"Well, escorts," Ernie timidly replied. The remark drew large smiles out on the two faces before him.

"Escorts, Ernie, escorts," Dee replied, playfully rolling her eyes. "We're not shameless tarts loitering about hotel lobbies. It seems you have us confused with those women of rather questionable morals. There isn't anything sexual about anything we're engaged in. As a point of fact, the slightest impropriety on the part of any of the men we accompany will land them in front of a magistrate. We're pleasant dinner conversation and thoughtful companions for an evening out with English gentlemen whose demanding lives have left them relationship bankrupt. Nothing more."

Jacque felt obliged to further define the difference, being ever mindful not to come across as a slap on the wrist. "Dee's right, there's no impropriety in what we do at all. And I might add, we're both reputable businesswomen. I'm a senior litigator with Anderson & Moody. Dee owns one of the finest millinery shops in London, and lives in a beautifully detailed flat above. It's nestled nicely amongst the bespoke tailors on Savile Row, around from Clifford Street, and holds two royal warrants. Her designs are always a topic of conversation at any social function and can be seen any weekend in the newspaper society pages. She's as well known as most of the men she accompanies."

"Sorry. I didn't—"

Dee waved off the compliment, along with Ernie's attempt to apologize for his innocent indictment. "Jacque's giving me more credit than I'm due. It's a small shop. I'm just fortunate to be able to work at what I love to do and thrilled people appreciate the results. As for the service we work for? Work consumes our lives also. It took a toll on our personal lives, having both lost husbands as a consequence. Jacque and I have no desire to marry again any time soon, but fully intend to continue enjoying the lifestyles we've become accustom to. The service affords us this little indulgence. It's a pleasant respite from our hectic daily lives. We're invited to top social events, meet incredibly interesting men, and travel in all the right circles." Dee settled back in her chair, her brown eyes once again sparkling above a bright smile. "What more could a girl ask?"

The waitress arrived back at the table. Dee held out her hand. "I'll take the check, please."

The waitress smiled, shook her head politely and addressed Ernie. "Your change, sir."

Ernie took his change and handed back a five-pound note. "Thank you, luv. And here's something for the pleasure."

As the waitress walked away, Ernie couldn't help but laugh at the confused look on Dee and Jacque's faces. "Here now, it wouldn't be right two fine women like yourselves buying a pint or two for the likes of me. Don't think I don't appreciate the thought, but I paid enough in advance when I arrived to cover the check."

"Dragonetti was right about one thing," replied Dee, rising from her seat, "he said you could charm the change from a blind man's cup, and now I see what he meant. It seems there's a great deal more to know about you, Ernie Bisquets."

Ernie and Jacque both stood up, Jacque leaning forward and kissing Ernie on the cheek.

Dee followed with a peck of her own on his cheek, taking Ernie's arm in the process. "Promise you'll stop by the shop when you've news about this business. Mary was our friend. Whoever did this must be caught."

"I will," replied Ernie sincerely.

Dee put a small folded piece of paper in Ernie's hand.

"What's this?" he asked.

Dee smiled. "It's our mobile numbers, just in case you have any further questions."

The three made their way out the door, back into the bright afternoon sun. Ernie gave a final wave, watching as the two women disappeared into the crowds milling about in front of the George Inn. He looked at the numbers on the paper, smiled and stuffed the note into his pocket.

14/ A Walk in the Park

Quite pleased with the information he obtained from Dee and Jacque, Ernie turned up Newcomen Street, walking briskly toward Borough High Street. Anxious to share the details of his meeting with Inspector Flannel, he waved down a taxi, giving Scotland Yard as his destination. It was a quick ride through Southwark, then over Westminster Bridge. Big Ben chimed the three-quarter hour past three o'clock as the cabbie maneuvered Parliament Square. The ambulatory of Westminster Abby glistened ahead in the late afternoon sun, blocked partially by the trees surrounding St. Margaret's. Coming around St. Margaret's onto Victoria Street, the traffic slowed a bit, allowing ample space for the tourists milling about Dean's Yard and the Sanctuary. It was a right turn on Broadway and the cab came to a stop in front of the visitor's entrance to Scotland Yard.

Ernie expressed his desire to speak with Inspector Flannel to the policewoman standing watch at the entrance. She was polite, but official, instructing Ernie to see the sergeant at the front desk. Ernie did just that, expressing the same desire. The sergeant tapped at his keyboard, eventually directing Ernie to have a seat, pointing with his pen toward a row of green plastic chairs along the frosted glass wall that looked out along Broadway.

A half hour went by before a policeman approached Ernie. "Are you Bisquets?"

The officer's burly voice echoed down the hall, catching Ernie by surprise. He abruptly jumped to his feet, stammering a bit as he answered, "Yes, sir. Yes, I am. Ernie Bisquets."

Ernie had absolutely nothing to be nervous about, yet he stood there fidgeting like a truant schoolboy caught at the arcade. It was nothing more than a lingering byproduct of his former life, but his nervousness raised an eyebrow on the officer's already suspicious face.

"Are you all right, lad? You seem a bit uneasy. Anything you'd like to confess?"

"No, no, fine really. Just fine. I'm here to see Detective Inspector Flannel. Is he about?"

The policeman gave Ernie a long, questioning glance, finishing with a cordial, though somewhat apprehensive, smile as he answered, "He's out. Said he would contact you later as time permits."

"Very good. Thank you. Thank you very much."

The officer nodded, giving him one last curious look as he left. Once back out in the fresh air, the casualness returned to Ernie's manner. He looked back at the shiny building and sighed. The information he gathered from Dee and Jacque would certainly help with the inspector's case, not to mention possibly freeing him from any further involvement. Somewhat disappointed, Ernie raised his hand, motioning at a cab bobbing in and out of traffic coming up Broadway Street. At the last minute, he changed his mind, waving the cabbie on, an action that prompted a sneer in return. He decided a walk back to Conduit Street was more in line with his current situation. It was not much more than a mile back to the West End. A leisurely stroll would exercise both body and mind, with the derivative effect of building up a good appetite along the way for the exceptional meal Mrs. Chapman had planned for that evening.

A pleasant afternoon breeze made the stroll up Queen Anne's Gate relaxing. The deep green foliage of Saint James Park was visible ahead at the end of the narrow alley adjacent to the private quarters of the St. Stephen's Club. The fresh scent of floral blooms beckoned to those who passed, drawing them through a wrought iron gate at the end of the passageway and across Birdcage Walk. Short iron fences stretched out along the edges of the wide walkways, marked at regular paces with ornamental lanterns atop slender posts. Mothers pushed their prams along, nodding in appreciation of the smiles generated on the faces of the tourists and business folks they passed. Children played together on the soft grass, forming arches with their arms held high, reciting the words to "Oranges and Lemons" as they prepared to capture their next victim. Young lovers casually walked the grounds, stealing a kiss or two when prompted by a silly remark or an engaging view. While still others rested beneath the shade of a Plane tree or Scarlet Oak, enjoying the writings of a favorite author or the company of a friend as they snacked.

Try as it might, nature was unable to capture Ernie's attention. He strolled along in quiet thought, unconsciously returning each cordial glance with his usual pleasant expression. As he mechanically maneuvered his way through small clusters of people and busy intersections his mind was busy elsewhere, cataloging all the information he had for the inspector. Along with that, Ernie was still wrestling with the idea of his actions being deceptive to his benefactor. He was so consumed in thought during his walk that he was quite surprised to realize somebody tapping a finger on the lapel of his jacket.

"You all right, Bisquets?"

Ernie didn't answer at first. Instead he looked from side to side, then up and down the street. Just beyond the rotund body attached to the finger tapping on his lapel, he finally recognized the black Gothic door to his flat on Conduit Street. "Sorry," Ernie stammered. "I'm a bit off. What was it you said?"

"I said," repeated Mr. Hayball brusquely, withdrawing his finger, "are you all right, Bisquets?"

Ernie grasped Hayball's finger and shook it. "Yes, always good to see you, too." Without another word, Ernie stepped around a confused Mr. Hayball and entered his flat.

"Mental, that one," mumbled Hayball to himself, shaking his head as he walked back into the stationery shop.

15/ The Unspoken Word

"There you are, Ernie," called out a cheerful Mrs. Chapman from the other end of the long hallway. She was busy polishing a carved walnut sideboard. "Wasn't sure we would be seeing you for supper."

"What, and miss your Lancashire Hotpot and pickled red cabbage? I think not. I just had a few errands to run. Nothing more."

Ernie wasted no time in assisting Mrs. Chapman with the last bit of her chore. He lifted the large Staffordshire vase, setting it down on the tapestry runner, and moving it about in accordance with the jerking motions of Mrs. Chapman's head. Her rosy cheeks drew up a big smile when just the right positioning was achieved, an action met with a wink and a nod from Ernie.

Ernie took a step in the direction of the staircase, hesitating for a moment before casually asking, "I don't suppose anyone called for me while I was out?"

"I've been here all day, dearie. Anyone special you were expecting?"

"Can't say there is. Just wondering. I'll just clean up a bit."

Before Ernie could walk away, Mrs. Chapman took his arm and sat him down on the chair next to the sideboard. "His Lordship—and no finer man walks this earth—

remarked earlier how something seemed to be troubling you. Concerned, he was, and I can't say I blame him with the way you've been acting the past few days."

"There really isn't–"

Mrs. Chapman took a step back, crossed her arms and interrupted Ernie's explanation with just a determined you-aren't-going-to-fool-me stare.

"I'm working on a case with Inspector Flannel," Ernie finally confessed.

"With my Derby?" Mrs. Chapman was astonished. She was quite aware of the inspector's feelings toward Ernie. She quietly walked in a small circle in front of Ernie, following the fringe around the oriental carpet. Stopping at the outer edge, but not looking over at Ernie, she asked, "He's asked for your help, has he?"

"Yes, mum."

"And you're not to tell His Lordship?"

"Yes, mum. I mean, no, mum."

Mrs. Chapman continued on her way around the carpet, stopping when she made the complete rotation. She looked over at the closed door of Patterson's study and then back at Ernie. "You know, he thought you were in trouble. He thought maybe something from your past had caught up with you and you were embarrassed to say anything."

"Oh, no, mum," cried Ernie, quick to dispute such a notion. "It's nothing of the sort. It's all about this murder off Brick Lane. The inspector made me promise not to say anything to anybody, especially His Lordship. I feel just horrible."

"Well, Derby Flannel has no right to put you in a position like this. Wait till I see him."

Ernie jumped to his feet, pulling Mrs. Chapman down the hall, away from the study door. "Please, Mrs. Chapman, don't say anything to him. He assured me it was a matter of life or death and he gave me a choice to help him or not. He'll tell the Guv'nor straightaway when the time is right. Until then, I hope you might keep this conversation just between us."

"Not sure I like the sounds of this." Mrs. Chapman's irritation eased into a comforting smile. "Well, I guess there's no harm in it. If my Derby has asked you not to share whatever it is you two have been up to, I'm sure he has his reasons. You know, he and His Lordship go back to the days when they traded salutes attached to the Green Howards. Men of honor they are, and neither would raise a hand against the other. You do what's been asked of you without worry. I'm sure my Derby will make it right with His Lordship."

"He'll not be happy. I just don't feel right keeping what I know from him. If it wasn't for him—"

"Rubbish," Mrs. Chapman interrupted, waving her hands about as if swatting flies. "There'll be no more talk about this. Off with you now. Get cleaned up and ready for supper."

"I thought I heard you two out here." Patterson was standing with one foot in the hall, peering out from his half-opened door. "Before you get cleaned up, Ernie, could I have a word with you?"

Ernie looked over at Mrs. Chapman, his expression posing the question. She leaned in close and whispered in his ear, quickly answering the worried look on his face. "Go on. He just wants to know you're okay."

Ernie walked over, entering the study, and finding Patterson seated at his desk. Patterson motioned for him to take a seat in one of the two leather chairs facing the desk. Ernie sat quietly, waiting as Patterson finished packing away what looked to be the last of the funerary objects he had been cataloging. On a sideboard in front of an open bookcase were twenty or so small boxes, sealed and ready to make their final journey to the British Museum. The stark white of the boxes, tied tightly with red twine, caught his attention, standing out against the dusty old volumes in the bookcase they rested against.

"Perhaps tomorrow?" Patterson said, peering at Ernie over the top of his reading glasses, "Perhaps tomorrow you'll help me transport those boxes over to the museum?" Patterson took his glasses off and pointed them at the boxes. "I'll be happy to have my study all to myself again. That's presuming you have the time. It seems you've been a bit preoccupied of late."

"I'm at your service, sir," said Ernie brightly. "Never so busy that I can't put a hand to a chore, especially for you, sir."

Patterson smiled, settling back into his high-backed leather chair. "Brilliant. And, at some point do you think you could call me Patterson?"

"I'll try, sir."

Patterson laughed, closing his ledger and tucking his reading glasses into his top pocket. Returning to a more serious tone he continued, "You know, Ernie, Marie will be here tomorrow. She's been having a bad time of it lately and could use a bit of cheering up. I'm not really at liberty to explain all the details, but there is a personal matter that has drained her emotionally. I just wanted to give you a few background facts in the event her emotions get the better of her while she's with us."

"She's a fine woman, that one. Hate to hear such a thing. It's fortunate she is to have such a fine man as yourself to lend a shoulder when needed. You can count on me, sir, to put a little cheer in her stay."

"I have no doubt you will," replied Patterson, with a satisfying nod of his head. "Now, about this other business."

Ernie was about to get up when this last remark abruptly halted the effort. "Other business, sir?"

"I wasn't going to say anything, but the inspector can't expect you to keep a clear head about you if you're consumed with the idea you're deceiving me in some way, can he?"

"You know?" Ernie slowly sat back down, resting on the front edge of the chair. "Sorry, sir. I wanted to say something, but he said it was better this way . . . for the girl's sake, he said."

"You've nothing to be sorry about." Patterson sat forward, his elbows resting on the desk, his hands clasped below his chin. "What I think about the inspector's suspicions is immaterial. What's important is finding out who was responsible for this despicable act. One thing I can tell you about Detective Inspector August Flannel, he has one of the finest detective minds in all of Scotland Yard. If he believes Lord Raventhorn had a hand in that girl's murder, I have no choice but to entertain the possibility also, no matter what my personal feelings are in the matter. I've read the newspaper accounts of the woman's death in Spitalfields. It smacks of that business eight years ago, so it didn't take much for me to put the two together. That murderer eluded capture then, tarnishing the otherwise exemplary reputation of a fine man."

"It wasn't right what they did to him in the newspapers," Ernie responded determinedly. "Just doing his job, I says."

"I'm afraid I was just as critical," said Patterson apologetically. He settled back in his chair and continued, "I'll not make that mistake again. You do what you can to help him. It cost him a bit of pride, I'm sure, just to ask you for help. I wouldn't be much of a friend if I hampered his investigation in any way, and that includes not questioning *your* motives."

Ernie smiled and stood up. "Thank you, sir. I feel much better now. I've too much to be thankful for just being here. I'll not do anything to spoil that."

Patterson stood up, walked around the desk and put his hand on Ernie's shoulder. "As I said before, Mr. Bisquets, you've earned your place here. Now, what say we both clean up and get ready for that fine meal Mrs. Chapman has simmering in the oven?"

* * *

It was five and twenty minutes past seven o'clock when they finished eating. A fine port was decanted, following Mrs. Chapman's insistence she required no assistance in clearing the table, leaving Ernie and Patterson engaged in a insightful conversation regarding the general state of affairs of the British Empire. Patterson remarked more than once how neglectful he had been in not engaging in such a spirited interaction before that night. He was genuinely impressed with Ernie's view on the current affairs of the day, fascinated at how impassioned he became over some topics, and amused by related anecdotes from Ernie's past that were peppered into the conversation.

"Pardon, sir," said Mrs. Chapman, putting down a tray of custard tarts on the table between the two overstuffed sofas. "Could I borrow Ernie for just a minute? I'll not keep him long."

"Well, of course," replied Patterson, "but I'll not promise there'll be any tarts left if you keep him too long."

Ernie followed Mrs. Chapman into the hall. She motioned with her head toward the stairs leading down to the front door and whispered, "He's down at the front door. Said you wanted to see him. Hush, hush, and all that."

Ernie responded with a laugh. He leaned in close to whisper in her ear. "All's right with the world, *he* knows."

"Off with you then," Mrs. Chapman responded playfully, followed with a sharp slap on the mischievous child's bottom. "It's all a woman can do to keep up with you and His Lordship. Wink. Wink. Nudge. Nudge. Like a couple of school boys after class you are."

Ernie found Inspector Flannel leaning against the white limestone wall, tapping at his pipe as he waited. He saw no reason to inform the inspector of his earlier conversation with Patterson. Instead, he maintained the charade by talking quickly, giving only basic particulars of his meeting with Dee and Jacque. Ernie suggested they meet and have a look round Mary Walsh's flat the following day and finish the conversation then, intimating it was best if he went back inside. Inspector Flannel appreciated the situation and one o'clock was agreed to for the meeting.

"What is it, lad?" asked the inspector in response to the drawn look on Ernie's face.

"She's the daughter of Sir Harlan Trevor. Dee said Mary was terribly fond of her parents. It's only proper they should know what has happened to her and that everything possible is being done to bring her murderer to justice."

Inspector Flannel respectfully nodded his head. "I suggested that to Godfrey the other night. He's made arrangements to meet with her parents tomorrow. He'll explain as much as he can about what we know without eluding to Raventhorn and this business about those other eight murders."

Ernie bid the inspector goodnight and made his way up the stairs and back to the sitting room. Patterson was exactly where Ernie had left him, though the silver tray was now light two custard tarts.

"Have it all worked out, have you?" asked Patterson, with the look of a Cheshire cat.

Ernie just smiled, picking up a custard tart.

16/ A Call for Help

Newcomen Street was a quiet street, with the exception of the occasional spillover from a celebration at King's College. With Guy's Hospital around the corner, traffic was more an issue rather than the endless pedestrian chatter one experiences along the more touristy thoroughfares.

In a five-story, redbrick apartment building, close to the corner of Bowling Green Place, was the unassuming flat of Miss Mary Walsh, secretary, Hanson and Bloom. The small wrought iron balconies were dotted here and there with hanging baskets and flower boxes, overflowing with a generous collection of petunias bursting with color. The façade was boxy and repetitive in form and appointments, a monument to post-war Britain, but a personal touch was added to each flat with a painted front door. There wasn't much of a view, but the street was quiet enough and situated between Borough and London Bridge tube stations. Further up the block, an ample number of convenience shops were located along the Borough High Street.

When Ernie arrived, he found the inspector waiting for him, leaning against the wall in front of a deep crimson door on the third floor. A small brass plaque next to his shoulder was embossed with #302 in black.

"Just what do you expect to find?" said Inspector Flannel, unlocking and opening the door. "I've been assured by Inspector Godfrey the forensic team has been all over this flat, nothing odd about it. No sign of a struggle. No indication of a jilted lover or other such nonsense."

"A journal," Ernie responded briskly.

The inspector followed Ernie inside. "What's this?"

He didn't get far when he became aware of what stopped Ernie only a few steps into the room. It was a mess. The room had been tossed about, cushions torn open; drawers pulled out and emptied on the rug; cupboards cleared out. From the looks of it, every room had been given the same treatment.

"I would hope your forensic lads didn't do this," remarked Ernie dryly.

"Don't be daft," barked the inspector. He pulled out two pairs of latex gloves from his coat pocket, handing one pair to Ernie. "A journal, you say? It would appear you're not the only person who knows about it. Just how did you come about this knowledge?"

"It was the two women I met with yesterday at the George Inn, Dee Parsons and Jacque Laine. They were mates of Mary Walsh, all three escorts with the same service. Dee, a terribly attractive woman, owns a millinery shop on Savile Row I'm told, said Mary had confided in her about what she was up to a couple weeks past. Said she was a journalist investigating those Brick Lane murders eight years ago. It was Mary what mentioned to Dee about notes she was keeping in a journal. She also said she was close."

"Close to what?"

"I asked the same thing. Dee said, and there ended the conversation."

The inspector started looking carefully through the books strewn about on the floor in front of a large bookcase along the right side of the room. Waving his hand in the direction of the bedroom, he indicated Ernie should do the same in there. "Do we know what this journal looks like?"

"She didn't say."

"There was no mention of a journal in the evidence log, I can tell you that. A few theater tickets, souvenirs no doubt, and an address book."

"Was there a personal computer?" Ernie called out from the bedroom.

The inspector stopped, slowly looking around the room as he scratched his head. "That's a bit queer, now that you say she was a journalist. There was no computer mentioned in the evidence log. Do you see one in there?"

"No." Ernie came back into the living room. "No journal either."

"I'll make a note and have Inspector Godfrey inquire about a computer when he visits the parents later today."

The inspector continued his search of the books. Ernie picked up a cushion, placed it back on the sofa and sat down. He spoke quietly to himself.

"What's that?" asked the inspector, thinking Ernie was talking to him.

"Nothing really," replied Ernie. "I was just thinking, the last thing Mary said to Dee was, 'She was close.' If she felt she was close, then she must have been aware of the danger she was in. I think it's quite evident looking around here, whoever she suspected was very much aware of her suspicions."

"I would say you're right," replied the inspector, taking his mobile phone from his pocket. "We'd best leave this for the forensic guys. I'll call Inspector Godfrey and suggest he send the lads back over. He'll want to know about this mess."

Ernie waited quietly on the sofa, listening to the inspector's portion of the conversation. After Inspector Godfrey got on the line, Flannel explained they were at Mary Walsh Trevor's flat, followed by a brief mention of the journal and a promise to fill in the remaining details back at the Yard. There was a pause in the inspector's conversation. Ernie was startled by a sudden outburst.

"What did you say the name was?" cried Inspector Flannel, looking over at Ernie. "Who found her? She had whose card in her hand?" The inspector continued to stare at Ernie, listening intently for a moment or two and then snapping his phone shut. "Come on, up with you. We've got to go."

"What's wrong?" asked Ernie, very much upset. He followed quickly behind the inspector, slamming the door shut as they left the flat.

"Another woman's been attacked."

It took all Ernie had in him to catch up with the inspector. He grabbed his arm, stopping him at the top of the stairs leading down to the parking area. "What's happened? You said someone's been attacked? Who was it? I'll not let go till you tell me."

"I'm sorry, lad. It's one of your new friends—Diana Parsons."

17/ A Case of Nerves

"Where have you been?" snapped Raventhorn, raising his gold topped cane and rapping it against the doorsill. "I walk up the front steps to find this door open and you nowhere in sight. It's a wonder I didn't find my possessions being carried up the street by a band of thieves, no thanks to you. I don't know why I waist my time with you, you ungrateful wretch."

"Sorry, sir." Prophet eased out into the hall from the kitchen area. He moved slowly along the wall toward the front door, stopping and cowering near the newel post on the landing of the ornately carved staircase leading to the upper floors. "Just back from the market. A few groceries, that's all. Thought your guests might like their salad makings fresh today. Very sorry. Thought I closed it."

Raventhorn sneered, turning and slamming the door behind him.

Prophet walked over, reaching out and grasping the leather satchel Raventhorn held in his hand. The action startled Raventhorn. He quickly jerked the case out of Prophet's hands, knocking him to the floor in the process.

"Sorry, sir," whimpered Prophet. He lay quite limp on the floor as he answered, his head tucked down upon his breast. With his good arm he pushed himself up to a sitting position. "I . . . I was just going to put that in your study. That's all. No harm meant."

"No harm, indeed." Raventhorn slowly drew out each contemptible word, ignoring the hand Prophet held out for assistance in getting back on his feet. "There's nothing in this case that concerns the likes of you. I'll not have you meddling in my private affairs. Is that clear?"

Prophet nodded his head briskly, mumbling his apologies once more as he pushed himself out of Raventhorn's way.

"Now, if you're done lounging about and making excuses, I'm sure there is more than enough to keep you occupied in the kitchen until my guests arrive. It's just past two and I expect them to arrive at seven o'clock. You'll serve promptly at eight, clear the plates when we've finished, and retire to your room for the remainder of the evening." He stepped over Prophet's outstretched leg, continuing down the hall as he spoke. "I'm sure I have no need to explain the consequences should you make a dog's breakfast of my engagement this evening?"

"No, sir. I'll have all in order." With the aid of the newel post, Prophet slowly pulled himself up from the floor. "Eight sharp, sir. Not to worry."

Raventhorn stopped at the door to the drawing room, turning his head slightly back over his shoulder towards Prophet. He clutched the satchel tightly under his arm. "There is a bit of work that needs my attention. I do not wish to be disturbed for any reason. Is that clear?"

"Quite clear, sir."

Prophet watched as the door to Raventhorn's drawing room slowly closed.

18/ Addressing the Wounds of the Past

Inspector Flannel and Ernie hurried down the antiseptic-washed hall of St. Thomas Hospital. It was a wide corridor, brightly lit through large windows at each end, dotted here and there with stretchers and rolling intravenous poles. Inspector Flannel led the way, nurses and orderlies hugging the walls as the official express barreled through the local stops. Ernie handled the situation and urgency in a far better manner, excusing himself and the inspector as he trailed closely behind. Their destination was just ahead, a room at the end of the hall on the right marked by a policewoman standing by the door.

The inspector stopped short as he entered the room, surprised by the visitor sitting in a chair next to the hospital bed. Ernie, still making random appeals for pardon to the people in the hall as he entered the room, found his face flat against the course, wool coat of Inspector Flannel. As he peered around the rigid figure of the inspector, Ernie quickly realized what brought him to such an abrupt halt.

There, looking up at the two men over the rim of his reading glasses, was Patterson Coats. After putting a finger to his lips, he pointed at the woman in the bed and shook his head.

It was Dee. Her fiery red hair flowed out from beneath a white gauze bandage wrapped around her head like a turban. The bright brown eyes that captured Ernie's attention at the pub the previous day were closed in a peaceful slumber. A soft, steady beep from the monitor on the wall kept a vigilant watch over her vital signs. The only other physical sign of injury was a dark bruise on her right forearm.

Patterson got up and, with a jerk of his head, suggested the two men join him in the far corner of the room.

"How is she, sir?" whispered Ernie, looking back at Dee.

"She's a very lucky woman, Ernie. The doctors have told me she is stable and resting comfortably. I suggest we keep our voices down so we don't disturb her."

Inspector Flannel was conspicuously silent, and just as conspicuously confused.

"Something wrong, August?" said Patterson in a mock-inquisitive tone, addressing the inspector's gape.

"No. Uh, no," stammered the inspector as he cleared his throat. "Just surprised to see you here." He looked over at Dee, then at Ernie, then back at Patterson. "Just a bit surprised, that's all."

"Funny that, I'm not at all surprised to see the two of you here," replied Patterson sharply, but giving Ernie a slight nudge with his elbow. "I was occupied with museum business back at my flat when Mrs. Chapman and I heard a commotion out front on the pavement. We went down the stairs, opened the door, and found this poor young woman unconscious on the marble sill. I called for an ambulance straightaway while Mrs. Chapman tended to the wound on her head." Patterson held out his hand, displaying a small card. "She was clutching this tightly in her hand when we found her. I decided it would be prudent for me to stay with her until she was awake. I was concerned for her safety and very curious about what had happened and what brought her to our door."

Ernie took the card from his hand. "It's my card. I gave this to Dee yesterday at the George Inn. I told her if she was in any danger she could find safety at our flat." Ernie paused, glaring over at Inspector Flannel. "This is just terrible. We've done this."

"Now, now, lad." The inspector was quick to put any unfounded blame or cause in perspective. "Whatever's happened here may or may not have anything to do with the murder of her friend. You told me the two of them wanted to help any way they could. I'm sure they both understood by doing so there was a risk involved. Let's not jump to any conclusions until we talk with the woman and find out what happened."

As they were talking a nurse came into the room. Patterson walked over and whispered something in her ear. Following the brief conversation, he motioned to Ernie and the inspector, indicating he was going out into the hall. Both men followed and continued down the hall behind Patterson. At the end, was a very pleasant waiting room, brightly lit and furnished with plaid covered armchairs arranged in small clusters.

"I've asked the nurse," started Patterson, taking a seat in one of the armchairs by the windows, "to inform us immediately when Dee awakes. So, August, I believe you were just about to explain what brought the two of you to her bedside?"

The inspector fixed his jacket as he settled back into the chair across from Patterson. "You're not going to like it, Pattie."

"No doubt," Patterson shrugged, calmly brushing at his coat sleeves, "but that's neither here nor there. What's important is what has put this young woman's life in jeopardy and what's going to be done to insure her future safety."

Ernie wasn't bashful at all about filling in part of the details. With short excited bursts, he got right to the basics. "It's all about that young girl murdered the other night off

Brick Lane. Mary Walsh, or Mary Walsh Trevor as we now knows her to be. Dee was a friend of hers. They worked at the same escort service, they did."

"That's right," continued the inspector. "With the help of Bisquets here, I've been conducting my own investigation. You'll not be harsh on the lad, it was me what got him involved, and me what told him to keep what he was up to from you."

Patterson looked over at Ernie and smiled. "To do what's right without fear of the consequence is a trait often sought but rarely found. The courage you two have shown to bring a murderer to justice has been enough to prove me in want of a good reason to question either of your actions." He addressed the remaining dialog to Inspector Flannel. "*I* understand what you're doing, I'm just afraid it won't be enough for your superiors if they catch wind of what you've been up to."

"I'm a bit worried about that myself," replied Flannel, rubbing the back of his neck.

The nurse poked her head into the room, politely interrupting the conversation. "Would one of you gentlemen be Ernie Bisquets?"

"Yes, miss," replied Ernie eagerly. "I'm Ernie Bisquets."

The nurse smiled. "The young lady is awake and asking for you."

Ernie was out the door before the nurse finished the sentence. The inspector and Patterson rose from their seats also.

Patterson took the inspector's arm, holding him back for just a moment. "You and I both know the injuries sustained by that young woman recovering down the hall have everything to do with that other woman's death. I don't believe Ernie understands the full extent of the danger you've put him in. You look after him, August. Whoever this murderer is they are proving to be ever more daring and treacherous. I'll only say this once. Be very sure of what you're doing. Wrongly chasing after an old ghost can haunt you for the rest of your life."

"Don't worry about the lad, I've got my eyes on him. As for us, I knew you wouldn't be too keen on what I was doing, that's why I asked the lad for help. Thought I would save us the row."

Patterson gave his friend a warm smile of encouragement. "I've known you close to 50 years, August. By now I'm sure you've figured out I've put most of the pieces of your little puzzle together. If you believe Raventhorn had a hand in any of this recent business I'll be the first to stand behind you. Forgive me, old friend. My haste to dismiss your suspicions eight years ago was foolish. I can't help but feel I'm as much to blame for that young woman's injuries as the hand that struck the blow."

"Rubbish," Inspector Flannel barked. "You did what you thought was right. We both did. He fooled us last time, but he'll not fool us again." A slight curl of his lip turned up the end of his moustache, followed by a wink.

"All I can say is tread very carefully. Raventhorn is not a man to cross."

"That's a lesson I'll not soon forget. Now, let's see what this young woman has to tell us."

The two men walked down the hall, entering the room where Dee and Ernie were busy talking.

"Is that him?" asked Dee, looking over and pointing at Patterson as he entered.

"Yes. Yes it is. Diana, this is Lord Patterson Coats. He's the man what found you at our door."

Patterson took her outstretched hand between both of his. "You gave us quite a scare, young lady. I'm glad to see you're alright."

"Thank you. Ernie said if I ran into any trouble I could count on finding help at your door." Dee looked over at the inspector. "And you must be Inspector Flannel?"

"Yes, miss. Diana, is it?"

"Dee. Please, all of you should call me Dee."

"Well, miss, I've got a few questions if you're up to the task."

Tears welled up in Dee's deep brown eyes. She turned her head, looking away as she spoke. "I was only trying to help. It was a favor, that's all, a favor for Mary. She gave me it for safe keeping and now it's gone." She looked back at Ernie. "I'm so sorry. After we spoke, I realized I had to bring it to you. Now look what's happened."

"You'll not blame yourself for any of this." Ernie took her hand. "You're fortunate to be alive."

"What was it that Mary gave you," asked the inspector impatiently, his small notepad in hand.

"The journal. It was Mary's journal. She said it had all the notes from her investigation." Dee began to sob. "She joked how she might be too close for comfort. I was to keep the journal. Mary made light of the situation, but I could sense she was scared. There was one last piece to gather and she was ready to expose that *Slasher*."

This last statement got the inspector's full attention. He rattled off questions as quickly as he could form the sentences. "*Slasher*, you say? Just when was this? When did you see her last? Where is this journal now?"

The barrage of questions overwhelmed Dee. As she struggled to sort them out and answer them a gabardine-clad figure rushed in, the light citrus scent of Annick Goutal's Eau d'Hadrien filling the room. She pushed the inspector aside, her attention focused only on her injured friend. "Oh my God. Oh my God," she mumbled aloud, hugging Dee briefly with restraint then clasping her friend's hand tightly between hers. Doing her best to hold back the emotions evident in her concerned eyes she switched her attention to Ernie, making a tender appeal. "Who would do such a thing as this?"

Ernie looked over at Patterson and then at the inspector, unsure of what he should say.

Patterson walked over, taking Jacque's hand from Dee. "My name is Patterson Coats. Why don't we step into the hall and allow the inspector a few minutes with your friend? I'll give you the details, as we understand them.

Dee looked up at Jacque and smiled, her soothing tone doing much to reinforce Patterson's request. "It's all right, Jacque, I'm fine. These men are here to help."

As Patterson and Jacque adjourned to the hall, Ernie stepped over closer to the hospital bed. Dee reached out to him. The action prompted a comforting smile from Ernie as he lightly grasped her soft hand.

"I'm sorry, Inspector," said Dee solemnly. "You had a few questions?"

Intimate displays of attention were lost on the stoic inspector. "Yes. Thank you. This will only take a few minutes then I'll leave you to rest. When did you last see Mary Walsh Trevor?"

"Last Thursday, past. She called early that morning, suggesting we meet for lunch. I suggested we invite Jacque but she politely declined, intimating it was important we met alone. I had the feeling it was about that conversation we had a few weeks past concerning those murders she was investigating."

"So she told you she was investigating those unsolved murders?"

"Yes. She said she intended to casually interview the man she suspected to confirm her suspicions. All the facts were in her journal."

"So that's when she gave you the journal?"

"Not exactly."

"Not exactly?" replied Flannel, his tone rising with impatience. The inspector wasn't normally so prickly when interviewing a victim, but he was ever mindful that what he was doing was going directly against the wishes of his superiors. It put him a little on edge. "If not then," continued the inspector, calmly drawing out each word, "then when did you come into possession of the journal?"

"When we met for lunch, Mary told me she had put the journal in the post. A bit of nonsense I thought then, all this hush, hush, cloak and dagger business. Nonetheless, I was to expect it early this week. It came in this morning's post."

"And what was in it?"

"I'm sure I don't know. I never opened it. With what happened to Mary, and after talking with Ernie, I decided it best to bring the journal to him. I was sure he would know what to do with it." The tears welled up in Dee's eyes once more. "I was just at the door to his flat on Conduit Street when that beast attacked me." Dee began to cry, her brave face giving way to the frightened woman inside. "He grabbed me from behind. I can still feel his heavy arm around my neck. It all happened so fast. I felt something strike my head. I fell back against the door. That's all I remember." Dee's crying became more intense. "He killed Mary and now he has her journal. He's gotten away and it's all my fault."

Dee's outburst caught the attention of Jacque in the corridor. She rushed back in, grabbing the inspector's arm and spinning him around to face her. Jacque was petite by most standards, but she rose up like a mother bear when it came to protecting her friends. She tapped her well-manicured finger on the lapel of the inspector's coat, using a judicious tone usually reserved for the courtroom. "I would hope you are going to do more than just stand here badgering my dear friend. There's a maniac preying on helpless women out there. I suggest you find him."

Despite years of dealing with the public, each new encounter could still bristle the hair on the back of the inspector's neck. Painfully proceeding with a well-rehearsed comforting voice he calmly replied, "I can assure you, madam, it's been my intention all along to apprehend this villain. If you'll permit me, I've only one more question and I'll be on my way."

"It's all right, Jacque." Dee wiped at her eyes with a tissue handed to her by Ernie. "He's only doing his job. What is it, inspector?"

"Did Mary mention where she was going or who she was meeting Thursday night past?"

Dee thought for a moment, sadness overtaking the usual playful brightness in her eyes. "I'm sorry, inspector. Mary said she only had one last piece of the puzzle to confirm. She was excited about meeting with someone that night. She said she intended to surprise him by showing up unannounced, not giving him time to prepare a story. I asked who it was, but she thought it best not to say."

"Thank you, miss." The inspector closed his notepad, tucking it down into his jacket pocket. "I'll keep an officer posted at your door, just in case. If you think of anything else, please tell Bisquets here and he'll get the message to me. I'm quite certain there'll be an Inspector Godfrey dropping by later today. He'll want to go over the details again and may have a few more questions."

Dee nodded. A soft smile of appreciation drew up the ends of her lips. "You'll catch him, won't you, inspector?"

The inspector made a motion to tip his hat to the ladies. "You have my word. I'll have the man responsible for all this in custody as quickly as possible." He followed with a nod to Ernie and went on his way.

In the hall, Patterson was waiting for his old friend. "Bit of a mess I'd say, aye, August?"

"A mess indeed," grumbled the inspector. "You'll be easy on the lad, right Pattie? If it's angry, you are, it's with me, not Bisquets."

"Angry? I think not. Actually, I'm quite proud of him for his willingness to help you, especially in light of your starchy attitude toward his past. As for you, if I didn't know better, I'd say you've become quite fond of the lad."

The inspector answered with a harrumph.

Patterson drew out a large grin, slapping Flannel on the back. "It's a pair, you are. A couple of curate's eggs, the both of you."

The inspector walked off down the corridor alongside his friend. "I've not time for your nonsense. I've got to report all this to Godfrey. I'll be lucky to have my badge at the end of this business."

"You'll let me know what I can do, August?"

A thoughtful smile came to Flannel's stern countenance. "Thank you, Pattie. I wanted to tell—"

Patterson smiled back and shook his head. "You don't owe me an explanation. No matter what, we both want the same thing—justice. Like I mentioned before, I can't help but think that if I was more open to your suspicions during the original investigation eight years ago all this may have been avoided. As a result of my stubbornness, I feel somewhat responsible now for that young girl's tragic death and the assault on this young woman. I'll assist any way I can."

The inspector stopped. "There is one thing you might do if you would?"

"And what might that be?"

"I know you're a close friend of Cynthia Carolls. Would you mind asking her about whom Mary Walsh Trevor might have been meeting? Inspector Godfrey sent a constable over to her agency, but she seemed reluctant to answer his questions. Without a warrant, she was not about to expose her clientele to any undo public scandal. She finally said, to the best of her knowledge, Miss Trevor had no appointments last Thursday evening. She might have been telling the truth, but one never knows."

"Certainly. I'll call on her this evening. I'm certain she'll talk to me."

19/ Just Desserts

The front doorbell rang just as the French Ormolu clock on the mantel in Raventhorn's study struck seven o'clock. Prophet was smartly attired in formal black trousers and matching waistcoat, a white shirt with French cuffs, and a thin, black silk tie. His dark hair, usually unruly, was a rich black and shiny, combed back with a generous application of Layrite pomade. Despite his deformities and usual tarnished look, he could easily be considered handsome when properly cleaned and polished.

"Please, come in," said Prophet to the striking woman standing in the portico. He stepped aside allowing her to enter, taking a moment to look down the walkway expecting to see a second guest coming up the stairs.

"Very nice to see you again, Prophet. You're looking quite well."

Prophet closed the door. He dipped his head down politely two or three times. "Thank you, mum. Thank you. His Lordship is in the drawing room. I'll take your wrap. Please, follow me."

Raventhorn's drawing room resembled a Turkish parlor, ornamented with an abundance of paisley prints and dark woods, devoid of a woman's touch in every sense. Brass floor lamps with pierced shades were stationed here and there around the room, casting trails of light outward along the walls in all directions, leading the eye upwards to the jewel-like colors of the plaster frieze that encircled the room. From the stenciled ceiling, hung matching gilt cast bronze chandeliers, their dark red shades drenching the room in a warm glow. A rich complement of antique photos adorned the walls depicting important events in British history, with a candid moment featuring Queen Victoria with her favorite horse, Fyvie, hanging in honor above the fireplace. Raventhorn was standing by the piano, himself a portrait cast against the busy backdrop, pouring a sherry as Prophet opened the door.

"Sir. Ms. Cynthia Carolls."

Raventhorn looked over, quite confused by the announcement. His usual grim face was quickly replaced with an expression of cheerfulness, a look he reserved for his social encounters. "Cynthia, this is quite an unexpected pleasure. Please, come in. I'm sure Prophet has made more than enough to accommodate another appetite at the table. He's my right hand, that one. I can always count on him to anticipate the unexpected. Thank you, Prophet. We'll be three for dinner."

"Wait," Cynthia called out. "I'm sorry, Alfred, Lindsay and Laura have canceled. This business in Brick Lane has them quite upset. Then another woman in the service was attacked earlier today."

"Another you say?" Raventhorn, unaffected by the news, looked over at Prophet who stood patiently awaiting his final count for dinner. "We'll be two this evening, Prophet. Sorry for all the bother. I know how much work you put into our meals, but not to worry, it will certainly be appreciated."

With a polite nod, Prophet left the two alone.

Raventhorn lost no time pouring a sherry for his guest. They made themselves comfortable in the green leather chairs that flanked the fireplace. The conversation started with compliments over Cynthia's three-quarter-sleeve, Léger bandage-style dress, flowed easily down to her

Zébulon black patent pumps, and eventually drifted off into political affairs of the day as they sipped their Sherries. It took a second glass before they were done solving the problems of the British Empire for the day.

Prophet had been busy in the kitchen making the final preparations for the meal.

A faint echo could be heard as the clock in the study struck eight o'clock. Raventhorn had just seated Cynthia at the table in the dining room, himself taking his seat at the head of the table. He pushed the button beneath the small mound in the rug below the table. A moment later, Prophet emerged from the kitchen, the sweet aroma of minestrone soup wafting from a covered tureen that rattled as he pushed the serving cart to the table.

"I hope you'll forgive them, Prophet," said Cynthia. "The girls were really looking forward to dinner. That's the other reason I came to deliver the news in person; I know how much you put into every meal. It would be such a shame to have such a fine meal go to waste. Lord Raventhorn has spoken often about your prowess in the kitchen."

Prophet smiled as he ladled out the soup into Cynthia's bowl, quite taken with the attention. "Quite all right, mum. Better they're safe until the police get to the bottom of things."

Cynthia looked over at Raventhorn, her expression concerned. "I'm not at all afraid to say this whole business has me unnerved as well. Just when the horrors of those other murders have been forgotten, this had to happen. It dredges it all up again."

With her soup served, Prophet finished by placing fresh baked bread on a plate next to her bowl. He then walked around to Lord Raventhorn's place, mumbling softly as he repeated the process for his master. "Has them all scared, he does. They say he's back. Not a woman safe till he's caught." Prophet suddenly realized both were focused on his ramblings. He froze, looking up at Raventhorn.

"Not to worry," replied Raventhorn brightly. "I'm sure the police will make short work of this business." Raventhorn waited until Prophet had finished serving the soup. With a casual flare, he continued, "Please forgive Prophet. I'm afraid he has allowed his imagination to get the better of him."

"Sorry, mum," said Prophet, his eyes cast down as he retreated from the table. "It's a foolish lad I am. Didn't mean to scare you."

Cynthia smiled, placing a napkin in her lap and picking up her spoon. "You're making far too much of this, both of you. Enough about that. I, for one, intend to turn my thoughts to this wonderful soup. And, if I'm not mistaken, I believe that's lamb I smell?"

"Correct you are, mum," replied Prophet, happy for the subject change.

"He had it cut special for this evening," added Raventhorn. "I'm sure it won't disappoint."

Prophet mumbled one last apology as he disappeared to attend to the next course.

Cynthia Carolls and Raventhorn continued with a light conversation as they enjoyed their soup. Raventhorn studied her countenance carefully, uneasy about the parallel she made between the old murders and the recent attacks. It was while Prophet was clearing the dishes from the lamb course that he broached the subject again.

"You seem a bit preoccupied, Cynthia," said Raventhorn. "Has something with the meal not settled right?"

"Not at all; everything just delicious," Cynthia responded, giving Prophet a wink of approval. "I'm sorry, I'm trying to separate myself from this terrible business of murder, but others have no intention of letting me do that."

Raventhorn sat up attentively. "Others? What others are we talking about? Maybe I should have a word with them on your behalf."

"The police, for one thing. They sent a constable around asking about Mary Walsh's social calendar. She indicated she was meeting with a client, but didn't write in a name. I thought she mentioned Sloane Square in conversation earlier that day. I can't be sure, so I didn't say anything to the police." Cynthia paused, lowering her voice to a whisper. "You didn't happen to see her that night, did you?"

Raventhorn hesitated before answering, glancing in Prophet's direction. Prophet felt the sting of his glance and quickly finished up, excusing himself from the room afterwards.

"Now that you mention it, I believe she was intending to stop by to introduce herself that very evening. I was called away at the last minute and never able to meet with her. I called, suggesting we reschedule for next week. Prophet can verify every moment of my evening as he was there with me." Raventhorn sighed, resting back in his chair. "If only I hadn't canceled, maybe that poor young woman would still be alive."

"That's why I didn't mention any of this to the police. I remember what the newspapers did to you last time when the inspector unjustly accused you of wrongdoing. It was just terrible the things he said and the way the papers hounded you. I didn't want to see that happen again."

Raventhorn leaned forward, patting Cynthia's hand gently. "That was so very kind of you. Rest assured, I had nothing to do with any of those despicable acts, or this one. I can't let it bother me; the police are just doing their job. I'm sure Scotland Yard will get to the bottom of this matter quickly. For now, why don't we put this business aside and enjoy dessert?"

Raventhorn once again stretched out his foot, depressing the button below the carpet.

* * *

It was just past ten o'clock when Prophet announced the car arranged to take Cynthia home had arrived. Raventhorn and Cynthia closed the evening with pleasantries at the front door. Prophet helped her on with her wrap. The car service had pulled up in front of the house. A light rain that had started earlier in the evening continued, leaving the pavement awash, the lights of the surrounding buildings reflecting like jewels strewn about without care.

"Allow me," said Prophet, taking a black umbrella from the ornately carved hall tree.

"Thank you, Prophet. You're so fortunate, Alfred, to have such a thoughtful valet."

"Fortunate indeed," replied Raventhorn, forcing a smile through clenched teeth.

After one last goodbye, Cynthia proceeded carefully down the steps toward the waiting car. Prophet followed close on her heels with the umbrella held high above her head.

As the car pulled away, Prophet paused, looking back up at the silhouette peering down at him from the door. He made no effort to return to the house with any speed. Slowly making his way back up the white marble stairs, his clubfoot making the slippery steps that much harder to ascend, Prophet took another moment or two to shake off the rain before he entered the house. He walked quietly passed Raventhorn, who, calmly closing the door as he passed, watched as Prophet replaced the wet umbrella in the hall tree. The kitchen door was just down the hall. He was almost safe. Without a word he started toward the door.

"You'd like that, wouldn't you?" Raventhorn said smugly, the words piercing Prophet's very soul. "Slithering away like a common garden snake. Come here. You've had your say, now I'll have mine."

"I meant no harm, sir," Prophet stammered. He took two small steps, reluctantly closing the distance between himself and his master. "Just a bit of talk, that's all. No harm meant."

Raventhorn peered out through the curtained window of the door, assuring himself the car was well down the street. He slowly turned back toward Prophet, his steel gray eyes fixed on the trembling figure before him. "You insufferable, contemptible little wretch. How dare you dredge all this up again and frighten my guest with your unfounded tabloid gossip. This is how all that business started eight years ago. Idle rumors. Idle rumors started by you. Fortunately, Ms. Carolls was prudent enough to withhold certain facts from the police, unlike the way you carelessly tossed me into that business eight years ago." Raventhorn poked Prophet repeatedly in the chest with his sinewy index finger as he spoke. "That's right, I've not forgotten I have you to thank for dragging my name through the gutter. I'll not stand for it again."

Raventhorn was furious. He snatched his cane from the hall tree, raising it high above his head. Prophet cowered at the action, sharply turning away so as to absorb the anger of his master on his back. Raventhorn leaned forward, rising up on the balls of his feet. With his cane clutched tightly in his boney hand, he readied himself to deliver what he judged was a well-deserved reprimand.

"No, please!" Prophet whimpered. "Please."

But Raventhorn abruptly stopped, venting a final burst of anger by tossing the cane across the hall. It ricocheted off the walnut sideboard breaking a vase of fresh flowers, then clattered down the hall toward his drawing room. "Clean that up!" he shrieked.

"Yes, sir. Right away, sir." Prophet stood shaking, his words were barely audible.

"Don't think me a fool, I'll not fall victim to your plans again. Nor will there be cause delivered from my hand to haul me before a magistrate for assault." Raventhorn leaned down, his face within inches of Prophet's. "Enjoy the rest of your evening, I'll deal with you later, but in my own way. Right now, I've got a matter that warrants my attention more than the sniveling likes of you."

Raventhorn snatched his keys from the small table next to the door. "I'm going out to the club for a few hours to calm down. You'd best not be within my gaze when I return. You haven't heard the last of this." Raventhorn slammed the door shut as he left.

Prophet, still frightened, his face turned down and away, continued to nod his head quickly to signal his comprehension of what was said and what was surely to come.

20/ Three's a Crowd

Inspector Flannel decided to walk back to the Yard. Despite the advances he had made in his private investigation of the case, and his eagerness to share those findings with Inspector Godfrey, he couldn't muster anything more than a leisurely stroll. On every stranger he passed on the street, he saw the drawn faces of disappointment of his superiors. There was no getting away from it. He had deliberately gone against the declaration handed him by Chief Detective Inspector Hardgrave to remain removed from the Brick Lane murder investigation. This wasn't the first time Flannel circumvented direct orders in pursuit of a suspect, but this one carried with it a potentially lethal consequence. Lord Raventhorn was a very powerful man. Crossing him a second time could surely end Flannel's career.

The walk back gave him plenty of time to think over his situation. At first he was anxious, which quickly turned to anger. The idea that his actions would be considered insubordinate weighed heavily on his mind. This was a feeling he had never felt in his long and judicious career with Scotland Yard. He was only doing his job, he continually told himself; a job he'd done brilliantly for so long. *How dare they question my motives; how dare they put politics before the lives of these young girls.*

As he turned onto Broadway, Flannel had already resigned himself to the fact he was going to continue his investigation with or without the blessing of his superiors and, if things took a turn for the worse, with or without a badge. No matter the outcome, he would continue to keep Inspector Godfrey informed, but that was quickly becoming more a courtesy than an obligation.

In Flannel's eyes, of all the new inspectors at the Yard, Godfrey showed the most promise. Flannel took him somewhat under his wing, sharing evidence during a case and explaining his train of thought. Flannel often said deductive reasoning was a skill that could be taught if the student had natural, intuitive insight and the ability to disregard all outside influences, including static from superiors. Clues most often present themselves as obscure, unimportant details. Connecting two seemingly unimportant details often solves the most perplexing of cases. It's the ability to recognize those details where Flannel excelled and where he concentrated his effort with Godfrey.

This was a condensed education in criminal investigation, something Godfrey would otherwise have to collect little by little, case by case over the course of his career. Flannel tied it all up with a neat little bow, presenting aspects of it to Godfrey as the opportunities presented themselves. The reasoning behind Flannel's attention was simple–he felt he and Godfrey were cut from the same cloth, though Flannel's was a bit more tattered from the years of service. Godfrey, in turn, was honored such a seasoned inspector would take so keen an interest in his career.

Inspector Wynne Godfrey came up through the ranks. Some say his rise to Inspector was due in part to his uncle being the Deputy Commissioner. Others, less jealous and certainly more informed, knew it was a direct result of his exceptional abilities as a police officer. Flannel was in league with the latter. To him, Godfrey had the makings of a first-class detective inspector; he only needed to ignore the schoolyard gossip and continue to do his job.

Out of respect, Flannel gave Godfrey the option to be a party or not to what could eventually be considered the Brick Lane Mutiny of Detective Inspector Flannel. Godfrey was quick with his answer. He explained to Flannel he was told by the Superintendent to *"...use whatever means necessary to apprehend the person or persons responsible for that poor girl's death in Brick Lane."* In the event the mutiny was so assigned, he assured Flannel this was the defense he would use, not just for himself, but for Flannel also. Cut from the same cloth indeed.

* * *

Ernie had remained behind at the hospital at Dee's request. Jacque had calmed down somewhat, her eyes filled with compassion, but her words still laden with concern. Somewhere out there was the fiendish brute that attacked Dee. Ernie's reassurances were met with a pleasant nod from both women, but it did little to convince them the danger was over.

* * *

Long shadows were making their way up Conduit Street, signaling the end of another day and the start of the evening as Patterson arrived back at his flat. He found Mrs. Chapman in the kitchen rinsing Brussels sprouts.

Mrs. Chapman looked up as he entered, anxious to hear his report on the condition of the poor young woman.

"You'll be happy to know she is awake and doing fine," said Patterson in response to her expectant expression. "It turns out, she and Ernie had met yesterday. Her name is Dee Parsons and she was a friend of the woman killed the other evening off Brick Lane. She was coming here to give Ernie the deceased woman's journal."

"Do we know who attacked her?"

"I'm afraid not. It all happened so quickly; it went completely unnoticed on the street. With any luck, the CCTV cameras at the ends of the block may have captured something useful."

"You may want to talk with Mr. Hayball in the stationery shop. He's always sticking his nose into everybody's business. It wouldn't surprise me if he could give a description."

"Not a bad idea, Annie. I'll mention that to the inspector. For now, I'm just relieved Miss Parsons wasn't hurt more seriously. They have a policewoman by her door at the hospital."

Mrs. Chapman turned back toward the sink and the colander of sprouts. "The poor thing. Terrible business. Terrible indeed. I suppose my Derby will get to the bottom of it soon enough."

Patterson saw no need to explain the delicate situation the inspector was cloaked in. Instead he agreed and quickly changed the subject. Marie was expected early that evening and he wanted to be sure everything was arranged for her visit. As he rattled off the arrangements he was giddy as a schoolboy, something that hadn't missed the attention of Mrs. Chapman.

"Shall I wait at the window and send up a signal flare when Marie arrives?" Mrs. Chapman chuckled.

"Is it that obvious?"

"It does my heart good to see you excited like this over something other than some dusty old mummy. She's fortunate to have a fine man like yourself, she is, to look after her like you do."

Patterson walked over to the sink, picked up the roasting pan and held it out. Mrs. Chapman meticulously transferred the sprouts from the colander to the pan as Patterson responded to the compliment. "In some ways, I feel responsible for her troubles. Had I just let her go completely all those years ago things might have been different for her. Your kind words are appreciated, but I don't feel I deserve them."

"Rubbish," Mrs. Chapman quickly shot back, looking up into his eyes. "It's worse she'll be for seeing you like this. It's a pitiful sight, it is, and not becoming of such a fine man as yourself—and no finer man walks this earth. She'll be here soon enough, looking for a strong shoulder. I suggest you wipe that discontent off your handsome face and prepare to offer up the comfort we all know lies behind those steel gray eyes of yours." Mrs. Chapman turned back to the empty colander as if there were still sprouts needing her attention, playfully raising an eyebrow as she continued, "Quite frankly, I sometimes wonder what she sees in you at all."

Patterson let out a hearty laugh and kissed the top of her head. "It's for certain at the top of that list is my ability to employ the most insightful woman in all of London."

Mrs. Chapman's rosy cheeks drew out a contented smile. "Off with you now, enough of this nonsense. You'll not be so happy with me when you're left waiting for your supper."

Patterson cleared his throat with Shakespearean flair. "Well, I'll just leave you to it then."

He left Mrs. Chapman in the kitchen humming an old Irish ditty. After shuffling through the post sitting in the silver tray on the table in the hall, Patterson retired to the sitting room, occupying his time with the day's paper until Marie's arrival. It was just after five o'clock when Ernie returned.

"How's our girl?" Patterson asked sympathetically, folding the paper and tossing it on the stack in the basket near the hearth.

Ernie's arrival back at the flat was a welcome diversion. Patterson was very much excited about Marie's visit, and it was hindering his ability to stay focused on even the most relevant of articles the paper had to offer. Here was a man who was on a first-name basis with the Royal Family, a man who stared into the eyes of death countless times and laughed, yet could be rendered helpless by the mere idea of a beautiful French woman coming for a visit. To her credit, Marie was no ordinary French woman. He and Marie had a past, a loving, tender past. It was by his choice that their relationship changed. Since then, he's kept her at arms length, and the idea of holding her close once more scared the hell out of him. His mind raced with thoughts of what he would say, what he would do, once they got past the awkwardness of her arrival. It took a moment before he realized Ernie had answered him. Twice.

"Forgive me, Ernie. You were saying?"

Ernie took a seat on the sofa across from Patterson. "Everything all right, sir?"

"Preoccupied, that's all. Please, how is Miss Parsons?"

"Dee was in much better spirits when I was leaving. Jacque is still in a bit of a two-and-eight about Dee's safety. Having the policewoman in the hospital corridor is one thing, but she'll be released tomorrow. What then? Jacque believes this lout will be lurking about, waiting to finish the job?"

"There is that possibility, but I doubt it. Whoever it was, they got what they wanted. This attack was all about the journal. Why risk being identified for something as petty as a street crime? The murder of Mary Walsh has definite similarities to those murders eight years ago, but this new wrinkle breaks away from the old pattern." Patterson stared off into space again, lightly tapping his reading glasses on his knee as he pondered the question. "Attacking a woman in broad daylight makes no sense. It's not the actions of the cold, calculated killer the police believed they were dealing with eight years ago. Something has changed."

Ernie was just as confused over the conflicting actions. "It's a desperate man that does something like that. He must not want what's in that journal to get into the hands of Scotland Yard."

"I don't believe the person who murdered those women and the brute who attacked Miss Parsons are the same at all. What I *do* believe is the latter was hired by the former for the sole purpose of acquiring the journal. I'll even venture to say the latter has no idea of the true identity or nature of the man who hired him. If he did, I doubt very seriously if even the darkest of villains would have taken the commission."

Ernie took a moment to consider the conundrum posed by Patterson. It didn't take long before a smile emerged on his face. "He's become a liability."

"Brilliant!" responded Patterson, tossing his reading glasses onto the table between the sofas. "If we can locate him first, explaining the situation as we believe it to be, we just might be able to put a name to this *Brick Lane Slasher.*" A concerned look overcame Patterson's face. "Miss Parsons has nothing to fear from the man who attacked her, but I'm afraid she has every reason to fear the man who hired him. For the time being, she should be watched closely."

Ernie smiled. "I felt the same way, but for different reasons. I suggested Dee stay with Jacque for the time being until the police get to the bottom of this business."

"Excellent idea, my friend. I hope they were agreeable to the arrangement."

"Very much. I also promised to stop by with any news."

Patterson did a horrible job holding back a sheepish grin. "Did I notice a fondness in Miss Parsons' eyes for a certain reformed scoundrel?"

Ernie's face went flush. "She ain't right for the likes of me. Don't get me wrong she's quite a looker, but we don't exactly travel in the same circles. I'm happy just to know such a lady as that."

Patterson shook his head and gave a lighthearted, disparaging sigh. "If you'll forgive my use of a well-worn idiom, you're a diamond in the rough, Ernie. Someone any woman would be proud to be seen with. You've done so much in the last six months since you've joined us, but it would appear there is still much work to be done in the confidence department. Are you certain you were the top pickpocket in London?"

Fortunately, the harsh buzzer from the front door interrupted the conversation before Ernie had the opportunity to address Patterson's last bit of teasing. Instead, he craned his neck, peering around Patterson toward the pillared doorways of the sitting room. He caught a glimpse of Mrs. Chapman gliding past on her way to answer the door.

"I'll get it," echoed down the hall.

Moments later, a joyful chatter drifted up the stairs, trumpeting the arrival of Marie Bussière. Patterson was on his feet in an instant, brushing at the sleeves of his cardigan. Ernie laughed to see the Guv'nor primp himself like a nervous schoolboy about to meet his teacher on the first day of class.

Patterson shot a sharp glance in Ernie's direction. Despite his effort to hold a stern look, Patterson couldn't help but smile. "Well, it's apparent you have an opinion, so how do I look?"

Ernie stood up, beaming with delight. He took the small badger hair clothes brush he kept in his pocket–a reminder of his incarceration and duties in the laundry of Edmunds Hill Prison–and lightly brushed at Patterson's shoulders. "Fit to meet the Queen, you are."

"And not a moment too soon," said Mrs. Chapman, escorting Marie into the room.

Patterson walked over, took Marie in his arms and held her tightly. Not a word was said. Finally, she leaned back, looking up into his eyes. Tears were running down her cheeks. Patterson cupped her head in his hands, gently wiping the tears away with his thumbs.

"I would have thought you'd be happy to see me," Patterson said playfully.

"Je suis, mon amour, je le suis."

Marie smiled, looking around to where Ernie was standing. She took the handkerchief Patterson held out to her and dried her eyes. "Bonjour, Ernie."

Ernie shook her outstretched hand. "So nice to see you again, Miss Bussière."

Marie drew her mouth in tightly, giving Ernie a stern look. "I thought we agreed last time I was here you would call me Marie?"

"I'll be sure to work on that, mum," Ernie replied determinedly, but with bashful hesitation.

"Come here. This will help."

Ernie stepped closer. Marie took his hands in hers and kissed each cheek. He stepped back, a rich, pink hue rising above an impish smile.

"Now what do you have to say?"

"Thank you, mum," was the reply.

Marie smiled and shook her head. "We're just going to have to work on that a little more while I'm here."

"Ernie," called Mrs. Chapman from the kitchen door. "I could use your help here, if you wouldn't mind."

Ernie looked at Patterson, whose eyes were fixed on Marie, and then over at Mrs. Chapman. Even a reformed scoundrel could tell when three was a crowd. "Can't say as I'd mind at all."

21 / L'étreinte douce de l'amour

Patterson took Marie's coat; unaware, or even remotely concerned, Ernie and Mrs. Chapman had left the room. He walked it over to the closet in the hall, allowing Marie an opportunity to gain her composure. The tears were running intermittently down her cheeks as she looked around the room, quietly commenting on changes she noticed since her last visit. Marie tucked the handkerchief Patterson gave her into one pocket and retrieved a small enameled gold compact from the other. She brushed a bit of powder on each cheek and returned the compact to her pocket. Afterwards, she plunged her fingers into her thick hair and gave a quick tousle, followed by a shake of her head.

Marie's breakup with Marc Lafarge–her husband of twelve years–had left her in quite an emotional state, despite her recent indifference to their marriage. It was the action of his leaving that distressed her more than the consequence. Marie turned to her work, something she had immersed herself in more and more as her marriage began to unravel. All the signs were there, but she chose to ignore them. Subconsciously, she was driving herself towards an end she was too afraid to initiate herself.

"I'm glad you're here," said Patterson softly, returning to her side. He led Marie to the dining table and pulled out a chair. "I'll pour us a glass of wine and we'll catch up. Are you hungry?"

Marie replied with a bashful smile and nodded her head.

"Wonderful. We were just about to sit down to dinner."

The table had been set in anticipation of Marie's arrival. Almost on cue, Mrs. Chapman brought out a fine roast, carved in thin slices and swimming in a shallow pool of au jus. Following close behind her was Ernie. He brought out the covered serving dish of Brussels sprouts and a basket of crescent rolls, carefully balancing one on each opened palm. Mrs. Chapman made one additional trip to the kitchen, returning with a plate of jacket potatoes and a second bowl of gravy. With the wine poured, the plates brimming with hot portions, and the group seated, the meal began.

Patterson kept the conversation light and focused on the details of his recent Egypt trip. Marie was fascinated with his descriptions of the funerary objects the group unearthed, asking to see them if possible. Patterson reluctantly explained they were packed and ready for delivery to the museum, which brought a disappointing sigh from Marie. Ignoring her resistance to the idea, he insisted on unpacking a few of the more unique specimens after dinner for her to examine. The brightness returned to her expression.

"You know, it's not fair manipulating me in such a way," said Patterson. "Those eyes of yours are dangerous."

Marie innocently picked at her potato with her fork, doing little to mask a playful smile. "I'm sure I have no idea what you're talking about."

Patterson looked over at Ernie. "A lesson well learned here is there is more danger in a beautiful woman's eyes than in all the dark shadows of London."

"Pay no attention to him, Ernie," Marie snipped blithely.

Ernie tossed a pensive glance at Patterson and then to Marie, appearing to weigh his response carefully. "I've spent a bit of time in those dark shadows, miss, and I would have to agree with the Guv'nor. You pretty much know what's lurking about in the shadows, but I'd be the first to fall victim myself to such beautiful eyes." Ernie finished his thought with a blush.

Marie smiled and patted Ernie's hand, thoroughly enjoying the compliment. "It seems my wiles are no match for the two of you."

Patterson was happy to see a sereneness return to Marie's face. He continued with his recounting of the more significant aspects of the dig in Cairo. Ernie filled in the gaps with his own antidotes, mostly amusing consequences of his first trip to Egypt and first encounters with mummies, scorpions, and the occasional overzealous fruit merchant. A pleasant jauntiness rose up from the conversation and was enjoyed by all three.

Coffee was promptly served at the conclusion of the meal, along with English Trifle prepared in individual dessert glasses.

"If you'll excuse me," Ernie said, rising from the table after finishing the last of his coffee, "I've an urge to walk up the avenue for a late edition of the paper. Anything I can bring back?"

Patterson looked over at Marie who was shaking her head. "I think we're just fine. Enjoy your stroll."

As Ernie made his way out to Conduit Street, Mrs. Chapman cleared the dishes and excused herself for the evening. It was obvious to all Patterson and Marie were in need of privacy.

"Why don't we retire to the sofa?" suggested Patterson once they were alone. "I think those relics can wait a while longer. I'll get us each a glass of sherry and maybe we can unburden that conscience of yours."

"I would like that."

Marie got up and walked over to the fireplace. She took the poker and jostled the logs about before tossing on a fresh oak log from the bin. As she sat down on the sofa, her eyes started to well up once more. The reality of her current situation was not about to be cast aside so easily. She looked over her shoulder at Patterson who was pouring sherry by the sideboard then turned back. With her face in her hands, she began to sob.

Patterson saw her lowered head and could hear her sobbing as he walked over. "Are you okay? We can certainly put off any conversation until the morning. Maybe a good night of sleep would be more in order?"

Marie shook her head, dabbing her eyes with the handkerchief she pulled from her pocket. "No, I've come here to tell you something and there is no reason to postpone any longer. I'm just sorry you have to see me like this; carrying on and crying like some silly schoolgirl disillusioned by a love lost."

"Nonsense," Patterson replied firmly. He sat down beside Marie on the sofa and handed her a glass of sherry. "We've known each other far too long to worry about such things. Now, what is it you've come to tell me?"

Marie paused for a moment and took a deep breath. "I'm hopelessly in love with you and I will not let you turn me away again." She took a sip from her glass, rested back into the soft oversized cushions, and continued in a gentle tone. "This has been festering inside me for years. I don't believe Marc and I ever had a chance at true happiness. I saw what was happening between us and did nothing to stop it. I didn't want to stop it. The love Marc and I once shared was more one sided than I was ever willing to admit to myself. My heart has always belonged to you. I was devastated when you broke off our engagement."

Marie put her glass down on the table in front of her. She shook with emotion, her fists clenched. "This is all your fault!" She burst into tears, pounding her fists into Patterson's chest.

Patterson pulled Marie close. She struggled for a moment but then fell limp into his arms. She continued to cry. Patterson rocked her gently back and forth. "I'm sorry, Marie," he murmured tenderly. "I'm sorry."

After a few moments, Marie looked up. His eyes met hers. He made no attempt to disguise the remorse tugging at his own conscience. "I blame myself for all this misery you now endure. What I thought years ago would release you to pursue a greater happiness has done the complete opposite. Can you ever forgive me?"

Marie wrapped her arms around Patterson's neck and whispered in his ear, "There is nothing to forgive, mon amour. I was a foolish young girl who should have spoken up years ago. There was no greater happiness for me than to be in your arms always."

Patterson leaned back into the sofa. Marie fell back against him, her head resting against his shoulder and the soft texture of his cashmere cardigan. "I've certainly made a fine mess of your life, haven't I?"

Marie looked up and smiled. "Non, mon amour."

"You're far too forgiving, Marie." Patterson softly caressed her long dark hair with his hand as he spoke. "Somehow, I always knew our parting was a mistake. I foolishly walked away, but I'll confess now my love for you never accepted the decision."

Marie ran her delicate hand over Patterson's cheek. "Why didn't you say something?"

"By the time I realized what a mistake I had made, it was too late. You had met Marc and you seemed very happy. I was not about to complicate your life any further."

"You misinterpreted my happiness. The happiness you witnessed was not a result of my life with Marc. It was the uncontrollable joy I felt every time we were together, no matter how brief that visit might have been."

Marie put her head back on Patterson's shoulder.

"Since we're being honest," Patterson confessed, "I'll tell you all these years apart have been filled with nothing but regret. Gallantry sometimes wears the armor of a fool. I've always loved you and I'm a right proper fool for not telling you sooner. I've had an emptiness in my heart these past eighteen years without you."

Patterson and Marie sat quietly, nestled in each other's arms. Patterson stared out at the fire. Visions of what could have been danced about the flames before him in the fireplace. Occasionally, the finger of regret directed his thoughts back to the woman he held tightly in his arms. The past was just that; it was time to correct a foolish error in judgment. He responded by kissing Marie softly on her head at first, then slowly moved toward her waiting lips. She moaned softly as his hand caressed her back through her silk blouse, his fingers slowly running along her spine.

As they kissed, Marie reclined back on the sofa, pulling Patterson down on top of her. The repressed passion they had denied for so many years was rising in both of them, aching to burst forth. Patterson gently kissed her neck as Marie quietly professed her love for him.

Patterson pushed up from the sofa with his hands. Marie held on tightly, her fingers intertwined behind his neck. "We shouldn't," Patterson whispered. "Not like this."

Together they both sat up. Marie was hesitant to release her grip, but understood he was right. "So, where do we go from here?"

Patterson stood up, pulling Marie up with him. He put his hands around her waist. "Well, we can unpack those funerary objects you've expressed such an interest in, or—"

An impish smile came to Marie's face. She was quick to interrupt him, her eyes expressing her desire. She took Patterson by the hand and led him toward the pillared doorway to the hall. Marie looked down the hall, finally pointing to an ornately carved door just beyond the staircase to the second floor. "If I remember correctly," she quipped, "that would be the door to your bedroom?"

22/ No Way to Treat a Lady

It was just past one o'clock Thursday morning when Inspector Flannel met up with Inspector Godfrey at the mouth of an alley off Gower's Walk. Gower's was a long, narrow street lined with modest brick flats along one side and the landscaped and fenced-in rear area of the Royal Bank of Scotland opposite. The north end opening onto Commercial Road was blocked off with construction equipment related to a group of glass-clad apartment buildings being constructed. The normally mild traffic was non-existent as a result.

The ME was already on the scene and a number of constables were milling about, keeping late night gawkers away from the crime scene. Two other constables were interviewing an older gentleman clutching a small white terrier, the lead dangling over the arm of his thick wool sweater. They were jotting down notes as the gentleman pointed here and there, apparently retracing his steps leading to his discovery of the newest victim.

"A bunch of nosey-parkers, they are," remarked Flannel to Inspector Godfrey, nodding his head in the direction of a group of onlookers, dressed in their nightclothes and clustered in small groups. "You would think they would be home in bed at this hour, not lurking about dark alleys. So, what do we have here?"

The two inspectors walked down the alley to where a tan sheet covered what looked like the body of a woman on the ground. A light situated near the roof of the building on the right should have illuminated the ally, but the lamp and the outer lens were shattered, shards strewn about on the ground below. Light from the construction site cast a bit of light down the Walk, but not far enough to reach the alley. The police had the situation well in hand, having two spotlights connected to a generator. This was enough to light up the alley more than if it was midday.

Inspector Godfrey bent down and pulled back the sheet revealing an attractive woman of about forty. She rested peacefully in a white gown, her hands folded in prayer on her chest. Her blond hair, which was curled under at the shoulders, rested in the halo of blood that glistened from the bright spotlights above. Around her neck, covering a deep gash, was the ever so haunting red scarf—a chilling signature Flannel recognized immediately.

"She looks familiar," grumbled Inspector Flannel. "Do we know who she is?"

"I'm afraid not," replied Inspector Godfrey. "This is the way she was found. The gentleman in that flat over there said he heard a bit of a dustup in the alley here about midnight. Afterwards, he took his pup out for a walk, thinking it was just a couple juveniles having a go at it. That's when he found the body. The police arrived a few minutes later. This is just how they found her. No purse. No ID of any type."

The inspector looked around the alley and gave a grunt. "No sign of a struggle either. Looks like someone dropped the body here, tossed that rubbish bin up in the air and took off."

"You think whoever did this wanted the body to be found?"

"Yes. I also think he's teasing us a bit. I won't be at all surprised if whoever killed this woman knew her. It's all a bit odd, and a bit too familiar."

"In what way?"

"I can't think of any reason why this woman would venture into this alley alone at this time of night. I think she was brought here after she was killed. It follows the same pattern as the others." Flannel continued, using a short yellow pencil to indicate the important aspects of the scene. "This white choir robe was put on her here, after the body was staged. Her arms are slipped in and the rest of the fabric is tucked under the body. The killer then places her hands together on her chest. Her throat is slit, providing enough blood to create the halo, afterwards the scarf is wrapped around her neck to cover the unsightly gash."

As the inspector detailed his thoughts to Godfrey the ME, John Deacons, had walked over. "We may have caught a break on this one."

"What do you mean?" replied Flannel. The drone of the generator forced him to cock his head and lean in close to hear Deacons' reply.

"I can't say for sure until I get her back to the morgue, but I'm relatively certain she fought back to some extent. I found what I believe to be skin under her fingernails."

"That's brilliant!" exclaimed Inspector Flannel. "We've got him this time."

"Got who?" asked Deacons.

Inspector Flannel hastily returned to his usual caustic look. "No one. Just get Inspector Godfrey and myself the results of that DNA as quickly as possible." The Inspector pulled a small card from his pocket and handed it to the ME "Here, phone me the minute you have anything."

Deacons nodded, picked up his case, and walked back over to the body. With a signal from Inspector Godfrey, the ME gave instructions for the body to be placed in the body bag and moved to the van.

"One minute there," Inspector Flannel called out. He walked over to the body and lifted the sheet. He paid particular attention to the victim's wrist and then replaced the sheet. "On your way now."

They watched as the body was removed. The alley was taped off with yellow police tape, and a constable was stationed on Gower's Walk and another on Back Church Lane.

With access to Commercial Road blocked, Inspectors Flannel and Godfrey made their way out through the entrance on Black Church Lane. There was a little more activity along this route, despite the hour. Small groups of college-aged kids gave the two inspectors only a passing glance as they walked by. Older brick buildings, once home to a sundry of commercial enterprises, crisscrossed the road and were now converted to flats, with newer construction filling in the gaps between them. An assortment of musical tastes drifted down from well-lit spaces above, though Inspector Flannel paid no attention to even the loudest of them. Not a word passed between the two men until they turned up White Church Lane.

"So what time was on her watch?" asked Godfrey.

Flannel gave no indication he heard Godfrey's question. He just continued along at the same pace.

Inspector Godfrey was a little irritated at being ignored. "You know, if you truly believe this was Raventhorn, you'll need to be one hundred and ten percent sure before you come forward with another accusation. I've given you as much rope as I can on this case and risked my own badge doing so, thank you very much. I have the greatest respect for you Inspector, but if you hang yourself, you'll hang alone."

Inspector Flannel smiled at the thought. He stopped and patted Inspector Godfrey on the back. "I have no intention of sharing a rope with you, Wynne. You have the guts and instincts of a first-rate detective and I'll not do anything else to jeopardize what I'm sure will be a brilliant career. Don't think I don't appreciate you letting me stick my nose in this business, because I do. Should this go pear shaped, I'll be the first to swear I've been poking about on my own without your knowledge."

"So you *do* think this was Raventhorn."

Flannel continued along his way. He was hesitant with a response, choosing his words carefully. "I think these two recent murders are directly related to those five other murders eight years ago. I made a mistake then and these two young women have paid dearly for it. I'll not make that same mistake again."

"What will you do now?"

"There's only room for one on the gallows I'm heading for. It's best we leave it here. I will promise to forward any information I uncover that I believe useful to your investigation."

Both men stopped in front of the glass door to the police station on Brick Lane.

"I'm going to write this up while it's still fresh in my mind," said Inspector Godfrey. "Are you coming in for a cup to warm you up?"

"You go on," replied Flannel. He pushed his derby back a little and scratched his head. "I've got a few problems to think through."

"I'll see you then."

Inspector Godfrey turned to enter, but stopped when Flannel tapped on his wrist.

"Quarter past," said Flannel, giving Godfrey a nod and tapping on the inspector's wrist once more. "Her watch was stopped at quarter past. Enjoy your evening lad."

* * *

There was a slight chill lingering in the air early that morning. Mrs. Chapman was up and about at her usual time of 6:45 and very surprised to see Ernie sitting at the island in the kitchen enjoying toast with jam and a cup of coffee.

"Must be something important has you up and fed this early," said Mrs. Chapman in her usual melodic voice. "I thought I smelled coffee brewing."

"I'm off to the hospital. They're releasing Dee Parsons this morning and I wanted to be there. Thought she might like a friendly face and a little reassurance."

"Why didn't you say something last night? I would have got these tired bones out of bed earlier and made you a right proper fry-up."

"You do far too much for me. I couldn't bring myself to disturb your rest for such a trivial matter as an early breakfast."

Mrs. Chapman smiled as she topped off Ernie's coffee. "It's a lucky woman for sure who lands the likes of you as a husband."

"I don't know about that," replied Ernie shyly. "I just feel responsible for what happened, that's all."

"Rubbish. It was fortunate for her she was on her way here to see you. What if she was home when that hooligan decided to attack her? Lord knows the poor thing might have been . . . well, you know. Have they any idea who?"

"No." Ernie hesitated before elaborating on the details, giving careful thought to the inspector's original instruction to keep this business secret. In light of recent events, he saw no reason to remain silent any longer. "Inspector Flannel believes all this is related to those murders eight years ago. Dee was on her way here to deliver a journal. It belonged to Mary Walsh Trevor, the woman killed the other night off Brick Lane. She was a journalist, apparently investigating those *Slasher* murders. From information given to him by Dee, the inspector believes Mary Walsh Trevor had put most of the pieces together. Dee said Mary had told her she made arrangements to meet with someone to confirm her suspicions about who she thought had committed the murders. That was the last time she saw her alive."

"Oh dear. That poor girl."

The front door buzzer startled both of them, causing Ernie to fumble the knife he was using to spread jam.

Mrs. Chapman looked up at the clock above the Imperial. "Who could be calling at this hour?"

Ernie shook his head as Mrs. Chapman went off to answer the door. A few minutes later she returned with Inspector Flannel close behind her.

"I'm sorry, lad," said the inspector, taking a notepad from his pocket, "but there's been another murder. It happened early this morning off Gower's Walk. I can't be certain, but the victim looked a great deal like that woman at the hospital yesterday." Inspector Flannel flipped through his notes. "Jacque, I believe she said her name was."

Ernie dropped his fork. He was speechless.

The three stood in silence for a few moments until Inspector Flannel looked up and realized the impact his news had on Ernie. "Let's not get ahead of ourselves here thinking the worst. Like I said, she only *looked* a bit like that woman. The ME has the body. I trust he'll make a proper identification with haste. Until then, our attention is best served other ways. I'm going to need a favor, Bisquets, if we're to stop all this."

Ernie was just staring off in space. He heard the inspector but was too distressed over the idea that Jacque may have fallen victim to this murderous fiend to answer. The look in his eyes quickly went from horror to anger. He pulled his mobile phone and the note Dee gave him from his pocket and began to dial.

Inspector Flannel took the phone from Ernie's hand, hit the disconnect button and handed it back to him. "In the event it isn't her, all this will do is terrify them more. Let the ME determine the victim's identity."

"This has to stop!" cried Ernie, jamming the phone back into his pocket. "Those two women are no threat to him. Killing them is just despicable. You have to arrest him, Inspector. You have to, before he kills one or the other of them . . . or both."

"He can't," Patterson softly replied from the doorway. He walked in and stood by his friend the inspector.

"But he must," Ernie replied sternly, glaring at the inspector. "You're the police. You know he did it. Just arrest him."

The inspector put his notepad back in his pocket. "I'm afraid he's right, lad. Without proper evidence it'll be balls up, and I'll end up with me head in me hands. We'll get him, but we have to tread cautiously. The wrong move now and we could lose him for good."

Ernie wiped his mouth with his napkin and tossed it on the countertop. He looked over at Patterson who confirmed the inspector's reasoning with an unenthusiastic nod.

Ernie gave a nod of his own, acknowledging he understood why it had to be. "You said you needed a favor?" he asked Inspector Flannel. "Will it help bring an end to this business?"

Inspector Flannel nodded his head. "I hope so, lad."

"What is it you need me to do?"

"Off with you now," said Mrs. Chapman, turning Ernie and the inspector toward the door. "We'll not have all this police business in my kitchen."

"Mrs. Chapman is right," agreed Patterson. "Why don't we go over the particulars at the table? Annie, could I bother you for a fresh pot of coffee and a few of those breakfast pastries?"

"Not a bother at all. I'll have them out to you in a shake."

The three men left the kitchen, taking seats at the dinning room table. The room had a soft glow from the early morning light streaming in through the front windows at the far end of the sitting room.

The troubled expression Ernie carried in from the kitchen was beginning to wane. Returning to a more placid frame of mind, he sat down across from the inspector, anxiously awaiting his instructions. With this latest development, he was consumed with a single-minded desire to do what he could to bring this murderer to justice.

Ernie folded his hands on the table in front of him. "What is it you need me to do?"

"I need you to interview Prophet Brown."

"Prophet Brown? Me?" Ernie cocked his head in confusion. "But I've never met the lad."

"Precisely." The inspector underlined his point with a sharp bob of his head and a tap on the table with his forefinger. "Every Thursday morning, Prophet Brown washes Raventhorn's car. Rain or shine, he's out there precisely at half past nine o'clock. If you could strike up a conversation with him and confirm a few facts, it might be enough for me to take what I know to my superiors. I'll plead my case and with luck we'll have Raventhorn across the table in interrogation before noon."

"Why would Prophet talk to me? He's no idea who I am."

"You just mention I sent you there. He'll talk alright."

Ernie sat back and scratched his head. "If he knows you, why send me?"

"Raventhorn doesn't know you," the inspector replied somewhat prickly over all the questions.

"Why would that matter?"

Patterson was quick to pick up on the inspector's line of thought and the rising irritation in his voice. "If Raventhorn happens to see you speaking with Prophet, he'll just think you are someone from the neighborhood stopping for a quick chat. I doubt he would connect you with the inspector or any type of investigation."

"Right you are, Patty." As the inspector concurred, his mobile phone rang. He looked at the screen to see the caller's name. "I'll need to take this."

Patterson and Ernie watched the inspector walk into the hall. They waited patiently for his return. Sadness lingered over Ernie's expression, his thoughts drifting off to concern for Dee. Being attacked over this business was tragic enough, losing a close friend as a result of trying to help would be devastating to her.

Patterson detected the disquiet Ernie was struggling with. "I know you're concerned," said Patterson soothingly, "but we don't know that it was Dee's friend Jacque in that alley. If whoever did this is the same person who attacked Dee for the journal, they would have no reason to attack Jacque. They got what they were after."

"But what if the murderer thought Mary had confided in them. What if the journal had the murderer's name in it? What if—"

Patterson held up his hand and shook his head. "I'll not go down that path with you. Emotional speculation is to deductive reasoning what weeds are to a garden—at first sight they appear to belong, but eventually they obscure that which one hopes will come into bud."

Ernie smiled, a bit embarrassed over his outburst. "Of course you're right. Sorry, not like me to be in a state over such things, especially without all the facts."

"You have no reason to apologize, it's obvious you care for these two women. You'll serve them best by keeping a good head about you."

"That was the ME," said Inspector Flannel in his official voice walking back to the table. "He's identified the victim. You'll be relieved to know it was not the young woman from the hospital."

Ernie released a big sigh of relief. "I don't mean to appear happy, I'm just glad it wasn't Jacque. Who was the woman?"

"Her name was Cynthia Carolls."

23/ Polishing a Bad Apple

The early morning sun threw long shadows across the quiet square. Ernie turned down Garret Way, a gated road off Sloane Square behind the row of houses on Lower Sloane Street. This private road allows the residents, accustomed to privileged admission on every level of life, access to their back gardens and drives. Each garden was impeccably manicured, the drives filled with expensive automobiles. Just ahead, about three quarters of the way up, he heard the clang of a bucket and saw water running off into the road. It was coming from a wide alley, which he assumed to be the drive behind Raventhorn's residence. As he approached, he heard someone mumbling to himself.

Ernie came up just behind a gentleman wearing a leather apron whose back was to him. The man was busy tending to the chrome wheels of an elegant black Jaguar. Ernie made a quick survey of the house overlooking the garden and drive just to be sure no prying eyes were fixed in his direction from any of the windows. With a deep breath, he stepped forward.

"A fine job you're doing on those spokes," said Ernie in a cheerful voice. "Tedious work, I'd say. Takes a proper hand to do it just right."

Prophet turned slowly. He took a moment to size up his admirer. Content he wasn't a threat Prophet cautiously returned a smile. "Not so tedious. Kind of you to say though."

Ernie was a bit nervous—something that didn't go unnoticed. "I was wondering if I might ask you a few questions?" he finally stated.

"Depends on who's asking the questions." Prophet stood up, tossing the wet rag into the bucket. He picked up a fresh rag from another bucket and dried his hands. "And who might you be?"

Ernie shook the nervousness from his expression. He identified Prophet by the deformed right arm curled up on his chest, a description Inspector Flannel had given him. "Bisquets, Mr. Brown. Ernie Bisquets." Ernie held out his left hand, leaned in close and finished his introduction with a whisper. "Detective Inspector Flannel thought you and I might have a common interest."

It was Prophet's turn to be nervous. He casually looked around, paying particular attention to the windows. When he walked out to tend to the vehicle, Lord Raventhorn was in his front study working on a speech he was to deliver that evening, but it did little to ease Prophet's mind. Raventhorn's library was in the back of the flat with windows overlooking the garden. The sudden need for a reference book would put Prophet and his curious new friend in full view of His Lordship, an act he felt certain would lead to punishment.

"Inspector Flannel, you say?" replied Prophet, shaking Ernie's hand. He scanned the windows of the house a second time. His cordial expression changed to one of concern. "Not right. It's just not right. You must go. I'll pay dearly for this if he sees us talking."

Prophet's head darted about. He grew more anxious by the minute. Ernie knew his actions would do nothing but draw attention to their conversation. He needed to do something quickly to give the appearance of just an innocent conversation.

"You have to stay calm," Ernie said through a smile. He knelt down and started retying his shoe as he continued. "Lord Raventhorn has no reason to think I'm anything more than a resident stopping for a quick chat. Go back to what you were doing and act like we're just talking about this fine automobile." Ernie stood up, pointing randomly at the Jaguar. "The inspector needs your help. I'll not be long, but I have to ask you a few questions."

Prophet went to scan the windows again but caught himself. He followed Ernie's lead by nodding and returning to polishing the spoke wheels. "What is it you want to know?"

Ernie alternated between a loud and soft voice as he posed his questions. "Brand new, is it? Did Raventhorn go out at any time last night?"

Prophet was quick to understand what was happening and followed suit. "Yes. He left for a few hours after dinner. It was after midnight before he returned."

Ernie bent down for a closer look at the bonnet. "Is that a blemish? Do you know where he went?"

"Just a water spot. Said he was going to the club. He was angry when he left."

"Of course, you're right," Ernie replied, walking around so his back was to the house. "You're doing just fine. You didn't happen to see a journal around recently? Leather bound I would say."

"I can't say I did." Prophet paused for a moment, thinking back to an incident from the previous day. He took a dry, wash leather from the bucket and began to polish a spot on the bonnet Ernie had indicated while he spoke. "The master came back yesterday afternoon with his leather satchel tucked under his arm. When I attempted to take it and put it away, he became very agitated. Knocked me down when he grabbed it back. Seemed very odd at the time; I always put his satchel away. There must have been something in that case he didn't want me to see. He went into his study and stayed there until dinner."

Ernie continued his way around. As he casually looked back toward the house, his attention was caught by something he thought moved in one of the windows. He made the mistake of letting Prophet see the alarmed look on his face. Prophet quickly turned, looking up in the direction of the house.

"It was nothing," Ernie said in a calming voice. "Just a shadow from a bird flying overhead."

Prophet wasn't listening. He began to shake. He knocked the bucket over in his haste to pick up the assorted cleaning supplies. "It'll be the head of his cane on my back for this. You must go. Go now! Go before he comes out and starts asking questions."

Ernie bent down, attempting to help Prophet put his cleaning supplies in the bucket with the clean leathers. "Sorry, I didn't mean to alarm you. I'm quite certain it was just a bird and not His Lordship. One last question and I'll go."

"No!" Prophet snapped. "You've done enough damage."

"It's important. It could help solve the case."

Prophet fumbled with the two buckets, finally getting the handle of the lighter one over his bad arm. He ignored Ernie and started toward the garage.

"Cynthia Carolls," Ernie called out in a hushed tone, but loud enough to get Prophet's attention.

Prophet stopped in his tracks. He turned, giving a quick glance up at the windows and then back at Ernie. "What about Miss Carolls?"

"Do you know her?"

Prophet nodded his head. "She had dinner here last night."

"A pleasure meeting you," Ernie called out in a cheerful voice.

Prophet didn't say another word. He walked over to the garage, walked inside, and abruptly pulled down the door.

Ernie casually walked once more around the well-polished Jaguar. After a nonchalant scan of the windows, he quietly made his way back down the road toward Sloane Square.

* * *

"I can see where this is going," Raventhorn grumbled to himself. He stood back from the window in the shadows just beyond the curtain, watching as Ernie disappeared around the brick wall along Garret Way.

Prophet emerged from the garage, looking nervously down the road before starting back toward the house. He gave another quick scan of the windows, trying not to be obvious by keeping his head down as much as possible.

Expelling a deep growl, Raventhorn stepped away from the window. He squeezed his sherry glass so tightly it shattered in his hand. He stared at the blood pooling in his open palm. "That miserable wretch has crossed me for the last time."

24/ An Arm's Length of Truth

Marie and Patterson sat quietly at the dining table, enjoying coffee, toast and jam, and the lingering bliss of the previous evening. Patterson's normal routine was to read the morning paper, something he decided to put aside until further notice and bask in the sheer delight of Marie's company. Besides general small talk and a bit of playful banter, he went over the particulars of Inspector Flannel's early morning visit, noting Ernie's absence as the result.

Marie reached over and took Patterson's hand. "From what you have told me, I'm very surprised you are not more involved in this matter. I hope this was not a result of my unexpected visit."

Patterson smiled. "Not at all. Quite frankly, I've just become aware of the investigation. It seems our good friend Inspector Flannel had begun an independent investigation after the murder of a young woman a few days back. He contacted Ernie directly, asking for *his* assistance in the matter."

Marie rested back in her chair. "That's rather curious. I was always under the impression the inspector had little respect for Ernie. What changed?"

Patterson's expression darkened as he sat back in his chair. "The inspector believes there is more to this case than the random murder of these two young women.

What changed was the inspector's prime suspect is a personal friend of mine."

"Le plus curieux en effet," Marie pondered. "So he didn't wish to risk your friendship?"

"It's frightfully more complicated than that; there is more involved here than just a friendship. His suspect is a very powerful and influential man. The inspector's wading through very treacherous waters, one wrong step could drag his whole career under."

"I would think that would give him even more of a reason to ask for your help."

"This has been a very touchy subject between the inspector and myself. We've since talked and his reluctance to involve me has passed. I've assured him I will help in any way I can, no matter where the investigation leads." Patterson paused. His determined expression faded to one of tenderness. "Enough about that. It's a rather ugly business and I see no need to upset you with the details. The inspector and Ernie have the situation well in hand, so we'll leave it at that."

Marie sat forward and once again took Patterson's hand in hers. "It would appear Ernie has wasted no time acclimating himself to his new life. You should be proud of yourself."

"I'm afraid I can assume little credit for Ernie's change in occupation; I did nothing more than offer him a choice. I will admit though how incredibly impressed I am with his decision and with his determination to contribute." Patterson looked back over his shoulder after hearing the street door close. "I believe that's him now."

As Patterson spoke, Ernie raced into the room.

"Sorry," Ernie coughed, somewhat winded by his run down Conduit Street and up the stairs. "I'll just wait in the kitchen for Inspector Flannel."

"Nonsense," replied Patterson. "Have a seat, catch your breath, and I'll pour you a coffee."

"That's quite kind of you. Thank you, sir."

"What's all the excitement?" asked Marie. "Have you a break in the case?"

Ernie looked over at Patterson standing by the sideboard, unsure whether to explain or not. Patterson met his glance with a cautious shake of his head.

Ernie looked back at Marie. "Not so much a break," replied Ernie with an unconcerned shrug, hoping to mask his hesitation.

Marie's raised eyebrow indicated his attempt to downplay his excitement was less than believable.

"I see you two are determined to shield me from this ugly business at hand." Marie relaxed back into her chair. "Your gallantry is commendable, but certainly not necessary."

"Sorry, miss, I was—"

"It's alright," replied Patterson placing a coffee down in front of Ernie. "Marie is well aware of how overprotective I can be at times." He sat down, taking Marie's hand. "You've had to deal with enough. I see no reason to upset you with the details of this business. When Ernie and the good inspector have brought this fiend to justice, I'm sure we can persuade them to highlight the particulars of the case for you."

Marie knew there was no sense arguing with Patterson over certain things. "Well, I guess you've made up my mind," Marie grumbled playfully. She leaned over the table toward Ernie. "But, I expect a full accounting once you've solved the case."

Ernie smiled and nodded his head, relieved.

Patterson sat back and slapped his hand on the table like an auctioneer. "Settled. Now, Marie, tell me a bit more about this presentation you have this evening at the museum. I would be delighted to escort you."

"It's a symposium on museum spatial capacity in relation to viewing the work of 19th Century Impressionists. I wouldn't think to bore you with such a topic."

"Nonsense. You can never learn enough about spatial capacity. Isn't that right, Ernie?"

Ernie coughed, choking a bit on a mouthful of coffee, unable to answer at first. The best he could do was a jerking nod of his head. By the time Ernie cleared his throat, a verbal response was no longer required.

Marie laughed. "No. After cocktails, I have a thirty-minute address to give to a roomful of curators. After a fifteen-minute break, I will join a panel for a thirty-minute question and answer session. That will conclude at 9:30 sharp, at which time I will be incredibly hungry and looking forward to a glass of wine and pleasant dinner conversation."

"Well, I can certainly provide that. I'll meet you at the museum at 9:30 sharp."

"Sorry to interrupt."

Everyone turned to see Inspector Flannel entering.

"Not at all," said Marie. "A pleasure to see you again, Inspector."

Inspector Flannel gave a quick nod and got right to business. "I'll not be long. I only need the lad for a few minutes, then you can return to your elevenses."

"I was just about to excuse myself anyway," replied Marie. She rose from her seat and gave Patterson a kiss on the cheek. "I've got to go over my notes for the address this evening, and then meet with the other presenters at the museum this afternoon. I'll leave you to your privacy."

"Sorry, miss," said the inspector, pulling his hat from his head. "Police business, otherwise I—"

"No need to apologize," Marie replied brightly. She patted the Inspector's coat sleeve as she walked by.

"Have a seat, August," said Patterson.

"I'll not stay long, Pattie. I just need to know what Bisquets here found out from his little chat with Prophet Brown this morning."

Ernie couldn't speak fast enough. "You were right, Inspector. Raventhorn was out for a while last night.

What's more, that woman you found dead? She had dinner at his flat last night."

"I knew it," cried the inspector. "I've got him now. He'll not get away with it this time."

"To quote Señor Santayana," Patterson remarked, "'those who cannot remember the past are condemned to repeat it.' If I'm not mistaken, it was Prophet Brown who led you down a very dark and similar path eight years ago. I would hope you will exercise a bit of restraint before charging forward once again into the darkness on the words of a disgruntled servant."

"Oh, I've learnt my lesson alright." The inspector took a seat at the table across from Ernie. "I have no intention of acting only on his word. As it is, I've received a bit of corroborating evidence on my way here myself on the matter. Inspector Godfrey searched the deceased woman's flat early this morning. A receipt for a car service was found on a table. It seems she was picked up by that car service at Raventhorn's address last night."

Patterson sat back, pulling lightly at his lower lip as he contemplated the relevance of the inspector's news. "That certainly is enough to raise a few questions, but not enough to condemn the man. What else do you have?"

"Bollocks, Pattie!" The inspector banged his fist on the table and rose from his chair. He paced back and forth snorting at each turnabout. He finally stopped, looking over at Ernie. His tone became accusatory at best, ending with a snide grunt. "There's a fine how are you. He says he wants to help but instead he's quick to rally round his own *kind*. You see now why I asked you not to involve His Lordship."

Ernie looked over at Patterson. It was the first time he saw anger in the compassionate gray eyes of his benefactor.

"Sit down you silly twit," Patterson shouted sharply. "You had best get your emotions off the boil before they drag you under the bus."

The inspector gave one last grunt and then flopped down into a seat.

"That's better," Patterson continued. "*My* own kind? Despite what you might think, I'm acting in *your* best interest. You came dangerously close to losing that badge of yours eight years ago. One false step this time and there'll be no saving you." He paused, giving the inspector a moment to grasp what he was saying. "Now, I'll ask you again, what else do you have?"

The inspector's silence more than answered the question.

"The journal," Ernie abruptly uttered. "I almost forgot."

"The journal?" said the inspector excitedly. "He saw the journal?"

The atmosphere at the table was very tense. Ernie hesitated answering, rubbing the back of his neck with his hand.

"Out with it, lad," barked the inspector.

Patterson shot the inspector a cold glance, which was enough to push the Inspector back down into his seat.

"Go ahead, Ernie," said Patterson in a calming tone. "What about the journal?"

Ernie looked over at the inspector. "I did what you said and asked Prophet if he saw a journal. At first he looked confused, but he finally said Lord Raventhorn had come back yesterday afternoon with his satchel under his arm. Prophet took the satchel to put it away—as was his custom—and Lord Raventhorn snatched it back from him. Knocked him over in the process, he did. Prophet said he didn't know what was in the satchel, but figured it was something Lord Raventhorn didn't want him to see."

"You say this was yesterday afternoon?" asked the inspector. "Did he say what time?"

"No."

The inspector stood up. "What do you say now, Pattie?"

"I must admit this does cast a very stark shadow of suspicion in the direction of Raventhorn. I would think presenting these facts to your superiors should at least raise the question of his possible involvement with this recent murder."

"That's all I need for the time being." The inspector became very animated, waving his hands and pacing about, as he spoke aloud about his next step. "I'll take this evidence to the Chief Inspector. He's a reasonable man. He'll understand the significance of these odd facts. I'm sure if I promise to proceed with prudence he'll allow me access to the case. With Godfrey's support, I should be able to secure a search warrant for Raventhorn's flat. As sure as the sun will rise tomorrow, I know I'll find the evidence I need and the man behind these crimes in that flat."

"A search warrant will also tip your hand," said Patterson cautiously. "Are you ready for what will eventually wash over the bow when this storm breaks?"

The inspector was quite pleased with himself. "Like I said before, Pattie, I'll not let this murderer slip through my fingers a second time. The car service receipt ties Raventhorn to the second victim and possession of the journal will tie him to the first."

"Not that I wish to add fuel to your fire," Patterson replied, "but I would imagine if the information in Mary Walsh Trevor's journal was enough to get her killed, then it would seem likely it's also enough to tie Raventhorn to those other five murders. It's a dangerous course you've plotted, August."

"What if he's already destroyed the journal?" asked Ernie.

The inspector's attention was once again captured by the seriousness of the situation. "It's possible, but I sees him as too cautious to just burn the journal. If it was me, I'd study every page just to be sure I had answers for any questions that journal might give rise to. He may have the journal, but I'll wager he is less than certain its contents weren't shared with someone else. He's too careful for that. No, he still has the journal and I fully intend to get at it before he has a chance to destroy it."

"And how do you propose to do that?" replied Patterson.

"Prophet Brown owes me, he does. And I intend to collect. It was jam tomorrow with him the last time, but I'll not stand for it again. He's scared. He'll get me that journal."

Patterson shook his head in disbelief. "Have you heard nothing I've said? You're taking a frightfully big chance relying on him like this again."

"I have no other choice. It's the only way I know to get the journal without tipping my hand." Inspector Flannel started toward the door, stopping after a few steps. "If it will ease your mind, I will at least present what I have to the Chief Inspector first. I'm on my way there now. I'll approach Prophet about getting me the journal *only* with his approval. Satisfied, mother?"

Patterson laughed. "Off with you now, and take that sharp tongue with you."

Patterson looked at Ernie after the inspector had left. His cheerfulness faded to one of concern. "Normally, I would only trust Nigel for this. In his absence, I'm hoping I could stretch the bounds of our friendship by requesting a favor of you?"

"Anything, sir." Ernie sat upright awaiting the command.

"Hear me out first before you answer. Something isn't right about these murders. I'm afraid our friend the inspector might be drifting into a raging gale. What do you think about this Prophet Brown?"

"He's a sorry lot, that one, with the bad arm and gammy leg. A bit nervous, always looking over his shoulders, but certainly seems pleasant enough though. The Inspector says he's been treated rather harshly?"

"Yes, I'm afraid there could be more truth to that than I ever cared to admit. If Raventhorn is as dangerous as Inspector Flannel believes, I'm afraid Prophet very easily could be the next victim if Flannel's interest in these two murders is exposed prematurely. I know you intended to visit Dee this morning, but could I impose on you to change your plans? Would you be averse to spending the afternoon in Sloane Square? The square should make for a good vantage point. You can watch over Raventhorn's flat without drawing any attention until the inspector can make it official that Raventhorn is a person of interest in the case."

"Not an imposition at all, sir," replied Ernie, quite pleased to be entrusted with the task. "I'll stop by the hospital briefly first and then head over to the square, if that's agreeable?"

"That's just fine." Patterson looked at his watch. "Keep an eye on things until around 5:00 o'clock, that should give the inspector enough time to put his plan into motion. Once he speaks to Prophet and secures the journal, I doubt Raventhorn would be foolish enough to harm him."

Ernie stood up. "I'll leave now."

"Since you're only making a brief appearance this morning at the hospital," Patterson continued, pausing Ernie's departure, "maybe your friend Dee would be agreeable to a more extended visit and dinner afterwards?"

A large smile came over Ernie's face. "Very good, sir."

With a lively spring in his step, he was down the stairs before Patterson topped off his coffee.

25/ When in Doubt, Adapt

Inspector Flannel waited patiently in the open area in front of Chief Detective Inspector Hardgrave's office. It was the northwest corner of the building, and very brightly lit from the wall of windows overlooking Broadway. Mrs. Harris, going on her thirty-second year as secretary to the chief detective inspector, gave Flannel a cordial greeting, nodding a suggestion for him to have a seat while he waits. He returned the greeting with a nod, choosing to pace a bit in anticipation of what he hoped to be a short wait. After a few minutes of pacing off his nervousness, he settled into one of the green, well-worn, wooden chairs lined up in a row below the windows.

There were voices coming from inside the office, at times sharp and loud, but not loud enough that anyone could make out the conversation. He snickered a bit to himself, assuming the raised voices were the result of a young recruit being called on the carpet. His amusement quickly vanished when his thoughts shifted to a previous encounter with the chief detective inspector. An uncomfortable feeling crept up the back of his neck as he recounted his last discussion regarding this topic in that very office. It was eight years ago, and despite a number of other conversations he and Chief Detective Inspector Hardgrave participated in, the sting of that particular conversation still lingered. *This time will be different,* he said to himself.

As he sat waiting, he went over the details in his head. *Cynthia Carolls was at Raventhorn's the night of the murder— there's a receipt from a car service to verify the fact. Raventhorn had left his flat not long after Miss Carolls departure, returning after midnight. The afternoon Miss Parsons was attacked Raventhorn had been out of the house, only to return with a satchel holding something he didn't want Prophet to see. Miss Parsons was in possession of a journal given to her by the first victim, Mary Walsh Trevor.* In his mind, Raventhorn had the journal, and his culpability for all the crimes related to the case, past and present, rested within the pages.

Flannel's thoughts were interrupted when the Chief Detective Inspector's door swung open. "Come in, August."

Flannel rose, following Hardgrave into the office. After only a few steps inside he stopped, unable to move forward another step. His face turned pale when he saw Lord Alfred Raventhorn standing by the window, his arms folded behind his back. Next to him was Deputy Commissioner Bullen-Smythe. Flannel was so stunned he almost didn't notice Inspector Godfrey sitting in one of the burgundy leather chairs facing the large oak desk.

"Is this him?" asked the deputy commissioner in a less than cordial voice.

The whole scene was surreal to Inspector Flannel. With the exception of Inspector Godfrey's attendance, it was as if he walked back into the very meeting he was called to and reprimanded in eight years ago.

Inspector Godfrey rose from his seat. As he walked by Inspector Flannel, he paused and quietly said, "I'm sorry Inspector. I did what I could for you." He continued out, quietly closing the door behind him.

Inspector Flannel was numb.

"Sit down, August," said Hardgrave sternly, pointing to one of the leather chairs.

Chief Detective Inspector Hardgrave was well tailored, with sharp edges and a chiseled countenance. He paced back and forth behind his desk as Flannel slowly approached the chairs.

"You've brought this on yourself," snapped Raventhorn, walking over from the window and stepping between Flannel and the chairs. He took the newspaper he held tightly in his hand and stuffed it into Flannel's overcoat. "I was tolerant the first time, but I'll not stand for it again." Raventhorn poked his boney finger into the inspector's lapel to underline his final point. "It's your meddlesome and misguided actions that's done this."

The deputy commissioner walked over and took Raventhorn's arm. "Enough, Albert. Hardgrave will handle this from here."

Raventhorn gave a final grunt and walked out, followed by the Deputy Commissioner.

The room was deathly silent. Flannel wanted to speak up in his defense but knew better. Instead he pulled the newspaper from his overcoat, hoping to find the reason for the hostility being shown him.

"Have you seen that?" asked Hardgrave contemptuously, pointing at the paper in Flannel's hand.

Flannel didn't answer. He opened the paper and it quickly became apparent why this particular group had convened.

The headline read: SLASHER RETURNS. The highlights of the accompanying article stated: *Old ghost has returned to claim more victims . . . Similarities to eight-year-old unsolved murders . . . Undisclosed source hints at scandal in Parliament . . . Original suspect once again on the short list of Detective Inspector Flannel.*

"What were you thinking?" barked Hardgrave. "I expressly told you to stay away from this case. You completely ignored my order, and worse, jeopardized the career of young Godfrey by conducting your own investigation. And for what?"

"Inspector Godfrey had nothing to do with my actions," Flannel quietly replied penitently. "He was against—"

"Shut up, August," interrupted Hardgrave bluntly. "I've spoken with Godfrey. I'll blame inexperience for his part in all this, but you have no excuse as far as I'm concerned." He resumed his pacing as he continued. "This rod in pickle you have for Raventhorn will be your end. Lord Raventhorn is a very powerful MP. I've been on the telephone since this story broke in the papers, and none of the conversations have been pleasant. You've put me in a terrible position, August. The commissioner is getting pressure from the PM and is calling for your removal from the force."

Flannel gently placed the paper on Hardgrave's desk. "I have no excuse, Bernard. And I have no idea where the paper got this information. I'll admit I was wrong conducting this investigation against your specific orders, but I was hoping to gather enough evidence before anyone became the wiser of my involvement."

With a shake of his head, Hardgrave ceased his pacing and took his seat at his desk. "I'm sorry, August, but I'll need your gun and badge. You're on suspension pending a formal investigation and disciplinary hearing."

Flannel took the badge from his pocket, slowly rubbing the shiny surface with his thumb as he reflected back through the years. Pulling the holster from his belt with his other hand he put both on the desk in front of him and slowly stood up.

"Where are you going?" grumbled Hardgrave. Flannel attempted an answer but was abruptly cut short. "Sit down, we're not done."

Hardgrave took the inspector's gun and badge and placed both in a lower drawer of the desk. "We came up through the ranks together, August. We didn't always agree on methods, but I've never known you to chase the wrong suspect." Hardgrave leaned forward on his elbows. "For the time being, you're a civilian, so I have no control over where you go or what you do, as long as you stay within the law. With respect for our friendship, I'll drag my feet for a day or two before assigning the investigation. It would be to one's benefit to use that time wisely. I would suggest, however, you stay clear of Raventhorn."

"He's mixed up in this, I'm sure of it, Bernard," Flannel responded, returning to his customary determined tone. "I'll stake my badge on it."

"You already have," replied Hardgrave gravely. "Now, don't think I haven't forgotten about your call this morning. You might be on suspension, but you're still a first-rate detective. You said you had information and it was urgent you speak with me; well, this may be the only chance you'll get. What was so urgent?"

* * *

"I see you're feeling much better," said Ernie, peering in from the hall.

"Ernie, what are you doing here?" said Dee. Her smile lit up the room. She was dressed and sitting on the bed with her long red hair pulled back in a ponytail. Next to her were a large handbag and an overnight bag neatly packed and ready to be zipped.

"I just wanted to see how you were getting on. They said you would be released today so I wanted to offer my assistance."

"How very thoughtful. I'll be staying at Jacque's for a few days, just until I'm feeling myself again. She called and is on her way here now." Dee rummaged around in her oversized purse, finally pulling out a folded piece of paper. With the dreamy eyes of a doting young schoolgirl, she held it out to Ernie. "I was hoping you would stop by. Here, this is Jacque's address on Gilbert Street. You already have my mobile number."

Ernie blushed, taking the note from her hand. "I've been a bit shy about chatting you up, so this certainly helps. If it's not a bother, I would like to call you when you're feeling up to it."

Dee laughed. "I would be very disappointed if you didn't call. Besides, I know where you live, so I would have just knocked up for you if you didn't." Her joy turned serious when the thought of the flat on Conduit Street came to mind. "Have they caught that brute who attacked me?"

"Regretfully, no," Ernie replied softly. "But, between you and me, Inspector Flannel has a suspect in mind and I believe he is close to an arrest. I'm afraid I can't say anything more than that."

"Do you think I'm still in danger?"

"The Guv'nor thinks it would be wise to keep an eye on you until this business is settled." Ernie sat down on the bed next to Dee. "But he also believes you've seen the last of that bounder that attacked you. The whole point of the attack was to get the journal. He has it now."

Dee took Ernie's hand. "What do you think?"

"I think he's right. Someone was willing to kill for whatever was in that journal. They have it now, so I don't think you're in any more danger from him."

"I wish I could be as confident as you."

"Well, there is something you could do about that." Ernie smiled, holding back a slight laugh.

Dee thought for a moment, then shook her head and laughed over her conclusion. "Not him?"

"I'm afraid so," Ernie chuckled. "I know you think him a bit brutish, but you'll be safe under his watchful eyes."

"I was hoping *you* might offer to watch over me," Dee hinted demurely.

Ernie blushed once again. "Under any other circumstance it would have been my first suggestion, but the Guv'nor has asked me to handle another matter."

"Well, I guess it's Dragonetti then."

"It does me good to hear my name uttered by such a lovely creature as yourself," remarked Dragonetti from the doorway, "but you could at least put a little enthusiasm behind it."

"We were just talking about you," said Ernie, very much surprised at the appearance of the big man.

"As if I couldn't tell, Bisquets. No need to look so surprised," Dragonetti said, answering the confused look on Dee's face. "It's the other bird what called me. Said she thought you might need a little muscle about for the next few days. Mind you, I've got other business I've put aside for this. Maybe you could toss a poor lad a small crumb of gratitude?"

"I'm sorry, Mr. Dragonetti," said Dee. "I was just surprised to see you, that's all. Of course I'm grateful. In fact, I'm a very lucky woman to have two such fine gentlemen to watch after me."

"There you have it, Bisquets," said Dragonetti, tapping Ernie's shoulder a few times with his finger. "A kind word, that's all I was looking for." He picked up the overnight bag, nodding with his head toward the door as he continued. "This way, miss. That other bird is waiting out front with the car. No sense being formal, you can call me Elgin."

"Elgin it is," Dee agreed. "Please call me Dee, and that *other bird* is Jacque." She looked over at Ernie and quietly whispered, "Call me the minute you have any news."

"I certainly will. Maybe I could stop by later this evening? That's if you're up to having visitors."

Dee nodded and kissed Ernie on the cheek. With a big smile, she followed Dragonetti out of the room.

26/ A Quiet Chat by the Lake

The early afternoon sun had slipped suddenly behind a dense, soot-colored bank of clouds blowing in from the west. A sleek black car was heading up Horse Guards Road, as leaves swept up and twirled about in its wake. They were just passing the Treasury building when Prophet felt a sharp tap on his shoulder.

"Go up a bit further and pull off the road in front of the Horse Guard Parade."

Prophet didn't answer; he just nodded his head and drove on.

As they approached the Parade, Prophet felt another tap. "Pull over there, where the bollards cut in on the Parade. Pull over and park. I think it's time we had a walk and small chat about your recent activities."

"Park?" Prophet asked. "If I park here, the police will have the car on a lorry and down the road by the time we return."

"Unlike you," Raventhorn replied in a course and calculated tone, "they wouldn't dare raise the ire of an MP. Do as I say and stop your arguing."

Prophet pulled off the road as requested and turned off the motor. He sat motionless in the front seat. Once or twice he glanced in the rearview mirror, only to be greeted with the cold stare of his master.

Across the road was St. James Park. The gates were open and people were scurrying about, doing their best to find cover as a light rain began. Some thought enough ahead to bring an umbrella and moved along at a regular pace. Others held tightly to their collars with one hand, heads down and holding a walking map over their heads with the other, wishing they had done the same.

Raventhorn placed a bowler on his head and cinched up his collar. "I would say this is an opportune time for us to have that chat, wouldn't you?" He got out of the car and crossed over to the park with Prophet limping along behind as quickly as his clubfoot could carry him.

They walked along the pathway against the current of sightseers hastily walking toward them, following the iron fencing around to the turf-roofed restaurant. Other lingering tourists who hadn't left the park in advance of the storm had ducked into Inn The Park for a quick bite and to wait it out.

By the time Raventhorn and Prophet had reached the edge of the lake, they were quite alone, save for the curious ducks swimming about, wondering what these two un-feathered fowl were doing in such wet weather. Raventhorn made himself comfortable on one of the wooden benches facing the lake. He was indifferent to the weather. Puddles grew quickly between the walkway and the lake, blurring the lines between where one stopped and the other started. The storm continued its performance and completed its overture, the light rain intensifying into a dramatic aria. Standing beside the bench, Prophet opened the dark gray umbrella he brought along from the car, holding it above Raventhorn's head. The sight of their dark silhouettes cast against the bleak gray curtain of rain whispered of a tribute to Monsieur Magritte.

"I want you to know, Prophet," Raventhorn began, staring out toward Duck Island, "I have a pretty good idea of what you've been up to. I've always known. Eight years ago, you all but tied the rope around my neck because of it. You think me harsh and yourself ill-used by me, but I never raised an angry hand to you because of it. I've been tolerant of these dust-ups at the pubs you seem to attract. They leave you bruised and me suspect to the origins of those bruises. You've continually undermined me, yet I provide lodgings and ample food without want of appreciation."

"I'm forever grateful, sir," Prophet stuttered.

"Hold your pitiful tongue boy," Raventhorn snapped, "I'm not finished. You betrayed me once and I'll not stand for your treacherous ways any longer." He stared up at Prophet, his eyes piercing the trembling lad's soul. "There are some secrets worth killing for, and some worth dying for. It is only the most heinous of secrets that could drive an otherwise sane man to do both. With that said, I wish to tell you a story. Take from this what you can, because it could most certainly be our last conversation. I'll leave you to decide that."

Raventhorn looked out over the lake and began. "I'm sure, given only a few moments thought, you would be quick to dismiss the idea of this placid lake as a theater for the evil that lurks within a malevolent heart. The thought of such evil skulking about in this beautiful setting would be more comical than probable to an innocent man, yet, I sense in you a fear known only to the condemned. A fear spawned not from threat but from the guilt of one's own actions.

"There is a little known and all but forgotten tale of a young couple who would frequent this very spot each Sunday afternoon at three o'clock. They braved the cold of winter and the heat of summer, never once wavering from their commitment to spend Sunday afternoons on this bench in each other's arms. This young couple became as much a part of this setting as the trees and flowers surrounding them. It was believed to be near the latter part of the reign of King George V, though the actual point in time is of no consequence to this narration.

"A more loving couple you could never imagine was said of them. He was understood to be a man of some wealth and she the daughter of a prominent merchant. The glow of this young woman's rosy cheeks and the gleam in the eyes of her handsome suitor when he looked at her would pierce even the coldest of hearts. Their good nature extended beyond themselves. A bright word or greeting was afforded to all who walked past, paying additional compliments to the infirm being wheeled along this very walkway. And every Sunday before leaving the park they would stand at the edge of the lake, make a wish and each toss a shilling into the water, celebrating their good fortune.

"Over time they married, the ceremony being held at three o'clock here in the park over by that tree, which at the time was merely a sapling. Being the only child to each set of parents, and having within their two-year courtship the misfortunate circumstance to commit their parent's departed souls to God, there were no family members left to invite. Yet the ceremony was bursting with guests, strangers wanting nothing more than to catch a glimpse of this loving couple they admired through the years and offer their good wishes for a long and happy life together.

"Their Sunday appointment with nature continued, and soon the gift of a child became obvious on the woman. Even the most casual of acquaintances were anxious for the birth announcement. The day finally arrived. It was in the spring of the following year that this loving couple was blessed with a healthy baby boy. He was born on a Sunday.

"They were conspicuously absent from their bench by the lake as the weeks turned into months. It was certainly understandable with the young girl having just given birth, but the park felt slightly askew without them. The birds chirped, but their song lost some of its joyfulness. The flowers blossomed, but their colors were muted, their fragrance less pungent. Even the sun cast longer shadows along the lawn during the late afternoons as if searching for a missing ray of light.

"It was four months to the day when the couple returned to the park. They made their way along the path to their favorite bench, but this time pushing a pram ahead of them. Everyone was anxious to see the baby boy. He was a beautiful baby, as bright and cheerful as the parents who brought him into the world. Those who were familiar with the couple stopped and offered congratulations, while others, newly aware of this extraordinary couple, were just as curious to make their acquaintance and see the baby everyone was talking about. All seemed right with the world once again.

"Then one dark Sunday some months later, a day I'm sure not unlike today, a change began to creep over the father. He became very protective of his young son, refusing to let strangers peer into the pram. He had little to say to those passing by, and the kind words he felt obligated to offer appeared forced rather than heartfelt as before. He was even noticed on occasion to chastise his wife without warning for what appeared little more than an innocent comment or gesture toward the baby. He was quick to apologize, but it made little difference to those who witnessed this darker side of a man they believed to be as gentle as morning dew on a delicate petal.

"It wasn't long before the interest in the young family waned to a point of indifference. Those who once gathered to catch just a glimpse of what pure happiness looked like now continued along their way. For the next seven years, the family continued to visit the bench by the lake, but with little acknowledgement by others enjoying the park."

"I'm not sure I understand why you're telling me this story," said Prophet. He was drenched and beginning to shiver from the cold, but continued to hold fast to the umbrella over his master's head.

"If you will allow me to continue," Raventhorn snarled, glancing up briefly at Prophet, "the point of this story will become quite evident."

Prophet didn't say another word.

"It was during that seventh year another rather curious change came over the family. It was in the latter days of summer during that year when the father and son began coming to the park alone. What became even more curious was the anger he had become known for, the anger that drove away all who once admired him, was now replaced with a deep sadness. Gradually, the curious once again stepped forward to offer a kind word with the hope the gentle, loving man they once admired had returned to the park. And so it was.

"As the months went by, he began to open up to certain people he felt comfortable with. He explained how his wife, overcome with brain fever, had run off without warning. He was left to raise his son alone. He cried more than once telling the story, always remarking how he was to blame for the void her departure left in his family.

"Gradually, routine resumed. Without regard to the weather, every Sunday he and the boy would be found seated on the bench at precisely three o'clock talking or playing at cards. After an hour or so, the father would walk over to the water's edge, bow his head and mumble a short prayer silently to himself. Afterwards he would take a shilling from his pocket and toss it into the lake. His grief rolled down his cheek in a single tear. Not wanting his sorrow to taint the otherwise bright future of the boy, he was careful to hide his emotion from him.

"Soon the boy was a young man off to University. The bench, once the meeting place of love's true devotion, now welcomed only one. The man put on a brave face for those who stopped on occasion to wish him the compliments of the day, but the heartache he carried was evident in the heavy, cheerless eyelids that hung low over his once bright eyes. It was during the second year of his son's studies that the father became quite ill.

"Despite the pleas from his doctors, the man continued to visit the park. He braved the drenching rains of summer and then the cold chill of winter, only to worsen his condition. By the following spring, he was near death. The doctor sent word to his son to return as soon as physically possible.

"It was the first Sunday in April when the boy returned. He had stopped at their flat first, but not finding his father, he ran to the one spot he felt certain he would be. It was just five minutes past three o'clock when the son arrived at this bench, out of breath, hoping desperately to find his parent."

"Was his father here?" asked Prophet, shivering uncontrollably.

Raventhorn casually glanced up. The companionate stare he maintained during his narration quickly shifted to a malicious smirk. "Much to his horror, he found them both."

"Both?" replied Prophet. "You mean the mother returned?"

"You'll catch your death of cold," growled Raventhorn, rising from the bench. "I know you think me heartless, but you couldn't be more wrong." Raventhorn jerked his head, indicating the chat in the park was over. "Let's walk back to the car. I have business to take care of this afternoon. It's best we return to our flat so I can change."

The two men walked at a curiously unhurried pace past the tourists watching them from the restaurant. The driving rain pushed them along, building up to a crescendo. The car was as they left it, parked and devoid of any traffic citations. Raventhorn sat quietly in the back seat waiting as Prophet shook off the rain.

Prophet closed the umbrella, climbed in, and started the engine. He looked into the rearview mirror for instructions. His master's eyes were staring back. Then he felt a tap on his shoulder.

"Here," said Raventhorn. He held out an old envelope, yellowed with age for Prophet. "Here is the answer to your question."

Prophet took the envelope from Raventhorn's outstretched hand. After carefully opening it, he extracted the single page letter it held and read the words to himself.

Raventhorn was amused by Prophet's reaction to the letter. He could hear the surprise in his short, shallow breaths as he read over the details left behind by the father to his son described within.

The confession detailed in the letter drained all the blood from Prophet's face. His eyes returned to the rearview mirror, but Raventhorn was preoccupied staring out the window of the car. "Where did you get this?"

"It was left with a solicitor by the man, to be delivered to his son in the event of his death." Raventhorn held out his hand and waited for Prophet to return the letter before he continued. "On his son's death—my father—it was delivered to me."

"So your grandfather is the man in the story?" Prophet barely got the words out.

"Yes. And the boy was my father." Raventhorn tucked the letter neatly into his breast pocket. "You see, that lake holds a family secret most people believe is nothing more than an old ghost tale. I look into that lake and I see my own fate. To quote the words of my grandfather: 'Once you've tossed the evil you bare into the depths of a dark lake, be prepared to one day rest beside that decision.'" Raventhorn paused, then drew out these final words in one slow course breath. "I can assure you now I am prepared to rest beside whatever decision you'll force my hand to take."

27/ Set Honor in One Eye and Death in the Other

Marie spent the early part of the afternoon at the British Museum going over her slide presentation with the other presenters. Around 4:30 she finished up. There was a certain uneasiness she felt on her way out of the museum. A feeling someone was watching her. She walked through the busy public areas doing her best to dismiss her rising concern. Quick glances into dark corners revealed lingering shadows that would not allow the feeling to disappear completely.

Once outside, she was quick to hail the first taxi she saw. Safely inside, Marie glanced over her shoulder once or twice to convince herself it was nothing more than the dark clouds hanging over the city causing her uneasiness. With a heavy sigh, she settled back, feeling foolish for getting herself all worked up over nothing.

By 5:00 o'clock, she was hanging up her coat in the hall closet at Conduit Street, convinced it was only nervousness about her presentation affecting her judgment.

"Is that you, Marie?" Patterson called out from the study.

"Oui, mon amour."

Marie walked into the study, greeted by the austere faces of the little men gazing up at her from the desk.

Patterson had unboxed a number of the funerary objects for her inspection, fulfilling his promise from the previous evening. She bent down to take a closer look at the exquisite carvings. "Sometimes I wish I could spend more time out in the field digging through the sands of time, rather than just digging through the paperwork on my desk. These objects are magnifique."

Marie spent a few moments with each object, carefully studying the workmanship.

Patterson smiled, spending the few moments studying Marie. "You are certainly more than welcome to accompany us whenever you like. I'll make a note to inform you when our next dig is scheduled."

Marie put her arms around Patterson's arm, pulled him close, and whispered into his ear. "There is a chance we might not get much accomplished if we go off together to some exotic corner of the world."

"One can only hope," replied Patterson, kissing her forehead.

"Forgive my intrusion," said a blushing Mrs. Chapman. "I'll just come back in a few minutes."

Marie and Patterson looked over and laughed.

"Nonsense," replied Patterson. "What is it?"

"I was wondering how many there would be for dinner this evening?"

"Marie will be off to her symposium in a hour or so and we're meeting afterwards for dinner. Ernie is out taking care of an errand for me. I don't expect him back until late. You should take the evening off." Patterson thought for a moment, looked at Marie and sheepishly added, "Why don't you call August and maybe take in a gushy love story this evening at the cinema?"

"Funny that," Mrs. Chapman quipped. "I phoned my Derby twice, both times got his voicemail. Not like him not to ring me back."

Patterson returned to a more serious tone. "I'm sure this latest case has him a bit preoccupied. Not to worry, it wouldn't surprise me to hear a knock at the door before too much longer."

"Of course you're right," Mrs. Chapman cheerily consented. "Will there be anything else?"

"Could I impose on you to arrange a car service for me this evening," asked Marie. "I'll need to be at the museum by 7:30."

Patterson was quick to interrupt Mrs. Chapman's cheerful acceptance of the task. "No need. I've made arrangements for a car to pick you up here at 7:10 and deposit you at the museum. He'll be back for me by nine. I'll meet you out front at 9:30 sharp, after what I'm sure will be a landmark discourse on the spatial capacity of 19th Century Impressionists. I'm just sorry I won't be there for the address."

Marie playfully smacked Patterson's arm. "The spatial capacity of the *museum*, not the Impressionists."

"Oh, that's right." Patterson smiled, giving Mrs. Chapman a wink. "My mistake."

The harsh buzzer in the hall sounded twice.

"That's probably your Derby now," said Patterson.

As Mrs. Chapman went off to answer the door, Marie helped Patterson repack the funerary objects in their boxes. Both took pause when they heard a strange voice in the hall. It wasn't Inspector Flannel. The voice was all too familiar to Patterson, as revealed by his expression.

"What is it?" said Marie, answering the look on Patterson's face.

"Nothing, darling," said Patterson. His concerned look eased into a soft smile as he patted Marie's hand. "That voice just took me by surprise."

"Who is it?"

Mrs. Chapman peered in from the doorway. "Pardon me again, sir. There is a gentleman to see you. Wouldn't give his name, but he had your card. He's in the sitting-room."

"Very good. I'll be right there."

As Patterson spoke, the tall, gaunt figure of a man stepped into view from the hall. The light streaming in from the etched glass dome high above the hallway behind him obscured his features, casting a long eerie shadow into the room. "Please forgive this intrusion, Patterson." The voice had a coarse yet pleasant character. "I hope my sudden appearance at your door hasn't offended. I'm afraid I may need your council on a rather delicate matter."

Mrs. Chapman stepped aside, allowing the man to enter the study.

"Thank you, Annie," Patterson called out as Mrs. Chapman backed away. He turned his attention to the man standing before him. "You haven't intruded at all, Alfred. Marie, allow me to introduce Sir Alfred Raventhorn. Alfred, this is Marie Bussière."

"A pleasure to meet you, mademoiselle." Lord Raventhorn shook her extended hand. He stared at her for an awkward moment, his brow furrowed in contemplation. "Marie Bussière, of course, acting curator of the Musee d'Orsay in Paris. I understand you're presenting this evening at the museum symposium."

His remark caught Marie by surprise. She quickly withdrew her hand.

"Forgive me," Raventhorn offered, most apologetically. "Besides intruding, it would appear my sudden appearance has added a level of discomfort to your afternoon as well."

"It's I who must apologize," replied Marie after an awkward moment of silence. She brushed away the hair and concern from her face in one swift motion. "Forgive my rudeness. Have we met?"

Raventhorn gave a slight laugh. "No, I'm afraid not. Your name is familiar to me because I'm on the board of the British Museum. I remember seeing your name in tonight's program."

Marie did her best to cover her embarrassment "Of course. I don't know what I was thinking."

Patterson quickly came to her rescue. "It would appear nerves have gotten the best of Marie. Why don't we retire to the sitting room for a sherry? I think it might do us all good."

"As delightful as that sounds, I hope you gentlemen will excuse me." Marie kissed Patterson on the cheek. "I had best get ready for this evening before my nerves make a complete fool of me." She held out her hand to Raventhorn.

Raventhorn raised an eyebrow and playfully remarked, "Are you sure you want to do that?"

Marie laughed. "Absolument."

Raventhorn gently shook her hand. "I'm sure you'll be brilliant this evening."

The two men bade Marie goodbye as she disappeared into the hall and up the stairs. Patterson repeated his suggestion about the sherry and soon he and Raventhorn were seated on the sofas in front of the fireplace.

"She's a delightful creature," remarked Raventhorn, looking back toward the hall as he sipped his sherry. "It would appear my sudden appearance must have taken you both by surprise."

"Yes, I guess you could say that. It's certainly been a while. If I remember correctly, our last conversation was across the aisle in Parliament, and rather spirited."

"I'm still fighting the good fights," Raventhorn reflected. "Keeping my fellow MPs on their toes as best I can."

"You mentioned this visit was prompted by the need for council. A delicate matter, was it?"

Raventhorn sat forward, placing his glass down on a porcelain coaster. "I was hoping I could impose on your friendship to look into a matter for me?"

"This wouldn't by any chance have anything to do with these two recent murders I've been reading about in the papers?"

Raventhorn lightly brushed at the crease in his trousers. "I've always appreciated your directness, Patterson. Not a bit on ceremony, not you. Yes, yes indeed, it has everything to do with that terrible business. I'm afraid there are forces working behind my back determined to dredge up evidence implicating me in the matter." A deep red hue crept slowly over Raventhorn's face from beneath his starched white collar. "It was all I could do to repair the damage those baseless accusations inflicted on my family name eight years ago, and I'll not stand for it again."

"So the police have contacted you then?" Patterson remarked dryly.

Raventhorn grunted. "A waste of funding that lot. No, I've taken care of that for now."

"If the police haven't labeled you a suspect, I'm not sure I understand your concern. What *forces* are you talking about?"

"It's that wretched valet of mine, that's what."

Patterson laughed. "Prophet Brown? Surely you don't believe he has any credibility with the police. I doubt very seriously he could play that card again."

The pleasant, albeit forced, expression Raventhorn had maintained since his arrival turned to a soulless stare. "You'd not think this so humorous if your man was in league against you with that bothersome police dog Flannel. I don't know what his game is, but he'll not have the opportunity to drag another innocent name through the gutter. I've seen to that."

Patterson's cordial manner abruptly shifted to a defensive posture. "What have you done, Alfred?"

Raventhorn pulled a copy of the morning paper from his pocket and tossed it on the table in front of Patterson. "Have you seen this?"

Patterson picked up and unfolded the paper. He read the headline, skimming the related story, shook his head, and tossed the paper back on the table. "No, I've been busy all day. You think this is a result of Inspector Flannel and Prophet?"

"It's gone past what I think. This Flannel has crossed my path for the last time; I've taken the matter up with his superiors." A slight smile curled up the ends of his thin lips, distorting his usual scowl as he finished. It was evident he was quite pleased with himself. "He's been suspended and he'll be a pensioner by the end of the week."

Patterson fought back the urge to reach across and slap the arrogance and self-serving impudence off the face of Raventhorn. If for no other reason than to help his old mate, he needed to remain calm.

Raventhorn was oblivious to the anger staring at him across the table. He stood up, walking over to inspect a small Chagall etching hanging next to the fireplace that caught his interest.

"You mentioned you needed my help," Patterson remarked, slowly and deliberately through clenched teeth. "I've a rather busy evening ahead of me, so I would appreciate you getting to the point of this visit."

The tonal shift in the conversation caught Raventhorn's attention. Before he could comment on the sudden change in Patterson's hospitality, Ernie interrupted the two men. He came bounding into the room, waving the newspaper about as he spouted off bits and pieces of the aforementioned article between labored breaths. "Lord Raventhorn suspected in murder on Brick Lane. They know about the inspector's investigation. Someone has tipped off the newspaper." Suddenly Ernie realized he and Patterson were not alone.

Raventhorn turned, immediately recognizing Ernie. "I see how it is," said Raventhorn passing an accusatory glance from Patterson to Ernie. "I saw you milling about this morning talking to my valet. Did you get all the information you needed? Speak up man! You had no trouble engaging in conversation this morning."

Patterson jumped to his feet, positioning himself between Ernie and Raventhorn. "I think we're done here."

Raventhorn ignored him, stepping to one side and continuing his verbal assault. The sharp edges of his features and tone froze Ernie where he stood. "It would appear you've gained the confidence of that pathetic wretch. Perhaps he confided in you where he's run off?"

"He's run off?" replied Ernie nervously.

"That's right. That's why I'm here. We came back from Scotland Yard and that's the last I saw of his miserable twisted self." Raventhorn lunged forward, jamming the gold knob of his cane up into Ernie's face, all but rapping him on the tip of his nose. "I came for Patterson's assistance, but maybe it's you I should be speaking with? Come now, boy, don't lie to me. Where is he? Out with it. Out with it I say or I'll . . ."

Patterson grabbed the cane, yanking it away from Raventhorn. "I think you better leave."

Raventhorn took a step back. With a grunt, he began to button his outer coat. "You seriously disappoint me, Patterson. I believed you to be a man of honor."

Patterson held the cane out in front of Raventhorn, pointing it toward the hall. "I am a man of honor, otherwise you'd find yourself broken and at the bottom of those stairs you'll be using to see yourself out."

Ernie cautiously stepped aside, allowing Raventhorn to pass.

"Very well," grumbled Raventhorn. "It seems I'll be handling this matter myself. I'll find Prophet, and when I do, I'll put an end to this nonsense once and for all." He started towards the hall, stopping at the doorway, and turned back to address Patterson. "With all that has transpired, I have nothing at all left to lose, Patterson. It makes me a very dangerous man to cross. Good day."

Ernie was visibly shaken by Raventhorn's display of anger towards him, unable for the moment to convince Patterson otherwise.

"Are you all right, Ernie?" said Patterson soothingly. He was still tense over the situation but years of experience allowed him to keep the upper hand over his emotions.

Ernie forced a small laugh. "He's a bit scary, that one, ain't he?"

Patterson echoed the amusement. "Scary, indeed. Have a seat. I think you could use a brandy."

By the time Patterson handed Ernie a small snifter, he was seated at the table and had regained his composure. "Thank you, sir. Sorry about barging in like that. I didn't see him there, lurking about in the shadows like he was. Pure evil, that one."

Patterson waved off the apology. "Quite frankly, I was happy for the interruption. I just about had enough of Lord Raventhorn and his disparaging remarks about our friend Inspector Flannel. Flannel may have been wrong in his execution, but it's becoming extremely difficult to find fault with his reasoning."

"So you think Raventhorn is involved in this mess?"

"Much to my concern, I honestly don't know what to think."

"I'm sure Inspector Flannel will make short work of that one's idle threats." Ernie looked over and saw the saddened look on Patterson's face. "What is it? Nothing has happened to the good inspector I hope?"

"Inspector Flannel has been suspended from the force."

Ernie was gobsmacked. His mouth opened but not a word trickled out.

"Suspended?" came a worried whisper from behind.

Patterson looked back over his shoulder. Mrs. Chapman was peering out from the kitchen door. "I'm sorry, Annie. Apparently Lord Raventhorn has used his political connections against August."

"Why ever would he do such a thing?" The usual bright expression was completely gone from her face.

"I'm afraid we're dealing with a very powerful and possibly dangerous man," said Patterson pensively. "I don't know what his game is, but if he's caught up in these murders there's no telling what he might say or do to cover his guilt. I'm afraid the two people we need to speak with, the two people who might be able to confirm his guilt and clear this mess up, appear to be missing."

"The inspector is missing?" Ernie echoed.

Patterson was cognizant of Mrs. Chapman's deepened concern for Inspector Flannel. He chose his words accordingly. "Mrs. Chapman has tried contacting him twice with no response. If what Raventhorn said is true, it's quite possible the inspector is off somewhere brooding. I see no reason to entertain foul play at this time. I'm sure we'll hear from him shortly. August Flannel is not a man to walk away from a fight."

A smile followed the comforted nod of Mrs. Chapman's head. She returned to the kitchen leaving behind the shadow of her concern in the capable hands of Patterson Coats.

"A bit odd though, the other one, ain't it?" said Ernie, when the two men were alone again.

"What's odd," repeated Patterson, a bit distracted.

"Prophet Brown disappearing like he did. I can't say as I blame him much."

Patterson leaned forward, drumming his fingers on the table. "I'm more concerned whether his disappearance is by choice or by design."

28/ Puff Pastries and a Walk in the Park

The Great Court in the British Museum, not at all new to hosting grand intellectual and formal events, was appropriately appointed for the evening's symposium. Rows of upholstered chairs, their seats cushioned with fine French tapestry, fanned out in rows in front of the Reading Room. Like a blank canvas before the artist as he lifts his brush, the court soon became awash with a bounty of color, the last remnants of the setting sun splashing vibrant streaks across the pale marble floor. A once largely ignored outdoor space, rarely used since the 1850s, was now a two-acre indoor venue of dazzling proportion. What better place to hold a symposium on spatial capacity?

The circular Reading Room stood majestically in the center, peering out over the soon to be enlightened. Facing the rows of chairs, below the double-arch windows circling the structure, was a raised platform, presented to the assembled between two flanking staircases. Two long tables rested along the front, broken in the center by a slender podium.

Along the perimeter, viewing the staff making final arrangements to the chairs, hors d'oeuvre tables, floral arrangements, etc., were a gaggle of curious onlookers peering in through the glass panels of the closed doors leading into the court. They were unsure of the nature of the event, but quite certain they would surely catch a glimpse of a celebrity or Royal milling about if only they could stay long enough. It wasn't to be. The museum was just about to close to visitors for the evening. A courteous staff politely pointed down the hall with one hand while making a gracious sweeping motion with the other to indicate the required movement. The remaining not-so-curious only glanced causally into the court as they passed by, continuing on their way out through the massive colonnades of Sir Robert Smirke's grand entrance on Great Russell Street.

Coming in the opposite direction were the invited guests for the symposium, making their way through the exiting visitors like well-dressed salmon fighting their way up stream. Ushers met them at the main door to the court, checking invitations and directing them in the appropriate direction. A hum started to rise over the assembled mass as fellow curators welcomed each other, each excusing their lack of correspondence since a last meeting in their own way over a glass of chardonnay.

A wait staff, jacketed in red velvet short coats over black trousers, white shirts and black ties, circulated through the chattering clusters throughout the court, tempting each with puffed pastries oozing delightful delicacies from both pasture and sea. The bar was equally busy, with wine leading the popularity contest over the assortment of exceptional British gins. In the background, a soothing collection of classical favorites filled the room with quiet elegance. As eight o'clock approached, the sun had dipped well below the rooftops, replaced by the soft glow of light emanating from high on top of the Reading Room. The windows of the adjoining galleries cast a warm glow into the court, rendering it more like the outdoor square of years past. The steel framing high above disappeared against the night sky, giving a sharp contrast of rich indigo against the white sandstone walls and pillars surrounding the audience.

The clusters chatted, the glasses clinked, and the hors d'oeuvre trays slowly emptied until order was called over the crowd by a commanding voice heralding from the podium. The attendees lazily made their way down the two aisles separating the rows, settling in for the commencement of the symposium. By 8:15, Marie had been introduced and had the audience completely engaged in her presentation.

* * *

The miserable rain that washed across the city earlier had continued on its way, leaving a pleasant evening behind. Brook Street was abuzz with residents and visitors alike taking advantage of the crisp night air, enjoying an after dinner stroll up to Grosvenor Square. As Ernie and Dee chatted in Jacque's flat about all that went on over the past two days, the light hum of traffic off Gilbert Street drifted off into the air like smoke.

Dee was thrilled to see Ernie. She and Jacque had a dozen questions, though they both understood Ernie could only say so much about what he knew of the police case.

"I'm so glad you stopped by, Ernie," said Dee. "You mentioned this morning about handling a small matter for Patterson Coats. How did that turn out?"

"I don't know whether you've seen the paper," Ernie replied grimly, "but Lord Raventhorn has been labeled a suspect in this nasty business."

Jacque glanced over from where she was standing by the windows overlooking Gilbert Street. "That's wonderful news. So Inspector Flannel has made excellent progress since yesterday?"

"What's wrong, Ernie?" asked Dee, addressing his cheerless expression.

"It seems the situation with the inspector has become a bit muddy."

"Muddy? In what way?" Jacque inquired, still studying the activity on Gilbert Street. "Yesterday in the hospital, the inspector seemed determined to bring an end to this business. I did some checking, he has an excellent reputation at the Yard. If he believes Raventhorn is behind these attacks, I can't imagine anything that would divert him from bringing this scoundrel to justice."

"You're right about one thing," Ernie quipped, "he's a bulldog, that one. There's a bit more to it than just bringing charges against Lord Raventhorn. It seems—"

As Ernie was explaining, Dee became distracted by Jacque's preoccupation at the window. "What's going on out there, Jacque?" interrupted Dee, repositioning herself on the divan so she could see past Ernie and maybe get a better idea about what had captured Jacque's attention.

"Nothing. Well, maybe nothing." Jacque let the curtain fall back into place as she continued. "I've been watching for Mr. Dragonetti since he brought us back from the hospital. He seems exceptional at surveillance. It wasn't until an hour ago that I actually noticed him watching the flat. I've peeked out the window a few times, waving discretely on occasion, but with no response from him."

"Wouldn't be like him to wave back," replied Ernie brightly. "He takes his work seriously, he does. If he's to keep you two safe, he won't let himself get distracted."

"Does he know you're here?" inquired Jacque. She walked over to a small bar area that was part of the bookcase to the right of the fireplace, poured bourbon into a glass with ice, and returned to the window.

"I gave a quick glance across the street as I came up your steps. He gave me a nod and leaned back into the shadows."

"Across the street?" Jacque exclaimed. She stared intensely out the window, then craned her neck to see up the street. "He's not across the street, he's up in that doorway on Brook Street."

Ernie jumped to his feet. He was at the window in a blink. "There's Dragonetti," said Ernie, pointing to a dark shadow barely visible in the portico of a building across Gilbert Street. "Where's this other bloke?"

Jacque pulled the curtain back and pointed up the street. The two of them leaned in close, their cheeks flattened against the glass. "See, up there. The white stone building with the *For Let* sign in the window. There he is, pacing back and forth."

At first, Ernie didn't see anything, only shadows. Then a passing car threw enough light into the gated area leading to the lower stairs for Ernie to make out a familiar silhouette. "Prophet Brown," he mumbled to himself.

"Who?" asked Dee nervously. Ernie's abruptness upset her, something he hadn't noticed until he turned to answer her question.

"Sorry," replied Ernie in a soothing tone. He walked back over and took her hand. "I didn't mean to scare you. There's nothing out there to fear. Dragonetti is right across the street. He won't let anyone near this flat."

"So who is this Prophet Brown?" both women said simultaneously.

Ernie's attention was elsewhere. He ran out the door of Jacque's building without answering the question. Dragonetti sensed something was wrong and stepped out of the shadows. Ernie waved him off, motioning for him to stay at his post. In an instant, he was on Brook Street in front of the building where he saw Prophet. He was gone.

Ernie looked up and down the street. There was no sign of him. Then, up ahead in the distance he could see Prophet at the end of the block nearing the corner of Davies Street; the bobbing of his head caused by his step and drag pace made him easy to pick out amongst the other pedestrians. By the time Ernie gained the corner, Prophet had crossed over Brook's Mews and was almost at

Grosvenor Street. Ernie was at a run now, doing all he could to close the gap between he and Prophet. The clusters of people walking up and down the street made his progress erratic.

By the time Prophet reached Berkeley Square, Ernie was held up by traffic on the other side of the intersection on Mount Street. He watched Prophet walk through the open gate into the park only to lose sight of him in the shadows of the stately hundred-year-old London Plane trees lined up in regimental rows. In a hail of horns and tires screeching, Ernie darted between an assortment of taxis and buses to cross the wide intersection. Once on the other side, he walked the length of the square, carefully following every dark shadow back to its origin. Making his way through, he stopped at the far end by the intersection across from Hay Hill. There was no clue to where Prophet had disappeared. Disappointed, he turned, intending to walk back to Jacque's flat. There was the sharp crack of a stick.

"Pardon me," said a trembling and exhausted voice from behind one of the trees. Ernie turned to see Prophet Brown step out from behind the thick trunk, panting, doing his best to catch his breath. "Bisquets, isn't it? We spoke this morning."

"That's right. Why were you lurking about that building? People are looking for you."

"Sorry, I was hoping to find Inspector Flannel." Prophet's labored breath was returning to normal.

"So why did you run?"

"I didn't know it was you until now. I must talk to the inspector. He's threatened me, he has. Can't go back. I must find Inspector Flannel. He'll kill again, he will. He'll kill again."

"You've got to calm down," said Ernie, walking him over to one of the benches. "Sit down and get hold of yourself. When you're ready, tell me what's going on."

Prophet plopped down onto the bench, nodding his head rapidly.

"You say he threatened you?" asked Ernie, slowly pacing in front of Prophet. "Raventhorn?"

"That's right. He knows I've been helping the inspector again. All those poor women, he's killed them, he has. And who knows who else. I'll not be next. I've got a few hundred quid put away. Once I tell the inspector what I know, it's a moonlight flit for me. Otherwise my life won't be worth praying for."

"What is it you know?"

Prophet looked around, eyeing the faces of the people in the park, making sure the wrong person wouldn't overhear his words. "It's tonight," he whispered. "He's going to kill again tonight."

"Tonight?" Ernie exclaimed. He sat down next to Prophet. "What are you talking about?"

"I saw it, I did. The choir robe. He was putting it in his leather satchel. The white choir robe." Prophet began to sob uncontrollably, gaining the attention of those passing by. "You must call the inspector. He has to stop him."

Ernie took out his phone and dialed. "I found Prophet," said Ernie after Patterson answered. "He's a bit under the harrow . . . We're in Berkeley Square . . . Says Raventhorn is going to kill again tonight . . . He said he saw him with the white robe . . . Ok, I'll bring him back to our flat . . . No, I haven't heard from the inspector either." He tucked the phone back in his pocket.

Ernie stood up and pulled Prophet up along with him. "We have to go. You'll be safe for the time being at our flat. It's not far from here, a block down that way and three or four bocks up."

"Was that the inspector?" asked Prophet, following Ernie out of the park as best he could.

"I'm afraid not. That was Patterson Coats. He wants to talk to you and then the three of us will go to Scotland

Yard and get this sorted out with Inspector Godfrey. If anyone can put a stop to these murders, it's His Lordship."

Ernie started up Berkeley Square toward the corner. "This way," called out Ernie. He looked back; Prophet was shaking his head. "What is it?"

Prophet pointed across to Bruton Lane and called out, "Conduit Street, you say? This way. We can cut through there, it's a bit faster than the main street."

Prophet started for the corner as Ernie came up behind him. Ernie made it across quickly, dodging traffic, but Prophet was less daring. He waited, walking across behind a small group of partygoers.

"Sorry," remarked Prophet, "with this limp I can only move at one speed."

"My fault. Not to worry, I'll try not to walk too far ahead." Ernie gave Prophet a wink and the two men started walking up Bruton Lane.

It was a narrow street, with six and seven story redbrick or whitewashed buildings looming high above it on either side. It sliced through the block like the long side of a right triangle, emerging at the other end a block away from Conduit Street. There were lights on in most of the upper stories, but the occasional carriage lamp next to a door or over a garage was the only light at street level.

As they walked along, the traffic noise melted away behind them. Ernie paced a few steps ahead of Prophet. An eerie silence settled over the lane, broken only by their footsteps. Ernie gained the first bend where the street narrowed even more; the footsteps muffled. He looked back to see how Prophet was getting on. To his surprise, he wasn't behind him. He started back toward the corner, but as he attempted to call out for Prophet there was a sharp crack on the back of his head. Everything went dark.

29/ No Way to Treat a Lady

As the applauds subsided, the lights around the top of the Reading Room came up, signaling a brief intermission before the Q&A portion of the symposium. The wait staff had resumed their well-planned sorties, armed with a fresh barrage of tempting delicacies.

Marie mingled amongst the small groups congregating in the aisles, promising herself not to linger too long as she made her way through to the bar area. Everyone she came in eye contact with expressed a gracious appreciation over her presentation. Even those normally known for nothing more than the obligatory platitudes seemed genuinely impressed. She smiled and nodded politely to the attendees whom she was not formally acquainted with, reserving bits of time and words of thanks for those curators she had met and remembered from previous events. It was all somewhat overwhelming, but the worst was over. A glass of sauvignon blanc was in order and would certainly take the edge off the remaining portion of the evening.

One of the ushers from the front door approached Marie as she was walking from the bar. "Excuse me, miss. You're Marie Bussière?"

"Oui."

The usher raised his hand. Between his fingers was a small, cream-colored envelope. "A gentleman at the door asked me to give you this note. He said it was urgent."

"Did he give his name?"

"No, miss. I believe he was from a messenger service. He gave me this envelope and 10£, asking that I deliver it to Marie Bussière immediately."

Marie took the envelope from his hand and opened it. "Merci."

The usher smiled and walked away, returning to his post.

Marie pulled a folded note from the envelope and read it to herself.

You're in danger. There is a car out front on Great Russell Street. He will take you to Scotland Yard. I'll meet you there. Talk to no one and leave immediately.
Patterson

Marie's face went pale. She handed her glass to the first waitperson she saw. She hastily made her way through the crowd to the coat check, oblivious to any attempted conversation directed at her. Running out the main entrance, she stopped at the top of the stairs to collect her thoughts. A chill came over her. She held herself against one of the immense columns in a naïve attempt to obscure her presence, surveying the outer courtyard carefully for prying or watchful eyes.

Marie's nerves were getting the better of her. There were small pockets of people standing about the courtyard, talking and smoking innocently enough. Occasionally, someone would casually glance up in her direction and then look away. These same people she looked on as colleagues thirty minutes ago, were now stared back at with a suspicious eye.

"Is everything alright, miss?"

Marie jumped, the voice from behind catching her by surprise. She turned and saw the same usher who delivered the note standing there.

Marie took a moment to catch her breath and then answered, "Yes. I'm sorry, you just scared me."

"Terribly sorry, miss. You just seemed upset."

The usher turned to walk back into the museum, but Marie grabbed his arm. "I'm sorry. You'll think me silly, but would you mind walking me out to the front gate?"

The usher could sense the trepidation driving her response; something terrible was troubling this young woman. "I would be delighted, miss," came the soothing reply.

Marie took his arm, continuing to scan the small clusters of people as they made their way to the front gate.

Beyond the black iron fencing, a black Jaguar waited on Great Russell Street with the rear passenger door open. Next to it, a tall man in a charcoal gray Chesterfield overcoat waited, his collar synched, his hat pulled down slightly concealing his features.

"This will be fine," said Marie, thanking her escort. "I believe this is my car."

"Very good, miss."

"Marie Bussière?" asked the driver holding the car door open.

"Yes, I'm Marie. Have you been sent by Patterson Coats?"

"Yes, mum," came the shallow drawn reply. "I'm to take you to Scotland Yard without delay."

Marie breathed a sigh of relief. She smiled and got into the car. As she sat down, there was a sharp pinprick to her neck. She became groggy and disoriented. Struggling to stay awake, she reached out to the man holding the door. Splinters of blue and white shot out in all directions from the diamonds on her bracelet blinding her. Her hand dropped limp to her side. The dark figure just beyond her reach was now a blur. He slowly closed the door. Another moment more and all went dark. She fell back onto the sculpted leather seat.

* * *

"Sorry, sir," said Mrs. Chapman peering into Patterson's study from the hall. "There's a Mr. Dragonetti to see you. Says it's important, he does." She took a step or two into the study, lowering her voice as she finished. "He's pleasant enough, but brambly just the same. He's got a mate with him. Not sure I like that one. Not sure I like that one bit."

Patterson was surprised but he smiled, assuring Mrs. Chapman they were both harmless. "It's alright, Annie. Show them in please."

Patterson looked up from his desk. Dragonetti and a brutish chap, dusty with hard edges as if chiseled out of a back alley somewhere, stood just inside the doorway. "Well, Elgin, I'm surprised to see you here. It was my understanding you were minding a pot for a friend."

Dragonetti cleared his throat, jerking his head in the direction of the other man. "I was doing just that when I sees this one off the corner where I was standing. It came to my attention a bit earlier he had a bit of knowledge about that business here on your doorstep. That pot's being looked after 'till I return, put one of my own blokes on it. Thought you might find what this chap has to say a bit more important. Go ahead." Dragonetti gave the other man a shove forward. "Give him your name and tells him what you told me."

"Alright, alright," replied the man. He was average height with a thick neck and matching arms. High cheekbones flanked a fighter's nose, resting just above an expressionless mouth. He had rough darkened skin, a result no doubt from years of hard living and a laborers situation when other, more lucrative work, wasn't available. His vacant stare was made more dramatic by the black eye he sported. "No need to get shirty. Cobley. The name is Cobley, but you can just call me Cobs."

"Well, Cobs, what is it you have to tell me."

Cobs threw a thumb over his shoulder in Dragonetti's direction. "He says you ain't with the cops." He waited for Patterson to confirm with a nod and then continued. "Alright then. I does work from time to time for this toffee-nosed swell over on Sloane Square. A bit snooty for my taste, but the money's cushy."

"Does this toffee-nosed swell have a name?"

"Yeah, Raventhorn. Just like it says on the plaque on his door. This bloke gives me a hundred quid and an address. Says I'm to watch for the mail. Says there's a packet being delivered he wants me to nick. I'm to bring it to him and he gives me another hundred quid."

Patterson's relaxed mood tightened. "And did you?"

"I saw a package arrive. I was going to burgle the flat, but then I sees this bird leave with the package under her arm."

"And that's when you followed her here to my door?"

Dragonetti gave Cobs another shove. "Go on. Out with it."

Cobs puffed out his chest. "Yeah. That's right. Mind you, I didn't want to raise a hand to such a pretty bird. Put up a fight, she did. Left me no choice."

Patterson rose from his chair, his fist clenched, his eyes focused on the brute before him. "There's always a choice. You put her in the hospital. Was that part of the deal? Maybe I should blacken that other eye so you remember to make better choices in the future."

Cobs took a cautious step backwards. "Like I says, she put up a fight. I just wanted the package and the other hundred quid. That's all."

Patterson looked at Dragonetti. "Get him out of here." The two men turned to leave but Patterson called out. "Wait. Did she give you that black eye?"

Cobs jerked his head in Dragonetti's direction. "No. It was this one here what had the honors. Seems he didn't like the way I treated that bird neither."

Patterson gave Dragonetti a nod of approval.

Dragonetti grabbed Cob's shoulder and spun him toward the hall. "Go on, you're done here. And if I sees you anywhere near those two birds I won't be so *gentle* next time."

Dragonetti watched from the doorway as Cobs made his way down the hall and the stairs to the front door. An abrupt slam indicated Cobs understood.

"His lot gives all us decent reprobates a bad name," said Dragonetti with a slight laugh. "You know, I saw Bisquets earlier."

Patterson was preoccupied. He sat back down at his desk. "I'm sorry, what did you say? You saw Ernie?"

"I said I saw Bisquets earlier. He came running out of that bird's flat. I went to ask what was wrong and he waved me off. He was up the street without so much as a how'd ya do." The expression on Patterson's face gave Dragonetti pause. "Are you all right, Guv'nor?"

Patterson slowly looked up at Dragonetti and in a concerned voice said, "I think it is of the utmost importance we locate Inspector Flannel. Would you do that for me?"

Dragonetti scratched his head. "Beggin' your pardon, but couldn't you just ring him on his mobile?"

"I've tried that a number of times." Patterson motioned with his hand for Dragonetti to move away from the doorway. "Mrs. Chapman? Are you there?"

After a moment, Mrs. Chapman walked in the study, a dishtowel and pot in hand. "Something I can get you two?"

"Have you heard from August?"

The pleasant look on Mrs. Chapman's face drifted off, leaving behind a brow of concern. "Funny you should ask. I just tried him not twenty minutes ago and still no answer.

I don't like to bother my Derby, but with a murderer on the loose I'll tell you it's got me a bit worried."

"It's true then?" Dragonetti asked Patterson in a hushed tone, as if Mrs. Chapman couldn't hear him. "Word on the street is Flannel was suspended from the force for sticking his nose . . . Sorry, mum, no disrespect intended."

With a gentle smile of compassion, Mrs. Chapman patted Dragonetti's massive forearm. "It's alright, none taken. He's a stubborn one, that one. Ain't the first time he's caught a harsh word for sticking his nose in the wrong pie." She paused, her concern welling up in her bright green eyes. "It's not to say he couldn't use the help of a resourceful man such as yourself now and again if he was to be in trouble."

Patterson gave a nod to Dragonetti. "See if you can locate him."

"Consider it done." Dragonetti made a motion with his hand like he was tipping his hat, bid them goodbye, and let himself out.

"I don't want you to worry, Annie," said Patterson after Dragonetti had left. "August and I have been through a great deal through the years. He knows how to take care of himself." Patterson's rationalization of the current state of the missing inspector was cut short by his mobile phone ringing. "What's that? . . . Where are you now? . . . I'll be right there."

"What is it?" asked Mrs. Chapman, a little less at ease by the concerned look on Patterson's face. "What's happened?"

Patterson forced a smile. "Nothing at all that would cause you any worry. I promised Marie I would meet her promptly at 9:30. I've got a stop to make first, so I'm going to leave now. If you should hear from August, please have him contact me right away."

Without another word, Patterson grabbed his coat from the chair next to the door and hastily made his way down the stairs and out.

Mrs. Chapman wasn't at all convinced with Patterson's explanation. Something was wrong. Something was very wrong.

30/ A Call to Action

"Alright, alright," cried out Mrs. Chapman, bounding down the steps to the front door faster than a woman her age and size should. At the bottom, she opened the door, very much surprised by who had been pushing the buzzer.

"Sorry, mum," said a somewhat dazed Ernie Bisquets. "Ran out with out my key."

"My word, son," exclaimed Mrs. Chapman as Ernie entered aided by a constable. She made her way back up the stairs, waving them along to follow her into the sitting room. "You look a fright. What's happened? Is everything alright?"

"I found this lad on my patch," replied the constable, "unconscious in a narrow alley on Bruton Lane. Lucky it's only a bump on the head, I say."

The constable had a boyish face, tall with a sharp edge to his posture. The black name badge on his crisp white shirt said *Thursby*, and the chevrons on his shoulder badges indicated he was a sergeant.

"Lucky indeed," said Mrs. Chapman. She took Ernie's arm and led him to the dining table. "You just sit here and I'll get you an ice pack for that bump."

Ernie smiled at her thoughtfulness, but waved off the offer. "That's very kind of you, but I'll be fine. It's important I speak with His Lordship. Is he here?"

"You've just missed him. I believe he's gone to the museum to collect Miss Bussière." Mrs. Chapman paused, recollecting the events. "Odd though. He got a phone call not five minutes ago and ran out of here without so much as a word to why or where. He says it was nothing."

"We saw the car service out front," Ernie replied, looking over at the clock on the mantel. "Says he's here to pick up His Lordship."

"He must have forgotten he called for the service," mused Mrs. Chapman. "Not like him though. Not like him at all. Said he had a quick stop to make first, then it was off to the museum."

Thursby waited politely for an opportunity to interrupt. "Well, if you remember anything else, just stop by the station. I'll be on my way then. I'll send the driver away if you like." He tipped his hat. "Mum."

As the constable spoke, the dispatcher's voice crackled through his police radio. He excused himself and walked over to the pillared entrance to the hall. They could hear bits and pieces of his response. It sounded important and they expected him to leave right afterwards. Instead, he came back over to where they were talking.

"Pardon me," said Thursby. "You mentioned on the way over here the other man you were with was Prophet Brown?"

"Yes, that's correct," replied Ernie briskly. "Have they found him?"

"It seems he called into the station to report an attempted murder. Says he's by the tracks below the abandoned Shoreditch rail station. Inspector Godfrey is on his way there now. I told him how we found you and he's requested I collect you and bring you down to the scene."

"What about Inspector Flannel?" Ernie asked. He looked from the constable to Mrs. Chapman. "Has anyone heard from the inspector?"

Mrs. Chapman slowly shook her head, as did the constable.

31/ The Rhyme and Reason

His eyes slowly opened. There was darkness all around. A throbbing in the back of his head held his attention for a few minutes as he struggled to ascertain where he was. He was lying face down on the ground, the sharp edge of a rock or brick cutting into his cheek. As his eyes adjusted to the darkness he could make out train tracks an arm's length away. They were rusted on top, indicating a lack of use for some time. Long, slender fingers of light stretched into the darkness from behind where he lay, reflecting off the glass and metal debris. His eyes were beginning to focus.

Off in the distance were the muffled sounds of traffic. The only other sound was from his labored breaths. Through a watery squint, and from the rough objects he could feel beneath him, he soon realized he was lying amidst brick and rubble. He was below street level, beneath a flyover of some sort. With one fierce movement, he rolled over on his back. Looking out toward the source of the dim light, he could make out a long, curved brick wall, ornamented with debossed brick arches beneath a row of ornamental squares. It ran off into the distance, disappearing around a bend into a tunnel or beneath another flyover. Resting along the top ledge, secured to bent and rusted metal armatures glistening from the streetlights above, was a tangled mess of barbed wire. Beyond that, silhouettes of tall thin trees and assorted buildings were cut out of a moonless indigo sky. The air was thick with the stench of decomposing rodents, excrement, and the assorted waste left behind by fly-tippers.

He looked back into the darkness, becoming eerily aware he was not alone. As he pulled himself up, he could make out a dark figure ten or so feet in front of him, kneeling down beside an object covered in a white cloth of some sort.

"You there," his raspy voice called out. "I say, you there. What is the meaning of this? Why have you brought me here?"

The dark figure paused for a moment, then ignored the questions, and continued with what he was doing.

"I don't know who you are, but I can assure you people will be looking for me." Doing his best with what strength he could muster, he managed to get to his feet. "I'll not ask you again. Where am I?"

As he took a step forward, a shaft of light caught the end of a revolver pointed straight at him. He stopped, not so much because of the revolver, but because of what else he saw. There on the ground, laid out at the feet of the dark figure, was Marie Bussière. A white choir rob was fitted neatly onto her body, her hands together in peaceful prayer.

"What have you done, you miserable wretch?" Raventhorn no longer required additional light to identify the dark figure before him. "Do you know who that is?"

Raventhorn began to step forward. Prophet cocked the hammer of the gun, once again halting his master's motion.

"You're at the west end of the abandoned Shoreditch underground station," Prophet replied shrewdly. His manner was determined, his speech flawless. He stood erect. With the exception of his deformed arm, there was little indication of the pathetic wretch Raventhorn had become accustomed to. "I can assure you we won't be disturbed, at least not until the police arrive. And yes, I know exactly who that is."

Raventhorn was taken aback by the transformation of the man he believed to be a twisted pathetic wretch. As he stared at Prophet, he cautiously sidestepped over to the body of Marie. Kneeling down he put his finger on her carotid artery.

"She's alive," Raventhorn stated, rising to his feet.

"Of course she's alive." Prophet laughed, motioning with the gun for Raventhorn to step back away from the body. "I need her to confirm my explanation of the events. And, as I'll soon be explaining to the police, it was fortunate for her I was able to overpower you, otherwise you might have killed her like the others."

"You're mad," barked Raventhorn. He rubbed the back of his head as he continued, "You've done this. You struck me from behind at the flat and dragged me here to this miserable, discarded corner of London. And for what? To cover your own murderous ways?"

Prophet began with a raised brow and an innocent pout, "I've killed no one. I've done nothing but try to prove to the police it's been you all along." He finished with the ends of his lips curled up in a baleful smile. "They'll believe me now."

Raventhorn looked around. Behind him were the dilapidated remains of a train platform, the cement edges chipped away from years of neglect, grass and weeds growing through the cracks. He stepped backwards and sat on the edge. "It *was* you," he mumbled to himself. Raventhorn looked up at Prophet, his voice deepened to a measured, indicting tone. "After reading of that young woman's death I had my suspicions, but I didn't think you capable of such a murderous act. So your debilitating disfigurements are nothing more than a sham? It would appear you're not at all the pitiful wretch you've portrayed yourself to be all these years."

Prophet's expression reflected an overall sense of pride in his deception. "Slightly crippled holds little weight in our society, but a twisted wretch enjoys a bounty of charity." He smiled wickedly. "Fooling you wasn't difficult at all, you were preoccupied with your own secrets. That journalist was a bit of a challenge though. It took all I had to convince her I was the ill-used servant of a loathsome murderer. She said she was going to help me, but I knew she was holding something back after we spoke."

A muted siren drifted in from beyond the silhouettes above the wall, barely audible in the thick night air.

Raventhorn returned a contemptuous grin. "That bothersome reporter came to me next fishing for information, foolishly admitting she was drafting an article detailing those murders eight years ago. She had gathered up the circumstantial bits of evidence you and that fool Flannel put together years ago. What I didn't expect was her accidentally implying she had a new piece of evidence she believed would expose the murderer. I realized that information could only have come from you. I could hardly contain my anger, but you already knew that since you were listening at the door."

"You are a clever one." Prophet sneered.

"Not clever enough to stop you from doing something foolish. I was going to deal with her my own way. A young woman alone in a city such as London, anything could happen. First, I had to find out what this new piece of evidence was. Unfortunately, she kept it safely in a journal, which she smugly declared to have mailed to a friend to protect herself. The original circumstantial implications were nothing new. It was this new evidence she hinted at that would finally substantiate a motive. All you've done by killing her has tied the noose around both our necks."

"But I'm a poor crippled wretch," Prophet sobbed in a mocking tone. "Who could ever think me possible of such a heinous act?"

"Who indeed," grumbled Raventhorn. "I wondered why you suddenly recanted your accusations to the police years ago. It's become painfully obvious what I attributed to the fear of my wrath was actually the first step in a premeditated plan. I had hoped our conversation in the park this afternoon would have loosened the grip on that dark soul of yours enough to confess what you've done. Sadly, it would appear you have no intention of doing anything of the sort. Before you complete this misguided act of vengeance, I only wish to understand why you did it. What possible reason did you have to kill that naive journalist and Cynthia Carolls?"

"Why?" Prophet growled. "You really don't know, do you?"

"Know what?" Raventhorn griped.

"The two of you tossed me aside like yesterday's rubbish. Those murders eight years ago, all of them, were at your hand. The first one was random enough, so were the last three, but they were all necessary to cover the motive behind the second." Prophet waited. He laughed when he saw the spark of recognition ignite terror in Raventhorn's eyes. "That's right, Margaret Morris."

Raventhorn stood up. "You . . . you knew?"

"Not at first, but I became curious why a prominent man like yourself would take such an interest in a pitiful cripple like me. Snatched me right from the street, you did, without rhyme or reason. Makes a bloke wonder. After years of digging, I finally got the truth. I found out from hospital records her full name was Margaret Morris Brown. I located her in Highbury eight years ago." Prophet tensed up. "She laughed in my face when I asked her about you and why she abandoned me. Said I was mental. Denied ever having a child and slammed the door in my face. Maggie Brown was my mother by birth, but that's where it ended. Both of you made sure of that. Isn't that right, father?"

Raventhorn's fear turned to rage. "I should have left you in the gutter. So what is it you want? Money?" Raventhorn snorted. "You're no better than that cheeky tart. This explains why she suddenly tried to squeeze me for more money eight years ago. I knew then, there would be no end to it." Raventhorn glanced over at the motionless body of Marie Bussière, continuing in quiet, proud reflection. "The *Slasher*. All of London trembled in their beds, consumed with the headlines of his seemingly insatiable blood lust, wondering when he would strike again. I recreated the perfect villain, adding, of course, my own ambiguous distortion to his raison d'être as he preyed on young women of a certain type. It was brilliant. They so wanted to call him 'Jack'." Raventhorn paused, the rage returning to his eyes, his attention back to Prophet. "Now, I'm afraid the elaborate theatrics I was driven to and employed years ago will be my undoing. It was a silly indiscretion, an indiscretion, I might add, that was instigated by her. I'm an important man. I was not about to be threatened by the likes of her." Raventhorn brushed the soot and dirt from his sleeves as he finished, his tone giving validation to his final action. "She left me no choice."

Prophet stepped forward, a shaft of light catching the intense resentment in his eyes as he spoke. A malevolent curl drew up the right side of his mouth, properly framing his response. "Earlier today, a reporter received an anonymous phone call suggesting you may have fathered a child with one of your victims. I'm quite sure hospital records, as well as bank records, are being checked *again* as we speak. In the end, it will all substantiate your merciless actions, applying the proper name to the villain you so carefully created."

"So that journalist, Mary Trevor? She didn't just stumble onto information about our past, did she?"

Prophet laughed. "And she felt so sorry for the abuse I've taken at your hand. Besides exposing a ruthless murderer, she was determined to establish my proper birthright. Imagine how surprised I'll be when they inform me of the estate I've just inherited."

"And I suppose it was you who leaked the story about Inspector Flannel's involvement to the newspapers?"

Prophet nodded smugly. "He was useful at first in pointing evidence at you, then getting him removed from the investigation would serve a greater purpose. Having you killed by the very man you ruined would have been a fitting end to your miserable life. I'm afraid his resistance to my plan has forced me to change my plans slightly since then."

"So it's revenge is it?"

"Revenge? If that were all it was, I would have just killed you myself years ago. I want all of London to see you for the loathsome man I know you to be. Killing one woman makes you a murderer; killing seven makes you a monster. They'll thank me for killing you. Then, when you're gone, I'll finally get what was denied me for all those years."

Raventhorn's eyes narrowed. His voice deepened to a harsh rasp. "I'll make no excuse for what your mother did in the past, but don't assume I was a conscious participant. It wasn't until years after your birth I was made aware of your existence. And years after that I found out your mother frivolously spent the money I gave her to give you both a proper home. She was never going to be satisfied. That's the rhyme and reason I *snatched* you from the street. Her greed and threats of exposure drove me to commit those murders, so I've earned the right to be resentful. I couldn't make up for your mother's actions, but I did what I could to make a proper home for you."

"A proper home, is it?" Prophet snarled, his voice cracking in anger. "Treating me like your servant is making a proper home for me? Raising your hand to a cripple is your idea of a proper home?"

A slight glint of compassion welled up in Raventhorn's eyes, though it was less than convincing. "You thankless ingrate. Nothing was asked of you, but you have no idea of the sacrifices I made because of you. I gave up what was probably a grand political career to protect my name from being splashed all over the front pages of the tabloids. Yet the first chance you get, you concoct an outlandish story of murder and deceit from bits and pieces you've picked up along the way and run off to that fool Inspector Flannel. You think me harsh, but my treatment of you is no different than how I was treated by *my* father. It doesn't make it right, but life is cruel. It was a stiff backhand that taught me that lesson and afforded us the life we've both enjoyed. I'm only sorry it wasn't enough for you. I've provided for you, without asking anything in return, and this is the way you repay me. The monster you say I became was to protect my good name and the fortune I amassed. But you? You're nothing more than a common murderer."

The faint sirens, moments earlier indistinguishable in direction, could be heard rapidly approaching the abandoned railroad yard from the west.

Prophet took off the long Chesterfield overcoat and tossed it at Raventhorn. "It would seem it runs in the family. Put that on."

The sirens were now above them on Brick Lane. Red and blue lights from the police vehicles danced through the dark windows of the buildings overlooking the abandoned tracks.

Raventhorn hesitated for a moment. He looked at the tag stitched into the lining, shook his head and tossed the coat to the ground. "That's my coat. I see what your game is. Since that journalist started nosing about in my business, you'll have the police believe the *Slasher* has fallen victim once again to his addiction for murder."

"That's something you'll be taking with you to the bottom of the lake."

"And what about her journal?"

"I have that safely tucked away. It should make for interesting reading."

Raventhorn ignored the glib response. "You're as dense as you are reckless. That new evidence you so foolishly placed in that young reporter's lap can serve two masters. It certainly implies motive on my part for the first five murders, but, ironically, it also implies the same on your part for her murder. You won't get away with this. You've played the police for fools, but the truth will surface."

"There are only two people who know the real truth," Prophet snarled, "and I'll be heralded a hero by the frightened people of London for killing one of them."

Enraged, Raventhorn lunged at Prophet. The two men thrashed about for a moment, staggering back and forth on the loose footing. A muffled shot abruptly stopped the struggle, the gun dropping to the ground. Alfred Raventhorn stepped backwards, his eyes squinting from the pain. His grip tightened on Prophet's arm. He took two short breaths then collapsed on top of the rubble, dead.

Down around the bend in the tracks were the first glimmers of torches streaking across the brick wall heading in Prophet's direction. He hastily pulled a knife from his pocket, wiping both the handle and blade with the end of his coat sleeve. He squeezed the knife in Raventhorn's hand and sliced across his deformed arm. The red scarf was already in the pocket of the overcoat. Satisfied everything was in place, Prophet laid down in the rubble, pulling Raventhorn's lifeless body on top of him.

The police were less than fifty feet away, chattering to each other about what they just heard and to proceed ahead with caution. After one last look to assure himself Raventhorn was dead, the contentment drifted from

Prophet's face. The cold, calculating eyes of a murderer slowly closed, soon to open as the frightened stare of a disfigured pathetic wretch who barely escaped the murderous clutches of his master.

32/ Here and Gone

"The woman's still alive!" one of the first constables on the scene called out. "The old one here is dead," shouted another.

Within minutes, an additional ten constables arrived, their torches illuminating the space. At first, they didn't even notice Prophet, Raventhorn's coat obscured most of his torso.

"Help! Help me!" a pathetic voice shrieked out from the darkness. "Tried to kill me, he did. Help!"

The constables flooded the area with their torches in the direction they thought the voice emanated from. Prophet called out again, this time managing to raise and wave his hand as best he could under the weight of the body. Three constables carefully moved the body of Raventhorn, exposing the frightened and bleeding wretch beneath.

"Who might you be?" one of the constables asked, helping Prophet up into a sitting position.

"Prophet Brown," replied an official voice walking toward them. "It is Prophet Brown, isn't it?" repeated Inspector Godfrey.

"Yes. Yes, Prophet Brown," Prophet whimpered, shaking uncontrollably. He gripped his deformed arm tightly, blood oozing out between his fingers. "He was going to kill that poor girl, he was. I knew it. Tried to stop him."

As Prophet continued to mumble short bursts of details, Inspector Godfrey moved his torch along the ground around the area where Raventhorn's body was. He quickly spotted the gun, his light reflecting off the shiny barrel. The torch also illuminated the blade of the knife still clutched in Raventhorn's hand. Godfrey nodded his head in the direction of the weapons, directing the constable next to him to cordon off the area around the body.

Running toward Godfrey was Patterson Coats. "Godfrey, where is she?" his commanding voice called out, echoing through the flyover. "Where is she?"

Godfrey nodded, pointing in the direction of the small cluster of constables behind him. It isn't often such a monstrous crime can be prevented before another victim is claimed. He gave a sigh of relief this was one of those occasions.

Patterson ran over to where Godfrey was pointing. He knelt down beside Marie, gently picking her up, wrapping his arms around her. Marie gradually opened her eyes, startled at first over her condition and the odious place she found herself. She quickly calmed down when she recognized the man whose arms she was in. Her eyes glistening with tears, she smiled looking up at him.

"I thought I lost you," Patterson whispered, brushing away the hair from her eyes. "I'll never let you go again."

Inspector Godfrey turned his attention back to Prophet. "Can you walk?" asked Godfrey looking down at Prophet, who nodded his head briskly.

Two constables helped him to his feet, walking him over to the cement platform. At that point, the EMTs had arrived. One went directly to check Raventhorn, but was waved off and redirected to where Marie was lying; another was called over to attend to Prophet's arm.

As the technician dressed his wound, Prophet watched Godfrey, being careful not to draw attention to himself. Godfrey spent a few moments on his mobile phone, then a few more minutes talking to the constables, pointing here and there as he spoke. At one point, he went over to check on Marie and have a word with Patterson. Satisfied she was being tended to, Godfrey returned to Prophet. As he did, the technician was just finishing up.

"How does it look?" asked Godfrey.

"A clean cut, not too deep. Ten stitches in all." The technician stood up. He looked over at the body of Raventhorn and then looked back at Prophet and smiled. "It's a lucky lad you are. Up with you now, and we'll get you to the hospital."

Prophet winced, slightly nodding his head in acceptance of his good fortune, then slightly shaking his head in refusal of the offer. "Don't like hospitals." He stared vacantly at the body of Raventhorn, tears running down his cheeks.

Inspector Godfrey shrugged his shoulders, unenthusiastically assenting to Prophet's wishes. He motioned for a constable to cover the body as they waited for the ME. After taking a notepad out of his pocket, he sat down next to Prophet, partially obscuring his view of the body. "I'd like to ask you a few questions if you're up to it."

Prophet wiped his nose on the sleeve of his coat and nodded his head. He shivered slightly, his head resuming the involuntary jerking motion as he spoke in a quiet, drawn tone. "Going to kill that poor girl, he was. Just like the others. I told the inspector. Why didn't he stop him? I had no choice. He would have killed me too."

"How did you know he was going to abduct Marie Bussière?"

"He went out somewhere. He came back angrier than I've ever seen. Kept ranting about how *he would fix him*. Saw her name circled on a program on his desk. I watched him put the white robe in his satchel." Prophet winced, making a motion with his deformed arm in the direction of Marie. "It's over there. He must have known I was listening at the door and I saw him with it."

"How did you get here?"

"He must have followed me when I went to find Inspector Flannel. I had to tell him what the master was up to. Found that Bisquets chap instead." Prophet's head twitch worsened as he continued, "He said he'd help. We were on Bruton Lane when he got the drop on us. He didn't kill Mr. Bisquets did he?"

Inspector Godfrey shook his head. "No. One of my men found him in the corner of the alley. A knot on his head, but alive just the same."

"A bit of luck that. He seems like a pleasant chap." Prophet took a deep breath and continued. "Next thing I knew, I woke up in that pile of rubble with a sore head. He didn't pay any attention to me at first. He was busy. That's when I called the station. Then I saw him pull the knife out of his pocket. He was going to kill her. I had to do something. I looked around for something to hit him with. He just laughed, stood up and walked over to me. He pulled a gun out of his other pocket. Said I was worthless and better off dead." Prophet shivered uncontrollably as he spoke. The tears again began to stream down his cheeks. "Said he would have no trouble convincing the authorities I was behind all those murders. We heard your sirens. When he looked away, I lunged at him. He slashed at me with the knife. It all happened so fast. I felt something poke into my ribs. As we struggled, he lost his footing. I grabbed at the gun and it went off. We both fell to the ground. I thought I was dead."

"It's a very noble and selfless thing you did," Patterson Coats interjected. He stood in front of the two men, his arm around Marie, his coat over her shoulders. "You very easily could have been killed. I'll be forever in your debt."

Prophet looked up, his head bobbing as he smiled in modest appreciation. "I'm glad you're alright, miss."

Marie forced a brave smile. She reached out, putting her hand on Prophet's lowered head. "Je te dois ma vie."

"If you have no objection, Inspector," suggested Patterson firmly but with respect, "I think it best to remove Marie from this dismal place and the frightening realities of this evening's events. You'll find her at my flat."

"Certainly," replied Godfrey with a considerate nod of his head. "I'll stop around after we finish up here to get your statement, miss."

Marie smiled and turned her face into Patterson's shoulder. They walked off along the tracks, disappearing around the bend. The ME was coming in the opposite direction, the red and blue emergency lights above glimmering off the stainless steel stretcher he and his assistant pushed along the gravel close to the wall.

Inspector Godfrey stood up, walking over to have a word with the ME. Running toward the scene, and outpacing Thursby, was Ernie. He had stopped first to have a quick word with Patterson and Marie before continuing toward all the activity under the fly-over. The inspector motioned for him to wait, pointing over to the rusted handrail at the end of the platform behind where Prophet was seated.

Prophet sat quietly, his head down, nonchalantly trying to catch a word or two of the conversation between the men. He hadn't noticed Ernie. After a few minutes, Inspector Godfrey returned to his seat next to Prophet.

"Are you sure you don't want to go to the hospital?"

Prophet ignored the question. He motioned with his head toward the black body bag the ME was zipping up. "It was him, you know. It was him eight years ago and it was him what killed those women in Spitalfields. Found out, she did. He knew I heard her tell him so."

"What do you mean?"

"He threatened me." Prophet motioned with his head once more toward the body bag. "That woman he killed up on Brick Lane knew what he had done eight years ago. Wrote it all down in her journal. Mailed it to her girlfriend for safekeeping, that hat maker. He killed that other nice woman, too."

"Yes, the journal," the inspector remarked purposefully. "What has come of the journal? Have you seen it?"

Prophet slowly raised his head, looking away from Inspector Godfrey. He glared at the motionless body with a momentary flash of contentment. "Burned it, he did."

The inspector finished his notes, tucking the small pad into his pocket. He glanced over to where Ernie was standing, surprised to find he was gone.

33/ One for the Road

"Is that you, Bisquets?" called out John over the crowd at the bar. "I said he'd be back to see his old mates and here he is. Ain't that right, Fie?"

Ernie gave a wink and a nod as he walked up to shake John Grimbald's hand. Fiona was waiting with a pleasant smile, dusting off a stool with her apron. Before he sat down, John leaned across the bar, jerking his head in the direction of the far corner.

"He's here again," said John in a hushed tone. "Brought some other bounder with him this time. I'll tolerate the big one, bein' he's your mate, but I can't say I like the looks of that other one. Ain't that right, Fie?"

Ernie looked down the bar. In the far corner, a small dim light above a well used and long since polished cash register illuminated Dragonetti's face, his stocky silhouette cast against the dingy white plaster wall about a foot behind him. He lifted his pint to acknowledge Ernie's glance.

"He ain't my mate," Ernie sharply responded to address the sarcastic section of the remark, "but he's not one to start trouble either. Sorry about the other one, I asked Dragonetti to bring him along. I just have a few questions and I'm sure he'll be on his way."

The Copper Needle Pub was quickly becoming a favorite nightspot of the young new artisans revitalizing an otherwise old and neglected neighborhood. John and Fiona smiled and served pints to the thirsty young patrons from five o'clock till closing. It exhausted them most nights, but it was a profitable exhaustion. The afternoons were still quiet, only the afternoon regulars and the occasional tourist looking to discover a hidden treasure.

Ernie made his way through the little clusters assembled along the bar. He gave a furtive smile to the people he passed, reflecting back on how in the old days a walk like that in a crowded bar would net him a half dozen wallets. He reached the heel where it turned and ended at the wall. Dragonetti sat on one of the two stools around the corner, quietly sipping his pint, winking now and again at the young birds cackling away across the bar. Standing next to him, leaning his elbows on the bar and impatiently ringing his hands, was the man Ernie was particularly interested in talking with. Sipping his whisky from a thick shot glass, he watched Ernie slip in and out of the clusters, like a needle along a seam.

"Cobs," Ernie mumbled under his breath as he approached the two men, "I should have known."

John ignored the empty glasses held out for a refill as he mirrored Ernie's progress to the far end of the bar. He pulled a fresh pint, placing it down on a bright red and gold Courage coaster in a narrow opening at the heel of the crowded bar. There was just enough space for Ernie to wedge himself in, his back to a young woman busy talking on her mobile.

"Could I get you lads another?" grumbled John Grimbald.

"I'll have another, thank you very much," replied Dragonetti unaffected by the dismissive tone. He pushed a 10£ note forward. "And I'll take care of Bisquet's pint while you're at it."

This gesture brought an expression of acceptance to John's face, despite his devout decision to dislike everything about Dragonetti. He picked up his glass, replacing it with a fresh pint from the tap behind him.

"I'll have one more, too," screeched Cobs over the din of voices.

John Grimbald sneered, taking the shot glass from Cobs' outstretched hand and turning it upside down on the bar. In an acerbic tone, sweetened with just an ounce of innkeeper pleasantry, he replied, "I'm afraid you won't be here long enough to enjoy another."

Dragonetti gave a hearty laugh as they watched John turn and attend to his other patrons. He leaned back on his stool, allowing Ernie a full view of the undesirable Pete Cobley next to him.

"Good thing you called when you did," Dragonetti remarked. "I was lucky to find him before he crawled back into whatever crack he crawled out of." He looked over at Cobs. "Go ahead, tell him what you know."

"Like I told that other bloke, this tosh Raventhorn gives me 100 quid to nick a package. He gives me the address of this bird what lives on Savile Row, just off Clifford Street. I never got the chance to burgle the place; she left all in a hurry that same afternoon. I followed her over to Mayfair—"

Ernie lunged forward, grabbing Cobs by the dusty lapel of his rough canvas jacket. Cobs reached into his pocket, fumbling to pull out a 38 revolver. As his hand came across the bar, raising the gun and pointing it at Ernie, the blunt end of a bat wielded by Grimbald crushed his hand. The gun slid across the bar, clinking against Dragonetti's glass. John Grimbald was quick to retrieve it, tucking it into his apron pocket.

The pub went perfectly still, everyone looking over to the dark corner of the bar where all the excitement was. John slowly lowered the bat; order was restored. The small clusters returned to their conversations and the fresh round of pints graciously provided by Fiona to help distract their inquisitive minds.

Cobs cringed, holding his hand tightly to his chest. "You've broken it. You broke my damn hand."

"I'll break more than that if ever you darken a stool in here again," replied the dark side of the otherwise pleasant and accommodating John Grimbald, his eyes reduced to slits, a single eyebrow raised. "Off with you now."

"Wait. I have one last question," said Ernie, stepping in front of Cobs.

"I ain't got nothing else to say," grumbled Cobs, attempting to push his way past Ernie.

John Grimbald leaned over the bar forcing the bat between Cobs and Ernie, stopping abruptly when it hit the dingy white wall behind them. "The lad says he has one more question and my wooden mate here says you have one more answer."

Cobs was in no position to argue. "What is it you want?"

"What did this Raventhorn look like?"

Cobs cringed from the pain. "He's a bit younger than you, drags that club foot when he walks. A quiet sort but a bit gruff for a cripple, what with that bad arm curled up like it is." Cobs looked over at Grimbald, pulling his injured hand away from view. "No doubt he's made your acquaintance."

"A cripple," Ernie quietly mused. He looked over at John Grimbald and gave a nod. The bat was promptly retracted. Ernie completed the transaction with a jerk of his head indicating the direction of the exit.

"This ain't over, Bisquets," sniped Cobs, looking from Ernie to Grimbald.

"Oh yes it is," replied Dragonetti steadfastly. He didn't turn around, he just reached out and grabbed Cobs' injured arm with his meaty grip. "These good people are close friends of mine. I'll hold you directly responsible if any one of them so much as breaks a nail. Do we understand each other?"

Ernie stepped aside

Cobs winced in pain and quickly bobbed his head in response. He pushed his way through the crowd, fielding a number of disparaging remarks about his character, and a few pointed suggestions on how he might sexually occupy himself, as he made his way out the door.

Ernie started to express his thanks, but was abruptly stifled when Dragonetti raised his hand. Instead, he was directed to sit down on the stool next to him.

Fiona walked down and stood next to her husband who was busy wiping down the bar with his rag. "Everything all right now, Ernie?" she asked politely.

"It will be, Fiona. It will be."

"I said that one was trouble, didn't I, Fie?" remarked John, looking toward the door. "I think we've seen the last of him."

Dragonetti laughed. "I believe you're right. I don't think he'll chance another meeting with the business end of that wooden mate of yours."

"Nice of you to stand up like you did for the lad here," said John apologetically, giving a jerk of his head in Ernie's direction. "We think a lot of Ernie, like he's our own family. Seems I might be carrying the wrong idea about you. Ain't that right, Fie?"

Fiona looked over and nodded, a brilliant smile illuminating her chubby face.

"It's kind of you to say, John," replied Dragonetti, uncharacteristically accepting of the praise. He took a long draft, finished his pint and stood up. "Well, enough of this maudlin nonsense. His Lordship has asked me to locate the good inspector and I've wasted enough time with the likes of you."

The tale end of the remark brought a smile to Ernie's face, but it was quickly dampened by the idea of Flannel still being among the missing.

"There's something I need to do also," said Ernie.

Dragonetti noticed the hint of anger in Ernie's eyes. "You'll not do anything foolish now, will you?"

Ernie didn't answer at first, his eyes focused down the length of the bar.

"Will you?" Dragonetti repeated, slightly sharper.

"Sorry," Ernie stuttered. "Sorry. No, no need to worry."

"Right then." Dragonetti had no trouble making his way to the door, his commanding size and somewhat menacing expression more than parted the sea of faces before him.

34/ Almost Home

Raventhorn's Jaguar was found close to the construction entrance off Pedley Street near Weaver. It was unlocked with the boot open. Inspector Godfrey instructed the forensic team to have a go at it. He explained to Prophet he would have someone from the Yard bring it round to the flat when they were done. Prophet once again refused another request to be taken to the hospital, resulting in Godfrey having one of the constables drive him back to his flat on Sloane Street.

It was close to eleven o'clock when Prophet climbed out of the police car. A bright moon was visible beyond the rooftops, illuminating a brilliantly clear cobalt sky. He hobbled up the marble steps, careful to secure firm footing for his clubfoot, and more careful of his appearance to the constable watching his assent, before continuing up to the next step. He paused at the top, giving a reaffirming wave to the constable in the car. Prophet watched as the car pulled away up the street, surveyed the length of the block for any other prying eyes, then continued into the dark portico. He fumbled with his key in the lock, eventually gaining entry. After closing the door, he leaned back against the carved panels of the oak door and breathed a sigh of relief. Afterwards, he took the sling off, tossing it on the floor.

The flat was as silent and cold as Death's sickle, with only the faint echo of the quarter hour chime from the French Ormolu clock drifting eerily down the hall. By the hall tree, rested the black leather suitcase Prophet had packed earlier. A small case was perched on top with a passport and cash inside. He picked up the case and started down the hall, his stature more upright, his gait more natural. At the end of the hall, a sliver of light pried open the door to Raventhorn's study. As he slowly pushed the door open, the light from the etched glass desk lamp illuminated the contented smile on his face. The corners of the room were relatively dark, save for the area around the desk.

Prophet checked his watch then walked over to the built-in bookcase to the right of the fireplace. He laughed to himself as he poured out a glass of Courvoisier L'Esprit—Raventhorn's personal cognac—from the Lalique crystal decanter. Next to the decanter was the silver bell Raventhorn used to call Prophet. He picked it up, violently shaking it as he growled in mocking imitation. "Prophet! You miserable wretch, where's my supper! Prophet! Bring the car around! Prophet!" He abruptly spun around, tossing the bell into the fireplace in the same motion. It clanked and clunked, finally settling into the cold gray ashes below the grate.

Prophet looked at his watch once again, then drank the cognac down in one unceremonious gulp. With his hand, he felt the underside of one of the shelves, moving along until he found what he was looking for—the button that released the recessed panel below the bookcase. With a *click,* a small panel popped open between a pair of four-light glazed doors. Prophet knelt down, looking through the books and papers lined up along the shelf. He was casual about it at first, then the casualness turned quickly to panic. He started rifling through erratically, pulling out small bundles and tossing them on the floor next to him.

"It has to be here," he mumbled, the anxiety rising in his voice. "Where is it? Where is it?"

"Is this what you're looking for?" asked a voice from a dark corner behind the open door of the study.

Prophet stood up. The two cast bronze chandeliers dangling from the stenciled ceiling came to life, causing Prophet to squint and shield his eyes as he looked toward the figure in the corner. "Who's there? What do you want?"

"I believe Inspector Godfrey would find the entries in this journal quite damning," replied Ernie, stepping out into the light, holding up Mary Walsh Trevor's journal.

Realizing whom it was, Prophet stood up, instinctively resuming his role as the ill-used, pathetic wretch Ernie expected him to be. He hunched his back slightly, turned his foot in and curled his hand to a more pronounced disfigurement. "Yes, yes he would," Prophet stammered. "Killed them, he did. I told the inspector as much not one hour ago. He was ready to kill me, too. Saved that young woman, I did."

Ernie listened patiently for Prophet to finish. He rambled on, very convincingly, until Ernie had finally heard enough. "I must be losing my touch," Ernie interrupted. "I even felt sorry for you, cowering to such an evil man as Lord Raventhorn. I think you might have gotten away with it if you hadn't tried so hard to convince me Raventhorn killed Mary Trevor and Cynthia Carolls. I think it's time Scotland Yard had a go at this journal."

As Ernie spoke, Prophet had knelt down, attempting to straighten up the mess of papers he tossed about on the floor. "It was him, it was," pleaded Prophet. "He killed those woman eight years ago. Mary Trevor said she was going to the police. He had to kill her. He killed Miss Carolls to cover up the motive." With a bundle of papers in his fist, Prophet reached into the cabinet. A second later, he jumped to his feet, a revolver in his hand pointed at Ernie. "I believe that journal would be better off with me."

Ernie froze. He slowly raised his hand, holding the journal out at arm's length. Prophet walked over, taking the journal from Ernie with his deformed hand.

"How did you know?" asked Prophet, cautiously stepping back to the desk. He placed the journal into the small leather case. "How did you know it was me?"

"There were a few things you said that got me thinking. The first was *Conduit Street*."

"Conduit Street?" Prophet repeated quizzically.

"That's right, Conduit Street. Earlier at the park, how did you know my flat was on Conduit Street? It didn't register at first; I was too busy pondering the other question of why you would be lurking about in the shadows outside Jacque's flat. I must admit it was quite a performance in the park—the frightened pathetic wretch hiding from his murderous employer, looking for the inspector. It wasn't until I was shaking off the affects of that crack on the head that I started putting the pieces together."

"If you must know," Prophet scoffed, "I *was* waiting for Inspector Flannel. He was the only other person who could possibly link me to the murders. I called him earlier, explaining I had new information about Raventhorn. I said he planned to kill again and I thought it might be the woman Mary Trevor gave the journal to."

"You spoke with the inspector this evening?" Ernie interrupted.

"I said I called him earlier," sniped Prophet. "It went right to voice mail. I said meet me on Brook Street, I'd be watching for any sign of Raventhorn. Imagine my surprise when I saw you looking out the window at me."

"So you had the whole scene in the park planned?"

"That's right. I had Raventhorn in the boot of the Jaguar and the French woman in the backseat. All I needed was the inspector to follow me out to Shoreditch. I fully intended to stage a dramatic confrontation beside those dreary and long abandoned tracks between the good inspector and Raventhorn, tragically ending in the deaths of both men. But your intrusion derailed that plan."

"Sorry to disappoint," replied Ernie glibly. "So why Marie Bussière?"

"She was another convenient link between Raventhorn and the murders. I was here when Raventhorn returned from your flat. He was enraged. Ranting about how I was in league with the police and anyone else who would listen. At one point, he mentioned her name, remarking how the intimate relationship she must have with Lord Coats was clouding his judgment. I remembered seeing her name in the museum program. The rest was easy. Now, you still haven't told me how you figured it all out."

Prophet's stare intensified as he listened, glancing away only once to check his watch.

"I was standing behind you in the rubble beneath that old station when you mentioned to Inspector Godfrey about Mary Trevor's friend the hat maker. Only the person who had the journal would know it came from her friend and that her friend was a hat maker. It made sense if you were behind nicking the journal, but you wouldn't do it yourself and chance being identified. You would need the assistance of a right proper villain. I will reluctantly admit I've had some experience with that lot." Ernie smiled, shaking his head. "You should really hire a better class of villain."

Prophet responded with a snort. "You're a clever one alright. So how did you know I didn't burn the journal?"

"Inspector Godfrey might have missed it, but I saw the glint of satisfaction in your eyes when you looked over at Raventhorn's body. I was certain at that moment you were behind all the *Slasher* murders, and just as certain you had the journal. So what was it then, Mary Trevor and Raventhorn figured out you killed those other five women? Is that why you killed them?"

"You're as daft as the police," Prophet grumbled, raising the 38 revolver. "Raventhorn killed those women eight years ago. He planned the whole thing thinking he would permanently seal a skeleton in his closet. Genius, really, the *Slasher* bit. While all of London trembled over the thought of this demented murderous fiend, he's pounding his fist in Parliament demanding justice for the victims. I've got to hand it to the old crow, that was a stroke of genius."

"But it was you who suggested to the police Raventhorn that was the *Slasher*?" Ernie responded in quiet perplexity.

Prophet laughed. "Funny thing, that. The evidence, if spun the right way, could have just as easily implicated me in the crimes, and Raventhorn was very quick to point that out. So I waited these eight years, enduring all the ill treatment he could inflict on me, looking for the right opportunity to resurrect the *Slasher* and finish what I started."

"Mary Trevor?"

"Exactly," boasted Prophet. "Once I found out she was nosing about in that old business, I dropped a trail of crumbs in front of her, eventually leading her to confront Raventhorn with the facts. Once that happened, it was time for the *Slasher* to claim his next victim."

"And Cynthia Carolls?

"An unavoidable necessity," Prophet remarked casually glancing again at his watch, his tone hinting slightly toward remorse. "I was rather fond of her."

"All this to expose Raventhorn as a murderer?"

"I don't expect you to understand," replied Prophet. He zipped up the small case, tucking it between his deformed arm and his chest. "He's not just a murderer, I've exposed him for the heartless bastard who thought nothing of casting his son aside like rubbish."

"Lord Raventhorn was your father?"

"That's right. It seems the stately and revered Lord Alfred Raventhorn fathered a son with a cheeky tart named Maggie Brown." His face flushed with anger. "I tracked her down. She laughed in my face and denied ever having a son. The only use she had for me was to confront him with my existence and demand money for her silence. He was no better, giving her the money to ease his conscience. Eight years ago, when she came back for more, he abruptly put an end to it, then took me in like some charity case."

As Prophet was ranting on about the abuse he endured throughout his life, Ernie was slowly backing toward the doorway to the hall.

"Stop right there, Mr. Bisquets," said Prophet coldly. He pointed the revolver at Ernie, cocking the hammer. "This is twice you've ruined my plans this evening, but there won't be a third. I'm afraid your intrusion into this flat has caught me by surprise, causing me to accidentally shoot you. I'm sure the police will understand, especially after the frightening events of this evening. Goodbye, Mr. Bisquets."

A shot rang out, followed by the thump of a body hitting the floor.

35/ Evil Seeks Its Own Level

From the hall, the sound of heavy footsteps approached Raventhorn's study. At first he didn't see the body, it had fallen back into the shadows behind the desk.

"Are you all right, Bisquets?" asked Inspector Flannel. He walked over, kicking the gun away from Prophet's outstretched hand. "Lucky I figured this out when I did."

Ernie stood staring at the body, speechless for a moment. The muffled sounds of sirens could be heard drifting down the hall into the study.

"Are you injured, Bisquets?" asked the inspector, his voice returning to its usual gruff edge.

"No . . . sorry . . . no," stuttered Ernie, finally breaking his silence. "What . . . what are you doing here?"

Inspector Flannel scratched his head and laughed. "Well there's a greeting. Save a lad's life and here's the thanks I get."

"Sorry, what I meant was—"

"I know what you meant, lad," said the inspector cordially. "You're welcome."

"Prophet Brown killed those two women. He confessed to everything."

"I know," explained the inspector. "I got here just as he was starting. The door was unlocked so I entered.

Heard the whole thing, I did. I've been in the hall with my gun on him the whole time."

As the inspector finished, additional footsteps were heard approaching. Inspector Godfrey and two other constables entered the study. Flannel pointed toward the body, pointing here and there as he briefly detailed the events he witnessed. When he finished, Inspector Flannel walked over to where Ernie was.

"They said you were suspended," remarked Ernie, his eyes still fixed on the body. "It's not right, I'll tell you. It's not right at all."

"Never you mind about that," replied the inspector matter-of-factly. "Just doing their job to keep the peace between the Yard and the politicians. What's important is we solved seven murders here this evening. Why don't I have one of these constables take you back to Conduit Street? I'm sure Pattie will want to know you're alive and well."

Ernie bobbed his head, his eyes still transfixed on the body. "I still don't understand how you knew I was here."

"Well, if you must know, your mate Dragonetti mentioned I might find you here."

"I don't understand. When did you see him?"

"Right after I got the ME's DNA report on the skin they found under Cynthia Carolls' nails. I half expected it to be Raventhorn's, but as it turned out, it belonged to Prophet Brown. He didn't know it, but we had both of their DNA on file. Dragonetti tracked me down, rambling on about how he thought you might be on your way here to do something stupid. Pretty resourceful, that one. By the way, all that talk about Prophet Brown being the illegitimate son of Raventhorn is a bunch of rubbish. They're no more related than you and I are."

This last statement was enough to distract Ernie's attention from the body. "You mean he lied about that?"

"No, I think he must have believed it. If Maggie Brown was Prophet's mother, it's more likely she convinced

Raventhorn he was his father for her own benefit. Whatever information she manufactured to support her claim must be what Prophet found. I don't see Raventhorn as a man who is easily made the fool. Was there an affair? Of that I'm sure, otherwise he would have dismissed her allegations. Whether he believed her or not about Prophet, we'll never know. He could just as easily have paid her off to sweep the whole business under the mat." The inspector motioned with his hand for one of the constables to come over to where he and Ernie were talking. "This officer will take you home. Tell Pattie I'll stop round in the morning to give him all the details."

"Thank you," Ernie nodded looking back at the body. "All that and he wasn't even related."

"They may not have been related by blood," stated Inspector Flannel coldly, "but it was blood that bound them together. Like water, evil seeks its own level."

36/ An Evening Out

"Absolutely incredible," remarked Marie, taking a glass filled with an interesting sherry from a tray held out by Patterson.

"Which?" replied Patterson, taking one himself. "The part where Inspector Flannel asks Ernie for help, or the part where the two of them solved seven murders in as many days?"

"They're both as remarkable as anything possibly could be," remarked Marie."

Patterson placed the tray down on the table between the sofas where they sat. There was one glass left resting in the center, as conspicuous as the absence of the person it was intended for.

"Well," Marie continued, "I for one am looking forward to hearing this whole story."

"As much as I would like to give you the details," said Patterson, himself settling back into the cushions and placing his arm around Marie, "I'm afraid this story is Ernie's to tell. It would be an injustice for me to take that away from him."

"You must have been terrified," pondered Mrs. Chapman.

"It all happened so quickly. One minute I was getting into a car and the next thing I know I was in Patterson's arms. I have no memory of anything that transpired between those two events." Marie looked up into Patterson's eyes. "I'm safe now and that's what matters."

"Remarkable," replied Mrs. Chapman. "This whole business has been utterly remarkable."

Patterson looked up at the mantel clock and then toward the hall. "Just where is Bisquets, anyway?"

Marie smiled. "He's met someone and they are going out this evening."

"And just who is this lucky woman?"

"Here now," Mrs. Chapman interrupted in her best headmistress tone, picking up the tray. "The lad is nervous enough without having to deal with this schoolyard gossip." She leaned in close to continue in a hushed voice. Marie and Patterson leaned forward in response. "I laid out the dark blue suit for him and a crisp white shirt. He'll look ever so handsome. He's mentioned the young woman in question will be meeting him here. Any minute now I suspect."

Mrs. Chapman smiled contently, leaving the solitary glass behind on the table, and retreated to the kitchen.

"Oh, there you are Bisquets," said Patterson, picking up the glass of sherry and holding it out. "We were just talking about you. Here, this should take the edge off. A date is it?"

Patterson's bluntness prompted an elbow to the ribs from Marie. "Pay no attention to him, Ernie."

"Quite all right, miss," Ernie responded brightly, taking the glass from Patterson's outstretched hand. "The Guvnor's right, I'm a bit nervous."

"Well, you look very handsome," said Marie. She stood up and proceeded to adjust his tie. "Whoever this young woman is she's fortunate to have captured your attention."

Ernie smiled in appreciation, his face flush with color. Marie returned to her seat as he finished the sherry off in one gulp then checked his watch.

Patterson threw caution to the wind—and by caution to the wind it should be noted he lowered his arm to protect his ribs from another assault—and exclaimed, "Out with it man, who is she?"

Before another word was uttered, or an elbow was thrown, the discussion was interrupted by the harsh buzzing of the front doorbell. Everyone looked at Ernie.

"I'll get it," Mrs. Chapman chimed in as she breezed past the pillared archway.

"As much as I'm itching to hear all the details of this Brick Lane murder business," Marie casually remarked, "I'm far more excited to find out who this mystery woman is."

Ernie was far too distracted to even realize Marie was talking to him. He took out his small brush and made one final pass along each arm of his suit coat.

"Here you are, miss," said Mrs. Chapman showing an attractive young woman into the sitting room.

She wore an elegant red Preen, one-shoulder, bandage dress, body-sculpted, giving height to her petite frame. A matching clutch, diamond and ruby pavé bangle, and tan leather pumps completed the outfit. Her makeup was modest and perfect, pale gold eye shadow highlighting inviting green eyes, a slight blush to her high cheekbones, and deep red lipstick. Her smile filled the room, though her raised brow hinted at being surprised by the curious group.

"You look lovely," Ernie quietly confirmed. He took her hand, an action that erased all her concern.

Patterson stood up, followed by Marie, as Ernie made the introductions. "Marie, Patterson, this is Victoria Littlebury."

"It's a pleasure to meet all of you. Please, call me Vicki."

"You know," Patterson remarked, shaking Vicki's hand, "you look terribly familiar. Have we met?"

Vicki gave a slight laugh and took Ernie's outstretched arm.

"If you'll excuse us," replied Ernie, "we're off to Queen's Theater to see Les Misérables."